I0620681

The Life and Death of
Lizzie Morris

Prairiescape Books

The Life and Death of Lizzie Morris

a novel

by Robert Hays

Prairiescape Books
an imprint of
Herndon-Sugarman Press
Savoy, Illinois U.S.A.

Copyright by Robert Hays 2009
First printing, Prairiescape Books edition, January 2014

This is a work of fiction. Names, characters, places, and incidents either
are the products of the author's imagination or are used fictitiously and
any resemblance to actual persons, living or dead, is purely coincidental.
Except as permitted by current U.S. copyright statutes, no part of this
book may be reproduced or transmitted in any form or by any means,
electronic or mechanical, including photocopying, recording, or by any
information storage and retrieval system without written permission
from the publisher. All rights reserved.

ISBN-10: 0-9899926-0-8
ISBN-13: 978-0-9899926-0-2

To Mary, as always

❦ Love is most nearly itself
When here and now no longer matter.
— T. S. Eliot

1

When Bradley Morris was ten years old, his father told him he could do anything he set his mind to. "If you want something bad enough," Randall Morris declared, "and you work for it long enough and hard enough, you can make it happen. Just don't ever give up."

He had never forgotten those words. They were the counsel of a man whose wisdom he respected, and over the years he generally had tended to have a good deal of faith in his father's advice. Some things, of course, were well beyond one's control—the war had taught him that, early in life—and had anyone asked if he truly believed he could command his own destiny he would have been quick to say no. But he was not a man who gave up easily, which was exactly why he and Lizzie found themselves in this strange place, driving a treacherous Sicilian highway in a cramped little Fiat they had rented at the Catania airport just a short while ago.

So far, Sicily was much the same as he remembered. The landscape was harsh and barren, uninviting. What might have been patches of green in the spring and early summer appeared now as hardly more than scorched brown spots on the rocky slopes, mute testament to the long, hot Mediterranean summer. There were scattered small fields of grain and parcels of arid pasture that looked barely able to sustain the herds of sheep that occasionally materialized as if from nowhere. Alongside the road, a steep bank dropped off to a dry stream bed fifty feet below.

Bradley Morris drove slowly. He respected the challenges of the unfamiliar, winding road, and he was finding it difficult to concentrate on his driving. Carson Streator was on his mind.

Decades ago, he and Streator had been thrown together by fate, and Streator had become the closest friend Bradley ever had. Streator's short life ended on a bleak Sicilian hillside when his heart was almost ripped from his chest by jagged steel shrapnel from the same artillery shell that left Bradley gravely wounded—their blood pooling collectively on the hard ground, the smell of their seared flesh indistinguishable, one body from the other. He had grieved over his shy, loyal comrade during the early months of his own recovery and vowed to visit Minnesota one day and look up whatever family Streator had, imagining that such a visit somehow might restore a vital connection that had been brutally severed. But getting back on his feet had taken what seemed like forever. Then he and Lizzie were married and quickly found themselves facing the struggles of everyday life. They always had too many other things to do.

On the whole, life after the war had been good, thanks to the love and companionship Bradley shared with Lizzie. Had he been a praying man, he would have thanked God every day for the gift of a perfectly matched soul-mate. But he still was haunted by a sense that Carson Streator had been cheated by fate, snatched away at such an early age that there hardly was a trace of his existence. Why had others, including himself, been spared to pass life on to future generations when Streator had not?

There were men in his rifle squad that he had not come to know nearly as well, and he tried to recall them now as a way to conquer the melancholy reminiscences of Carson Streator. He thought about the two boys from New Jersey, Potter and Mathieson, who didn't like one another, and a hulking Georgian whose name he could no longer remember. And Potter's bitterness toward women: "You go ape over the end of a gut and think it's a lifetime deal. Forget about it. Some other guy's shoes will be under her bed when you get back."

"But you don't know my Elizabeth," Bradley had argued, and he could tell that the other men hoped he was right.

He thought about Greer, who thrived on the regimentation

of army life, and the big, boisterous Raynor from Louisiana. Raynor claimed the biggest dong of any man in Pointe Coupee Parish and told fanciful tales about drunken brawls and passionate women and hunting alligators in the swamps. They all knew that his stories were exaggeration at best, and in many instances outright lies, but Raynor had offered entertaining diversions to routine barracks life and merely played the role they had cast him in to the best of his ability. And he thought about Sykes, the first among them to die.

Streator, Sykes, Greer, Raynor, Potter and Mathieson, the dull Georgia boy—all of them had learned to depend on one another when survival was at stake. They had been joined through a spirit of allegiance such as Bradley Morris never had experienced since.

And he remembered Caldwell, who stood out because he was different. Caldwell was a fellow Kentuckian, a coarse mountain man from the east. Others in the squad never had trusted him, considered him malicious and sneaky, and nobody complained when Potter dubbed him "that goat-fucking hillbilly." Nor had anyone shed a tear when he disappeared during their rough Atlantic crossing. Knowing Caldwell, they assumed that he had challenged the wrong man and got himself thrown overboard.

Bradley had tried briefly to be Caldwell's friend but was coldly rejected. Now he wished he had tried harder. Lizzie had taught him that there was good in everyone. Sometimes you just had to dig deeper to find it.

All this had happened more than a half-century ago and Bradley Morris himself found it hard to understand why it still mattered. But besides his life-long grief over the death of Carson Streator, he could not help but wonder what had become of Greer and Raynor and the others who were still alive the day he was hit. There probably were more who didn't make it, but at the time he had been in no condition to find out; all order had disappeared from his life in the explosion of a single artillery shell. He had been carted from the battlefield in a state of semi-consciousness, a morphine Syrette pinned to his collar, and then he was on the hospital ship and eventually on his way home.

Some months later, he heard through the army grapevine—usually reliable, but not always—that Potter had been charged with the rape of a teenaged Italian girl in Palermo. He never knew if it was true.

Lizzie's soft voice urged Bradley back to the present: "What are you thinking about, Brad? You haven't said a word for miles."

"I'm sorry," he said. "I was wondering about some of the men. I should have tried harder to track them down after the war."

"But you didn't have any way to do that." Lizzie's tone was sympathetic.

"None that I knew about at the time, anyhow."

"How many do you suppose are still alive?"

"It's hard to say. We're all old now. And I expect there were other guys I knew who didn't make it back. The day I was hit I would have said anybody that lasted till sundown was lucky. We took a pretty good shellacking."

"I think that may be as much as you've ever said about that day."

He knew she was right. For all these years, he had refused to make his personal ordeal in the war an issue of any consequence. He rarely talked about his final battle. Not even with Lizzie. If others raised the subject, he was resistant, like a patient diagnosed with a fatal illness who couldn't bear to discuss his disease.

At the same time, though, Bradley had made no bones about the pride he took in his generation of Americans. He would praise their sense of commitment and determination at the slightest pretext, to anyone willing to listen. His generation had given no thought to how long the war might last, he proclaimed freely; they had signed on for the duration. They had been willing if not eager to fight and there was no dissent or protest, no second-guessing, as he and fellow infantrymen of the 45th Division were herded aboard crowded troop ships embarking for North Africa. When their ships dropped anchor at Oran, Algeria, on June 22, 1943—a place and date tattooed on his brain—they were prepared to accept whatever fate had in store. And this is where his proclamation ended.

As far as the rest of the story was concerned, those few who had heard bits and pieces of it through the years would never charge Bradley Morris with trying to make it sound heroic. And they had not found him bitter, even though some resentment might have been justified. He had endured the darkest hours of his life in Sicily, and on bad nights that came too often he relived in his dreams the most haunting scenes from his long-past stint in hell.

Although the years had helped him come to grips with his mental wounds, there still were times when his war dreams left him depressed and anxious and difficult to live with for days. Even Lizzie, the center of his universe, could not lighten this darkness. She deserved better. For her sake, he had vowed to do whatever it took to fix this problem once and for all.

Seeing Sicily again was one of the last things he ever wanted to do, but just a few weeks ago, after a series of particularly bad nights, Bradley had gone through a wrenching epiphany. There was a key somewhere that would open the door to inner harmony, destroy his demons and erase the graphic images of carnage that vibrated through his subconscious mind. It was up to him to find it. He vowed that, like a knight of the Dark Ages, he would face his fire-breathing dragons head-on. It might be a desperate last resort, and it might not work, but he hoped that retracing his grisly wartime path would help bring an end to his nightmares.

Bradley expected no miracles; even a modest level of healing would make the trip worthwhile. Give him the slightest crack in that elusive door and he would kick it open wide. He was confident that he had the power within himself to accomplish this mission—especially with Lizzie at his side—and it was one he was determined to see through to the end.

Lizzie, as always, had been a rock of support. She had taken the initiative to find out about passports and immunizations and the other things they would have to take care of, then put her foot down. They were not getting any younger, she declared.

And perhaps worrying that he needed a final inducement, she had proposed that they return by way of Chicago and visit Matthew and Sarah and the grandsons. When he agreed, her smile was all the reward he could have asked for.

Lizzie could not read his mind, but after all their years together she knew him as well as he knew himself. It often seemed as if his thoughts were her thoughts, her words his, like two musicians reading notes from the same page.

He need not try to explain why he wanted to stand on the beach somewhere east of Gela where his invasion force had landed and walk in sunshine where once he had suffered unimaginable terror in the black of night. She understood. And she would hurt as he hurt, crouching silently on the forbidding hillside where the din of war had dulled his senses—the battlefield, if he could find it, where German and Italian artillery and rifle fire had snatched the lives of young Carson Streator and who knew how many others and left Bradley with wounds that by any mea- sure should have been lethal.

At the last minute, though, Bradley had suffered cold feet. An intense panic attack left him awash in doubt. What if seeing the battleground again made things worse? But there was no turning back. He could not disappoint Lizzie, and anyway they already had put themselves wholly into the hands of a pretty, infinitely patient young woman in a shopping-mall travel agency who had made their reservations, bought airline tickets, and outlined their schedule to Rome and then to Sicily and then back to Chicago and finally home again.

They would spend five days on the island. They had no detailed itinerary beyond a single night's reservation at an unpretentious Gela hotel, but a modest travel guide Lizzie bought at a Memphis bookstore would serve their needs well enough.

Now they were here. They would make the most of the time they had.

It was late afternoon when they reached their hotel and the check-in process went awkwardly. Their room's "first floor" designation led to some confusion until they understood the Sicilian innkeeper's explanation that this meant one flight up. A man who had been sweeping the sidewalk in front of the building lugged their small bags up the steep, narrow stairs. The room was poorly lit and sparsely furnished, the only touch of elegance a worn but exquisitely brocaded bedspread.

The man dropped their bags in the middle of the room, rebuffed Bradley's efforts to give him money, and left them alone.

Bradley turned to Lizzie with an expression of surprise. "Why wouldn't he take a tip? Did I do something wrong?"

"Of course not. I think he's just a janitor or something. Janitors don't expect tips."

Lizzie hurried into the bathroom while Bradley sat on the bed, rocking and bouncing to test the firmness of the mattress. "Couldn't we maybe walk around the block before dinner?" she called. "Unless you've already done too much walking today."

Bradley agreed. He had spent much of the afternoon on his feet, but so far his bad leg was holding up pretty well and it would be good to get their bearings and gain a better feel for this place before dark. They were, as Matthew might have said, "a far piece from Memphis."

They left the hotel by the front door, paused to marvel at the antiquity of their setting, and set off to circle the block. They turned at the first street corner. Just ahead, an old woman sat hunched behind a small, bright-green wooden table that nearly blocked the sidewalk. She watched intently as they approached and motioned for them to come.

"*Buongiorno,*" she said as they drew closer, smiling. "*Desidero parlare con lei.*"

"*Buongiorno,*" Lizzie said. "And I'm afraid that's all the Italian I know."

"Ah, tourists," the old woman responded. She said the word benevolently. "It is good. I speak English. Come, and let me tell you things."

Bradley glanced across at Lizzie warily, but she just laughed. "Please," she said to the old woman, "what things do you want to tell us?"

"I know your future. Show me your hands. The gentleman first, please."

Lizzie nudged Bradley with her elbow. He reached out stiffly to the woman behind the table, palms down. She grasped his hands gently and turned them over. "You have had big things in your life," she said, after studying his palms a few seconds. "But I believe your best story is yet to be told. Your palms read well. You are strong. You will face troubles, but you will overcome." Then, to Lizzie, "The lady has beautiful hands. May I see?"

Lizzie held out her hands, palms up. The old woman looked closely at one, then the other, then back to the first, squinting slightly while her eyes moved over Lizzie's palms as if she were reading a page of fine print in a book. When she spoke, her voice was low, barely above a whisper. "There is happiness," she said, "and also shadows. Forgive me. I think that I am not reading you well."

"Let's just go with the happiness," Lizzie said. "Brad is going to overcome his troubles, and I will be happy."

Bradley handed the old woman money he thought to equal about what they had paid for sandwiches and soft drinks in Catania, though he still was uncertain about the Italian currency. It seemed to be more than she expected. She accepted it with self-conscious expressions of gratitude. "I'm sorry for the lady," she said, and there were tears in her eyes.

The softly lit hotel dining room was nearly empty. The only other diners were three men they assumed to be locals, seated some distance across the room from their small corner table. A thick-bodied, rust-colored fly settled briefly on the white tablecloth, crawled across a dinner fork, and buzzed around Lizzie's hair. She swatted at it with a napkin and it flew away, the drone of its wings audible until it escaped to the outside world.

"My aim's a bit off," she said, and laughed at her own failure.

"Back home that'd be a horsefly," Bradley said. "I don't know if they have them here, though."

"It looked like a horsefly to me," Lizzie said, serious again.

"But there's a lot we don't know about Sicily, and I doubt we'd have studied up on its flies even if we'd had time."

"I know, but maybe we should have taken more time to study up on other things."

"We know enough to do what we came for, and that's all that matters." There was an element of finality in her tone.

Their waiter, a tall and slender young man whose name was Carlo, brought generous plates of pasta 'ncasciata. "I hope you will like it," he said in heavily accented English. His reddish-blond hair and pale blue eyes and fair skin made him look more Irish than Italian, and he was incongruously clad in badly faded jeans and a semi-formal black jacket. His white shirt, buttoned at the collar with no tie, was dingy but clean.

"It looks delicious," Lizzie said.

Carlo beamed with pride. "My mama is the cook," he said. "She's famosa all over this part of Sicily for her foods."

Lizzie asked about the music they could hear, playing elsewhere in the hotel. She told Carlo the singer's voice was wonderful.

"It's Bocelli," Carlo said. "You couldn't mistake it."

"Bocelli?"

"Andrea Bocelli. The greatest tenor ever, I think. By the new millennium he will be known all over the world."

"The new millennium—you mean 2000? That's only five years away, now."

"Si, 2000. Bocelli will be the greatest by 2000."

"Even greater than Caruso?"

"Ah, si—the Great Caruso. Who can say? The old people say Caruso was the best can ever be. But me, I never heard Caruso. I say Bocelli will be the greatest."

Carlo insisted on pouring more wine for Lizzie. Bradley's glass was untouched, which he had hoped the young waiter wouldn't notice. He asked for coffee, and Carlo soon returned with a pot of steaming, strong-flavored brew. Lizzie sipped the wine. Then she tried the water, in a glass with no ice, and wrinkled her nose. "This tastes terrible," she whispered.

"The first time I tasted Sicilian water we dipped it out of a dirty little creek," Bradley said. "All the halazone tablets in the world probably wouldn't have made it safe. But I guess when you get thirsty enough, you'll drink anything."

"I'm not sure some halazone, or whatever you said, wouldn't help this."

"They gave us phenobarbital, too."

"Who gave you phenobarbital?"

"The medical officers on the ship, before the landing. They said it was for seasickness, but it really was a tranquilizer. They had a bunch of scared young boys facing war for the first time. I couldn't tell that it made much difference, though."

"I don't think you ever told me that before."

"Well, it wasn't very important, I guess."

"Does Gela look familiar?"

"We never actually saw Gela," Bradley said. He paused, thinking back. "They probably brought me back through here after I was hit, on my way to the hospital ship, but I suppose I wouldn't have known."

"But we're close to where you landed?"

"Yes. It can't be more than a few miles up the coast, toward Ragusa. We'll find it tomorrow."

They were tired and hungry after the short but bumpy flight from Rome to Catania and the slow drive to Gela. A quiet time to enjoy their first substantial meal in two days came as a pleasant respite, and their dinner was good—less exotic than they had expected it to be, not too different from the food they occasionally had at an unsung Italian restaurant back home. The meatballs, cheese, and sausage were better, though, and the sauce a great deal more tasty. They ate leisurely.

Lizzie looked about the room. Weariness marked her pretty face. "It's hard to believe we're really here," she said quietly. "I want us to make the best of it, Brad. We'll be in Chicago with the children in a few days, and then back home in Memphis. In no time at all this will seem like it happened a long time ago."

"I hope this trip's worthwhile."

10

She reached across the table and put her hand on his. "It will be," she said. "I'm sure of it. I don't know how things are going to play out, but I know that coming here was the right thing to do. You'll see."

"I don't know what I'd do without you, Lizzie. You always make me feel better. And I think just coming back was the first big step in facing up to my problems. I don't know how it will play out, either, but we'll take it one day at a time and whatever happens, happens. We've got lots of good years ahead of us. I'm going to beat this thing, Lizzie. I swear I will."

"Yes, you will. The price you've paid for doing what you had to do already has been much too high."

The other diners were gone. Wary of abusing Carlo's hospitality by sitting too long, they reluctantly bade him good night and went upstairs. There was a tiny balcony outside their window, but they could reach it only by climbing over the high sill and decided against this physical challenge. No matter, Lizzie rationalized; it was too dark to see anything, assuming there was a view to begin with. She pulled the shutters closed and drew the faded draperies and they made ready for bed.

The hotel was quiet, with few of its rooms occupied.

"I guess we really are getting old," Lizzie said. "Look at us. Here we are, our first night in the most exotic place we've ever been, and we're too tired for sex."

Bradley groaned, good-naturedly. "We've put in a lot of miles together," he said. "I don't mean this trip. I wish we had traveled more, and come here sooner, but we did get around some. Besides, I don't know that this place is all that more exotic than Kentucky in the moonlight. It's funny that I can still remember that night like it was yesterday, but I can barely remember what we did last week."

"Are you looking forward to tomorrow?"

"Sicily may not be easy for me, Lizzie."

"But like you said, Brad, you've taken that first step. I know how hard you've tried to overcome the bad memories, and I know you won't give up. You never have."

"You know something, though? I'm going to worry about what that old woman said—the fortune teller. I'm not really superstitious, but I wish she hadn't said what she did."

Now Lizzie groaned, deliberately mimicking his earlier expression. "Oh, pay no attention to her," she said. "They just make things up. Don't worry, Brad. I'll be around for a long time yet."

Lizzie was soon asleep, but Bradley lay awake. This was Sicily, and the place where he had lived through an invasion and fought his short-lived war could not be far away. He lay still and quiet, concerned that he might disturb Lizzie, worried and tense from all the thoughts racing through his mind, afraid to sleep because he feared his dreams. But weariness overtook him at last and he no longer could fight off his body's determined need for rest.

The dreams came fast. He was in a landing craft, awash on a rough Mediterranean that tossed the boat around like an empty tin can, crouched in a huddle with other soldiers dreading what was to come. Tracer bullets fired by anti-aircraft batteries on shore painted a red arc overhead as German and Italian gunners searched out the planes that carried American and British paratroops and the midnight sky suddenly was illuminated by the beam of an enemy searchlight.

The voice of their lieutenant was no match for the roar of the craft's over-matched engine, but they all knew that their orders were clear and simple. They were to hit the beach running, cross the open space as fast as humanly possible and, in the remaining hours of darkness, establish a beachhead and rapidly form up in units ready to attack in full force as daylight broke.

Then, in a mad swirl of shouting and confusion, the landing craft's ramp was down. Men were spilling into the inky water....

"It's all right, Brad. You're safe now. It's all right." Lizzie cradled his head in her arms and gently stroked his face. "It's just one of your nightmares," she said softly. "You'll be all right."

"It's always so real. The water . . . cold and black . . ."

"Yes, I know. It must have been terrible. But it happened a long time ago. Someday you'll be able to forget and then maybe the nightmares will end. I certainly hope so."

"I'm okay now, Lizzie. As long as you're here by my side, I know everything is going to be all right."

"And I'll always be here."

Bradley Morris slept soundly for the rest of the night.

2

They woke later than they had planned, the noise of traffic in the street below rumbling into the room through the open window. Gela was hardly the quiet town they had seen on the day before, when they arrived after much of the day's commerce was finished. Now there was a steady growl of heavy trucks and the intermittent blaring of automobile horns, intermixed with the noisy whir of motor scooters. When they went down to breakfast, they were surprised to find the dining room nearly filled with people.

Carlo spotted them immediately. "*Buongiorno*, my friends," he said, escorting them to one of the few vacant tables. "I hope you slept well."

They were happy to see him again, a familiar face in this roomful of strangers. He also offered good service; they soon had breakfast on the table. For Bradley, the centerpiece was a pot of the rich Sicilian coffee he already had decided was considerably better than the drink he brewed at home or found in any of the prosaic Memphis coffee shops.

"Please tell me if you need anything," Carlo said. "We want our American friends to have a nice visit."

"We'll be leaving Gela this morning," Bradley told him, "but you've been very helpful. It's not easy sometimes when you don't know the language."

Carlo smiled. "Just talk with your hands," he said. "That's one thing they say about us Italians that happens to be true. Even we Sicilians. We may look like we're carved out of stone sometimes, but we understand the hands."

"I'll have to try that and see if it helps. I know my Italian's not going to get any better."

Carlo looked pleased, as if recognizing that his advice was being taken seriously.

They finished breakfast and left Carlo what they hoped was a generous tip. After they had carried their bags downstairs and sorted out the bill to be charged to their American Express card, Lizzie stood by with the luggage while Bradley brought the rental car around to the front of the hotel. With some inelegance, she lowered herself into the front passenger seat while he opened the hatchback and started to load the bags.

Carlo spied him from the dining room and hurried out to help. They engaged briefly in sober conversation, then Bradley wedged himself behind the wheel and they drove away as Carlo stood at the curb and waved a final goodbye.

"He's a nice boy," Lizzie said. "Not at all what I expected for an Italian waiter."

Bradley nodded in agreement. "He sure made it easier on us, our first night in Sicily."

"It looked like he was telling you something important."

"He said we might run into a roadblock. He said the police and the army set them up sometimes to keep check on the Mafia, and they've been active around here in recent weeks. The police, not the Mafia."

"Are you serious?"

"That's what he said. But he said if we get stopped, they'll send us on our way as soon as they know who we are."

They were getting their first good look at Gela, and finding it surprisingly ugly. Ancient, yes, but there was an inescapable atmosphere of modern dilapidation. The primitive Greek fortifications built by Timoleon at Capo Soprano, the sacred precinct and archaic temple of Athena on the Acropolis—those places listed in Lizzie's travel guide as the sights tourists ought to see—apparently lay somewhere beyond the rundown, graffiti-scarred shops and unsightly industrial plants that lined the little city's streets.

They drove to the outskirts of town without incident and

found a coastal road to Scoglitti. Off to their right, the glassy surface of the Mediterranean was ruffled only by an occasional moderate swell. Waves rolled ashore in constrained whitecaps that broke timidly on the beach and left ragged lines of mocha-colored foam on the sand. The early September sun already was high in a sky without clouds.

"Arnold Calder told me Sicily had people for nearly a thousand years before the Greeks," Bradley said, "and the Greeks were here hundreds of years before the time of Christ."

"How in the world would Arnold Calder know that?" Lizzie asked. Her tone was not doubtful, but reflected wonder.

"Don't ever be surprised by Arnold. He reads all the time. He knows everything. When he found out I was here in the war he studied up on the island and told me all about it."

"You've always liked Arnold Calder, Brad. You should get up to Simpson's Ridge one of these days and see him. You'll have lots to tell him, now."

"Arnold's an interesting fellow. Remember the first time you saw him, Lizzie? You said he looked fearsome. I think that's the word you used: fearsome."

Lizzie's reaction probably was not unusual, Bradley thought at the time. Arnold was a large, broad-shouldered, barrel-chested bull of a man. Had there been any meanness in his nature he indeed might have been fearsome, but Arnold always wore a wide grin that drew attention to his weathered face, dominated by kind green eyes. He and Bradley became acquainted when an instance of minor car trouble led Bradley to Arnold's garage.

Although they had little in common on the surface, they liked each other from the beginning. Arnold was a man without pretensions who still slid easily into the Appalachian colloquialisms of his native eastern Kentucky. Bradley enjoyed his openness and self-deprecating candor and over time learned more about him than any other man he ever had known except Carson Streator—even men he had worked alongside for years. He heard how Arnold went into the coal fields at the age of twelve as a pick-and-shovel miner, how hard times in Kentucky and the promise of steadier work eventually drove him to the deep-shaft mines of southern Illinois, and how he eventually found himself left out again as the underground mines lost markets to surface strippers and the demand for high-sulfur Illinois coal dwindled in favor of low-sulfur coal from the West.

After a decade of short-term jobs in assorted St. Louis industrial plants, Arnold arrived in Simpson's Ridge with a wife, two daughters and no money. When the people of Simpson's Ridge found out how good Arnold was at fixing things, though, they wondered how they ever managed without him.

But for Bradley, the most surprising thing about Arnold Calder was his intellect. He soon learned that Arnold was remarkably well-informed and could discuss virtually any topic with great insight. Arnold apparently had become an avid reader to make up for his lack of formal education, subscribed to two or three big-city newspapers at a time, and had an insatiable appetite for lit-erature of all kinds.

"I know Arnold's smart," Lizzie said. "But I still say he could look pretty fearsome if he wanted to. I'm just glad to have him and Glory in the old house. I know he'll take care of it."

Bradley didn't answer. As he looked out over the Mediterranean, his thoughts turned from Arnold Calder to a troop ship that had sailed these waters at another time. In his mind's eye he could see Carson Streator and other young soldiers squatting among mountains of supplies and equipment lashed down on a heaving deck, about to be thrown into war. Only hours before, after days of landing rehearsals in North Africa, they had heard for the first time that their mission was the invasion of Sicily. He remembered Sykes's frustration when no one could answer his urgent query: "Where the hell is Sicily?"

He recalled how desperately he had hoped that his courage wouldn't fail at the critical moment when they hit the beach. There was little doubt that the men around him, as the reality of their situation sank in, were as scared as he was. And although the same ships they had made the grueling Atlantic crossing on dotted the water as far as the eye could see in every direction, they found little consolation in the strength of numbers. How many thousands of young Americans would become fodder for enemy guns?

Bradley gazed over the calm, blue water and wondered how far it was to North Africa. Undoubtedly an easy crossing on clement days like this when the ocean lay at peace—so unlike that earlier time, when it had been driven and tossed into a white-capped frenzy by a rare summer windstorm. Their ship wallowed through thirty-foot waves and troughs, leaving the troops to bunch together below decks, paralyzing fear clawing at the pits of their stomachs, at insides already screaming for relief from the retching and vomiting brought on by seasickness.

The storm died down in the late afternoon and they were called on deck for final briefings. They would be in their landing craft by midnight, and shortly after that they would be churning toward the beaches.

"It was here." He suddenly recognized unmistakable landmarks. "This is the beach where we landed," he said to Lizzie. "I remember exactly how it looked that night, lit up by flares and artillery. See that ridge over there—it still looks the same, with those two little peaks. I remember thinking it looked like a two-humped camel. This is where we came ashore."

He stopped the car on a narrow, sandy shoulder only yards above the water line. To the left, the ridge he pointed out to Lizzie rose away from the beach as a gentle slope that gave way in turn to the low hills farther inland. Lizzie stood beside the car without speaking, and he limped slowly down toward the water's edge, alone.

As Bradley Morris thought back, that July day in 1943 was as vivid in his memory as his conversation with Carlo only hours ago, just before they left Gela. An uncontrollable physical wave flowed upward through his torso and into his chest and shoulders and arms and became a shudder. His hands trembled. *I can feel it . . . it's like I'm there.*

It was as if he could hear one of the battalion's majors reading a letter from General Patton. The letter was addressed to the men of Seventh Army, to be delivered at sea in the waning hours before the battle commenced. The major was some distance from Bradley and the other men of his squad and because of the noise of the ship and the crashing waves they could catch only some of his words. But they heard enough.

The temper of the general's message was clear: ". . . German and Italian soldiers whom it is our honor and privilege to attack and destroy . . . retreat is impossible . . . must retain this tremendous advantage by always attacking . . . honor of our country, the future of the whole world rests in your individual hands . . . God is with us . . ."

Carson Streator cupped his hands and yelled in Bradley's ear, "Where do you suppose old Patton is right now?"

"Probably loading up his gear, ready to go over the side right along with us."

Streator apparently enjoyed his sarcasm. They both laughed. It would be many hours before either laughed again.

The major finished reading and Bradley and his squad-mates clustered in a small knot. Their cocky young lieutenant tried his best. "The navy's been pounding them with their big guns and our bombers have been blasting them," he shouted. "The 82nd Airborne has a ton of paratroopers in there already. Hell, there won't be many dagos and krauts left to kill." Not a cakewalk, he admitted, but all they would have to do was go in and mop up.

The bravado of the young lieutenant rang false. Like the rest of them, he had never experienced war.

On shore, they could see the fires ignited by naval artillery and air strikes. The flames effected a reddish glow on their faces and exposed the apprehension in their eyes.

Then it was time.

Their chaplain, a brawny Infantry captain with the flattened nose of an ex-prize fighter, called for them to join in prayer. "God is on our side," he shouted. "Be proud that you're Americans, remember what you're fighting for. Think of your wives and sweethearts at home, your sisters and brothers, and your mothers and dads. Keep yourself safe so you can go home to them.

"Some of you aren't sure you can kill a man. Well, the Scripture says there is a time to kill—and this is it. God Himself mustered an army, the book of Isaiah tells us. He had one purpose: 'I will punish the world for their evil, and the wicked for their iniquity; and I will cause the arrogance of the proud to cease, and will lay low the haughtiness of the terrible.'

"If that sounds like Hitler to you, I don't think God would have any quarrel. That German soldier you face is Hitler's man and if you don't kill him he sure as hell will kill you! Don't look him in the eye. Shoot him in the guts. This is the job you trained for, and the job your country called on you to do. The future of the free world is in your hands tonight, men, and I know you won't fail."

The incongruity of a chaplain exhorting them to kill was lost on Bradley that night. The chaplain might have been reading his mind. He was telling the young soldiers what they needed to hear; if God was on their side, surely they would come through this ordeal safely and be victorious. In the chaplain's words he found a small measure of comfort and security.

The chaplain raised his arms and turned his face skyward. "Almighty God, hear our prayers," he intoned. "Hear our cry for mercy and give us strength as we prepare to do battle."

His powerful voice hovered over the silent troops. The sound of waves breaking against the surging ship interrupted briefly, then he spoke again. "Lay your hand on our shoulders and guide us as we face an evil enemy that plunged the world into cruel and merciless war. Let theirs be the heritage of oppressors, as promised in your word, Lord, that their generations may not prosper. Give us stout hearts to do heroic deeds, unwearying zeal to smite the enemy and win quick victory, all to your glory. And protect us, merciful God, by the shield of your righteousness that we may return from battle unscathed, and go home to our loved ones and live out our days in the blessed light of your everlasting benevolence. Amen."

And Bradley Morris recalled exactly how he felt as he went over the side of the ship in the darkness and clambered down a rope scramble net into a pitching landing craft. He had barely been aware of the men around him. His mind was on Lizzie, waiting for him back in Simpson's Ridge. Would he ever see her again? A determined enemy, as bent on killing and surviving as he was, waited on the beach. His fate no longer was in his own hands and he might die before his feet touched land again.

"We're going to make it, Morris," Carson Streator shouted in his ear. "God is on our side, just like the chaplain said."

Bradley Morris was an old man alone with his memories. Across the distance of time, he could feel the cold water and powerful drag of heavy, wet gear just as he'd experienced them on that terrifying morning decades before. This time, though, the fear was not so great.

This time, he knew the outcome: His squad made it safely to the beach and lived to fight another day—except for Sykes. Sykes had been running somewhere behind him, over sand Bradley had just crossed. There was a flash and Bradley heard a small explosion. Those bringing up the rear said Sykes never knew what hit him. That was merciful, they said. Land mines usually tore off your legs and left you to die slowly.

"Why wasn't it me?" He said this aloud, even though Lizzie was too far away to hear. "I had to have run past that mine, but I missed it. And Carson Streator was right beside me when he was hit. I don't know why it wasn't me."

He knelt on the sandy beach, looking out to sea as if on watch. How quiet it was. The only sounds were the gentle lapping of the surf and the occasional cry of a seabird.

It was an hour or more before Lizzie approached and gently put a hand on his shoulder.

"Are you all right, Brad?"

He reached up and cupped her hand in his. "It could have been me, Lizzie," he whispered hoarsely. "And then we'd never have had our life together. You would have found someone else, a good man, and had a good life. But he couldn't have loved you the way I do, Lizzie, never the way I do."

3

The terrace of the Mediterraneo Palace Hotel in Ragusa was sparsely peopled, most of those in the breakfast crowd choosing the air-conditioned comfort of the dining room. A sultry African sirocco blew from the south, across the Mediterranean, and already the morning air was oppressively warm. Lizzie had asked for outdoor seating because she loved the view. Their table was shaded by a bright orange patio umbrella.

After a restless night, Bradley Morris was eager to get started. "Somewhere this side of Caltagirone is where the war ended for me," he told Lizzie, carefully studying a detailed Touring Club Italiano road map of southern Sicily. "Near Vizzini, I think. But to be honest, I'm not overly certain I can find the battlefield the way I found the beach."

"If we get close, something may look familiar," Lizzie said. "Do you know how to get there?"

"Yes. We can drive from here down toward Comiso, then take this highway to Vizzini." He traced the route with his finger, and paused to sip his steaming coffee. "There aren't many roads so I don't see how we can get lost."

"Famous last words!"

"You'll see. We'll go straight to Vizzini, and from there to Caltagirone. When we get to Caltagirone we'll be almost back to the road we came down on from Catania to Gela." "Whatever you say. But this is such a beautiful place. It's too bad we can't stay here a while longer." She looked about, almost wistfully.

"I'm sorry my problems are taking up all our time, Lizzie."

"Don't be foolish. We had one reason for coming to Sicily, and it's important. First things first, as Papa would say."

"Maybe we can come back some day."

"Like ordinary tourists?"

"Yes. Like ordinary tourists."

Lizzie smiled. "That would be nice," she said. "Let's plan it for this time next year!"

They hurried through breakfast, checked out of the hotel and soon were on the road. Only a few miles out of Ragusa Bradley was forced to admit that he wasn't sure where they were. They had meandered through the city and turned onto what he hoped was the right highway, yet there had been no clear marker. He was afraid to go much farther without a better sense of direction. When they passed a man on a bicycle, pedaling leisurely in the morning sunshine, he agreed with Lizzie's suggestion that he try and ask the way.

"I just hope I can make him understand," he said. He guided the Fiat to the side of the road and stopped, got out of the car and stood waiting on the edge of the pavement.

The man braked his bicycle to a halt, leaned it to the side and swung his leg over the saddle. After shifting the weight of a cumbersome wicker basket filled with empty wine bottles that was strapped to his back, he stood erectly in front of Bradley with a pleasant smile. He looked to be middle-aged, his face blotched and leathery as if from years in the sun. Bradley raised his hand in a friendly gesture of greeting.

"Can you tell me if this is the way to Comiso?" Bradley asked, with exaggerated slowness.

"*Spiacente,*" the man replied in a rasping voice. "*Non capisco.*"

"Comiso? Is this the right road to Comiso?"

"Ah, Comiso! *Avanti diritto,*" the man said, pointing ahead. "*Si, avanti diritto.*"

With that, the man mounted his bicycle and pedaled away, waving an amicable farewell. Bradley turned to Lizzie in the car with an expression of exasperation and made a gesture of futility.

"What do you think he said?" Lizzie asked.

"I don't know, but I hope he said we're going the right way."

"You should have used your hands more, like Carlo told us."

"Well, if Carlo can figure out how to say 'Is this the way to Comiso?' with his hands, then more power to him. I couldn't."

They drove on, again passing the man on his bicycle. They waved as they went by and he waved back, still grinning broadly. Some miles farther on they came to the clearly marked Vizzini-Caltagirone road.

Bradley was greatly relieved. He was struck by a surprising sense of urgency as he turned north, into the Sicilian mountains. Somewhere ahead lay the place of his final battle, that one dreadful day of combat that still played out in tormenting dreams like an old war movie. He wanted to find his nether world and confront it. And this time he would drive away unscathed with Lizzie at his side.

"I'm sorry I doubted you," Lizzie said. "You may know where you're going, after all."

"Don't forget, I've been here before."

"Yes, but that was a long time ago. And you're always complaining that your memory isn't so good anymore."

"Depends on when I learned what I'm trying to remember. If I learned it when I was young, I probably still remember it. If I learned it last week, well . . ."

"Seems to me you're still pretty sharp for a man your age. I was about to say, for an old man. But they say age is relative. You know what I've always wondered—relative to what?"

Bradley's tension soon eased with Lizzie's happy chatter. No doubt she was inflating her cheerful mood for his benefit, but she was getting the result she wanted. He always had found solace in the sound of Lizzie's voice, and he was content to drive in silence and let her talk. She talked about the Sicilian countryside and the hotels they'd stayed at. She speculated about Carlo and what kind of family he came from, and repeated that he was much different from the stereotypical Italian waiter she had expected.

After a time, she came back to the mission at hand. "Is this beginning to look anything like the place we're hunting for?" she asked, studying the passing landscape. "Or can you tell?"

"It sure does. I remember it was really tough to get our heavy stuff in here. No way to go around, with hardly any roads. This was a hell of a place to fight a war."

"I don't think there's ever been a good place to fight a war."

"That's true, but there must be places better than this."

Sharp curves marked the highway's unnatural intrusion into the mountains. Bradley looked about. He was careless for only an instant, gazing off toward a distant range, and the car bumped off the pavement onto a rough shoulder. He tried to right his mistake but it was too late. They were in the ditch, the little Fiat crunching to a stop as he plied the brakes hard. The vehicle tilted awkwardly and felt as if it was about to roll onto its side.

"Are you all right, Lizzie?" Bradley called out excitedly. "My god, I've done it now!"

"I'm okay. Let's see if we can get out before we turn over."

They pushed open the high-side door and crawled carefully from the car. Bradley got down on hands and knees and studied the situation. He inspected the front of the car, then went to the rear and did the same. He stood up and dusted himself off, all the while with an expression on his face that Lizzie would describe later as both sorrowful and funny.

"Damn it all," he said. "How could I have been so reckless!"

"We weren't hurt," Lizzie said. "That's the main thing. And it doesn't look like there's any damage to the car."

"None that I can see. But I don't know how we're going to get it out of the ditch. Maybe I can find a phone and call the rental agency in Catania, but I don't know how to explain to them where we are."

"We'll get help. If we wait here long enough, someone's bound to come along."

Lizzie had barely finished speaking when they heard an automobile. It rounded a curve and came into view, a highly polished green Chrysler sedan that looked out of place on the narrow Sicilian highway. Bradley stood with his hands raised in a signal of distress. The car made a hasty stop and a back-seat passenger stepped out. He was tall and heavy-set, well-dressed, with black hair and mustache.

"*Avete un problema?*" he said pleasantly.

"I'm sorry," Bradley responded. "I don't speak Italian. Do you by any chance understand English?"

"I not only understand English, I speak *American* English," the man said. "And it's not by chance. I'm from Detroit. And I'm guessing you're Americans, also. Correct?"

"We sure are. Brad and Lizzie Morris from Memphis, Tennessee. I'm afraid I was careless and took my eye off the road."

"It happens. My name is Jack De Luca." He extended his hand to Bradley first, and then to Lizzie. "It looks like the two of you are all right, though. Is there any damage to the car?"

"Not that I can tell. But I don't know how we're going to get it out of the ditch and back on the road."

"We'll get you some help," Jack De Luca said. "Come, get in. We'll have you on your way again in no time."

De Luca held a rear door open and Bradley and Lizzie crawled into the back seat. The only other occupant of the car was the driver, a rather good-looking but serious young man who studied them in the mirror. De Luca went around and got in the front door, seating himself beside the driver.

"This is Paolo, who drives me where I need to go so that I don't end up in the ditch the way you did," he said, turning to face the back-seat passengers. "Paolo, these are some new American friends of mine. Brad and Lizzie from Memphis, Tennessee."

Paolo nodded by way of the mirror, but said nothing.

"Now if it's all right with you, I'm going to have Paolo take us to a farm house up the road here and see if we can get some help," De Luca said. "I think a tractor will do it, if they happen to have one. If not, maybe a team of stout horses."

"We'd appreciate that," Bradley said. "I didn't know what we were going to do, except maybe try to find a telephone and call the car rental agency."

"Have you tried the Sicilian telephone system? This is the only advice I'm going to offer: Don't use it if you don't have to!"

Jack De Luca turned to his driver and said something in Italian. The young man listened intently, nodded, but said nothing.

"Your Italian sounds perfect," Lizzie said. "And you're from Detroit?"

"I get by," De Luca said, and smiled.

"What do you do back home in Detroit, Mr. De Luca?" Bradley asked.

"Please, call me Jack. I'm in the import business. I specialize in high-quality products from Italy."

"Are you here on business or pleasure?"

"A little of both, actually. My business brings me to Sicily a couple of times a year, usually. But if you go back a generation or two my family roots are here, so it's also something of a homecoming."

As the car neared a side road, De Luca spoke to the driver and pointed to the right. The driver slowed almost to a stop, and cautiously turned into a country lane that proved little more than a rutted path up the side of the mountain. The heavy car bumped along slowly, like a ship wallowing in a rough sea.

"There's likely a farmer up here somewhere who will help us," De Luca said. "We'll get you back on the road so you can be on your way again."

They soon were at the front door of a farmhouse, a modest stone structure built low to the ground with small windows and a red tile roof sloped at such a slight angle that it appeared almost flat. There was no porch—not even a step, as the doorsill was at ground level. Two small outbuildings behind the house completed the farmstead. There was no fence or other enclosure and three scraggly olive trees and what looked to be either an orange or lemon tree provided the only shade.

The front door stood open.

Jack De Luca again said something to Paolo, who got out of the car and went to the door. Momentarily, an old man emerged from the house. The young driver engaged him in brief conversation, then the two strode toward the car, the old man smiling brightly. Although the day was hot, he wore a heavy black suit with a white shirt open at the collar. He was a handsome man, of medium height and strong build, with thick, unruly gray hair and piercing black eyes set deep in a bronzed face with classic Sicilian features.

"*Buongiorno,*" Jack De Luca said through the open car window. "*Come state?*"

"*Sto bene, grazie,*" the old man replied.

De Luca alighted from the car and occupied the farmer in an energetic discussion. After a minute or two of conversation he opened the rear door and addressed his back-seat passengers.

"He says he'll be glad to help. Please get out and come inside while he gets ready."

The old man, after saying a few words to a woman who stood in the doorway, went around the end of the house toward one of the outbuildings. Bradley and Lizzie followed Jack De Luca to the house, where the smiling woman beckoned them inside. She was short and round, with silver-gray hair pulled in a tight bun at the back of her head. Her drab gray dress was covered by a white apron overprinted with brightly colored flowers.

"*Buongiorno,*" the woman said, standing aside and motioning them in. She pointed the way to a table by the window and four wooden straight chairs, two at the table and two standing sentry-like against the wall. She spoke rapidly to De Luca, then stood smiling shyly at Lizzie.

"She wants the lady to stay and visit while her husband helps with our problem," De Luca said. "She says she doesn't get much company, and she'll welcome the opportunity to get acquainted. Her name is Donata and her husband is Silvestro."

Lizzie returned the woman's smile. "Please tell her I'll be delighted," she told De Luca. "Tell her we'll have an interesting conversation, even if neither of us understands a word the other says. Does she speak any English?"

Jack De Luca and the Sicilian woman engaged in a brief dialog, after which De Luca turned again to Lizzie. He seemed to enjoy his role as a go-between. "She speaks no English," he said. "She says language is not as important as feelings, and she hopes you will enjoy her hospitality."Lizzie reached out and touched the woman's arm. The woman guided her to a chair at the table and motioned for her to sit. Lizzie said "thank you," and turned to Bradley, who had stood by silently while the conversation went on among the other three. "You go with the men and get the car out," she said. "You can come back and pick me up here. I'll be fine."

Silvestro, as it turned out, had neither the tractor nor the team of stout horses Jack De Luca had hoped for. Instead, he produced a single mule, old and tired-looking, harnessed with little more than a collar at the shoulders and a rope halter. A coil of rope swung from the collar. When the four men arrived back at the scene of Bradley's mishap, the farmer surveyed the site ruefully. Then he spoke with De Luca, gesturing and pointing, and waited for De Luca to transmit his findings to Bradley Morris.

"He wants to pull you out forward, the way the car's facing," De Luca told Bradley. "He's afraid that if he pulls you out from behind you'll run over his damned mule!"

"I don't think we can get it out that way," Bradley declared. "It seems to me our best hope is to pull it out backwards. The brakes work just as well in reverse as they do going forward!"

De Luca passed that information on to Silvestro, who listened impatiently and shook his head, then said something that obviously restated his own position in quite forceful terms. Irritation was clear in his voice.

"He says not to be impolite, but his mule is the most valuable thing he owns. He says it must be the way he says or he won't do it," Jack De Luca reported. "I think you're right, but you may as well let him try it his way."

Bradley capitulated. He was certain the mule wasn't strong enough to pull the car out of the ditch from the front. The wheels would gain little traction and the vehicle's own power would be of only limited benefit trying to move forward. But De Luca was correct: They might as well let the old man try, and hope that if his plan didn't work he would come around to their point of view.

De Luca gave the go-ahead. Silvestro got down on hands and knees at the front of the little yellow Fiat and scraped away dirt and rocks until he found something to tie his rope to. After giving the rope a hard yank to test his knot, he straightened up and looped the other end twice around tie-horns on the mule's collar. Bradley got in the car and started the engine. Jack De Luca and Paolo got behind to push.

The old farmer tugged at the halter. The mule dug in and hunched its back. Bradley put the car in gear and released the clutch.

"Avanti, mulo, avanti," Silvestro shouted.

The car's drive wheels spun impotently in the loose dirt and gravel. The farmer yelled again at the animal, urging it forward, and pulled at the halter. The mule strained. The rope stretched until Bradley was sure it was about to snap. Then the car moved forward ever so slightly. The drive wheels made contact with solid rock and the Fiat and the mule both lurched forward. In the blink of an eye the car was back on the roadway.

The sudden movement took De Luca and Paolo by surprise. Paolo was able to maintain his balance but Jack De Luca sprawled headlong in the dirt.

"Bravo!" he shouted, picking himself up and knocking dirt off his trousers. "Bravo!"

The old farmer said nothing. Bradley saw an expression of fulfillment on his face, though, and noted that he patted the mule with great affection. There was no discernible smugness, only satisfaction.

Back at the farmhouse, all offers of compensation were summarily rejected. Jack De Luca explained that Silvestro would be insulted if Bradley persisted in trying to pay for his services. Helping those in need was something one was expected to do, De Luca said, whatever the need might be. The farmer had little material wealth to offer, but he was honored to be able to put his stout mule to work for Bradley and happy to extend hospitality to the visiting Americans. Silvestro and his wife would be pleased if all the visitors would stay for supper.

"He said he will kill a chicken," De Luca said. "Paolo and I will have to be getting on, but I assure you that the two of you would be most welcome to stay and visit for a while."

"Would it be an insult if we don't?" Bradley asked. "We need to move along, too. But I'm so grateful for his help, I'd hate to insult him by not accepting his invitation."

De Luca talked briefly to Silvestro. The old man shrugged his shoulders in a "don't care" gesture, then responded verbally. He stood by expectantly as De Luca translated.

"He understands," De Luca said. "He wonders, though, if you can't find time to at least stay and have a glass of wine?"

"Surely we can take time for that," Lizzie said, turning to Bradley. "They've been so nice to us, it's the least we can do. And maybe Mr. De Luca and Paolo could manage just a while longer, to help us understand."

Bradley agreed. Jack De Luca and Paolo conferred quickly and De Luca said the two of them could stay a few minutes more. Paolo was highly skilled at driving the mountain roads and probably could make up time if need be. Anyway, he was more on vacation than business and didn't have anything too important on his schedule.

Donata brought clean glasses and replenished a bowl of olive oil and plate of bread she had fixed earlier for Lizzie. Silvestro opened a cabinet and brought out a bottle of deep burgundy-colored wine. He poured six glasses. Everyone joined in a round of salutations.

Bradley put the glass to his lips without drinking, hoping his host would not notice.

"He asks if you've ever been to Sicily before," Jack De Luca said after the formalities.

"Tell him I was here in the war," Bradley said. "And tell him I've come back to see the places where I fought."

When De Luca passed that information along, Silvestro's demeanor abruptly changed. His friendly smile was replaced by a dark scowl. Could this be a reflection of old enmity? Bradley wondered. The Sicilian had known all along that his visitors were American. Surely the fact that Bradley had fought in the war would not of itself have brought the sudden change.

Donata quickly explained. Her husband had bitter memories of the war, she told Jack De Luca. He had been forced to fight in the Italian army, even though he hated the alliance with Hitler. And more important, his younger brother was killed in battle only kilometers from where they stood. He had no quarrel with the Americans, she said, but rather with the Germans, who used Italian soldiers as little more than human shields.

While De Luca repeated Donata's explanation to Bradley and Lizzie, the old Sicilian couple stood silently. Donata took her husband's hand and gently patted his arm.

"Can you tell him how sorry we are?" Bradley asked De Luca. "And please, let him know we'd like to hear his story if he doesn't mind telling us."

Even as Jack De Luca translated Bradley's request, Silvestro turned to a cabinet in a corner of the room and picked up three pieces of silverware. Carefully, he placed on the table two forks, about a foot apart.

"*Americano,*" he said, indicating one of the forks. And the other: "*Tedeschi.*" Germans.

Positioning it carefully between the two forks, he laid a spoon on the table. He looked directly into Bradley Morris's eyes and paused, as if questioning whether he needed to explain. The others were quiet until he spoke again.

"*Italiano.*"

"Tell him I understand," Bradley said to De Luca. "The Germans put the Italians between them and the American forces. We knew that. The German's did it all the time."

Jack De Luca and Silvestro conversed briefly. Tears welled up in the old man's eyes and his shoulders slumped forward. His wife again took his hand and patted him soothingly. While the old couple was occupied, Bradley surreptitiously switched glasses with Lizzie.

"He says the Germans mined the field behind the Italians and retreated," De Luca said. "That left the Italians in no man's land, facing the Americans in front and German mines in the rear. He says it was a German mine that killed his brother—not an

American bullet. That is why he bears no ill will toward the Americans. Many Italians were killed and wounded, and many more captured. He says the Americans treated their prisoners well."

"Was he captured?" Bradley asked.

Again, Jack De Luca queried the old farmer.

"He says no, he was not captured. He simply found a bicycle and rode away—away from the army, away from the war, away from the death of his brother. He says he just quit and went home. He says the battlefield was no more than twenty kilometers from where we stand, as the crow flies, but he's never been back."

Bradley saw tears in Lizzie's eyes, and even Paolo momentarily dropped his reserve and put a sympathetic hand on the old man's shoulder. Jack De Luca put a hand on his arm and said something gently in Italian. Silvestro responded to them all by raising his wine glass.

"*Amici,*" he said simply. "*Grazie, grazie.*"

Jack De Luca said it was time to go. He would have to change his plans a bit, no matter how fast Paolo drove. But he did not mind. He had enjoyed this day immensely and he would remember it for a long time to come. He spoke generous words of thanks and farewells to their hosts for the Morrises as well as for himself and Paolo. There was a final round of handshakes, then Lizzie and Donata embraced for a last time. The old Sicilian couple stood in the door and waved as the visitors walked to their cars.

"Till we meet again," Jack De Luca said cheerfully. "Here's my card. By all means look me up if you're ever in Detroit. Drive carefully, Mr. Morris. Next time we might not find a friendly farmer with such a stout mule!"

"I can't tell you how grateful we are—or how lucky you happened by when you did."

"Funny how life works out sometimes, isn't it? Just glad I was able to help." Jack De Luca waved and Paolo tipped his cap as the big Chrysler pulled away.

As Bradley eased the little Fiat carefully down the rutted lane, he felt almost exultant at the way things had turned out. "I guess old soldiers have a lot to commiserate over, even if they don't speak the same language," he said to Lizzie.

"What a wonderful old couple. I think Silvestro may be as sturdy as his mule!"

"They give me hope that we can do as well."

"Donata showed me a picture of her grandson, if I understood her right. It was a little boy, but I think she said he's twenty now. Neither of us understood a word the other said, but I talked about our grandchildren and I could tell she knew what I was talking about. I think mothers—and grandmothers—share their feelings, even when they don't understand. I'll have a lot to tell Anna when we get home."

When they reached the end of the steep lane, Bradley gunned the Fiat back onto the highway and once again they were on their way to Vizzini.

4

The terrain changed dramatically as they traveled farther inland from the coast. They no longer were climbing to higher altitudes. The mountains leveled off into a barren world of granite and limestone with sporadic vistas of imposing beauty. The highway generally ran parallel to the ridgelines, but to Bradley's chagrin there often were stretches where it wound among small peaks, edging deep gorges, a precipitous drop-off on one side and sheer rock outcroppings on the other. Steep grades taxed the modest power of the Fiat.

He shifted to a lower gear. "These hills are almost too much for this little car," he said. Lizzie nodded agreement. "And I think I'd feel safer in a bigger one, like Mr. De Luca's," she said.

"A big car would be good out here, but we'll be happy with this one when we hit town again. The streets in these old cities don't handle cars very well."

"I think it's safe to say they didn't plan for automobile traffic. The travel book says Vizzini and Caltagirone have been here for centuries."

"I suppose so. The last time I saw this part of the world, Vizzini and Caltagirone were nothing more than dots on a map—objectives we were fighting like hell for. You'd have thought the whole future of mankind depended on us capturing those two little dots on a map."

"I think maybe it did, in a way. It was something that had to be done, but like I've said before you paid a terribly high price."Bradley shifted in his seat. "I don't know," he said. "For a man who left Sicily more dead than alive, I've done all right. But

I still can't help thinking what a waste it was to lose young men like Carson Streator."

"Yesterday, on the beach—that had to be hard."

"Yes, it was. But I got through it okay. I guess I expected there to be visible scars from the fighting, but the earth seems to heal better than we do. What I'll remember now is a beautiful beach. This trip's brought some surprises, Lizzie. We stay in nice hotels and meet nice people and see a peaceful countryside, and then in two or three days we'll go home and Sicily will be a pleasant memory."

"The trip will be worth a lot if it leaves you with pleasant memories," Lizzie said. "That's what we hoped for, isn't it?"

"Yes, and I think it will work. I was afraid that seeing these places again might just bring it all back and make things worse. But that didn't happen on the beach. I can't quite explain it, but I felt a big sense of relief. I'm not afraid of the battlefield now."

Lizzie did not respond, but reached across and put her hand gently on his knee.

When prominent road signs warned of a dangerous highway intersection ahead, Bradley slowed abruptly, and had ample time to see that directions to Vizzini and Caltagirone matched his expectations. Vizzini was close by, to the east, and Caltagirone lay in the opposite direction. "I want to see Vizzini, though I don't think there's much to it," he said.

"We need to get something to eat. Anyway, I have to pee!"

"So do I. And I'm getting pretty hungry."

A few minutes later they were in the small city. Compared to Gela and Ragusa, it was even more exotic—its streets the worst they had encountered, choked and narrow, built on a town plan that surely was ancient even by Sicilian standards. They found a modest side-street *trattoria*, where they were warmly welcomed by a woman who served as cook, waitress, and cashier and who from all appearances lived upstairs. She offered no menu, but quickly had focaccia and generous bowls of caponata on their table, along with basins of olive oil and a decanter of full-bodied wine.

"I wish I could drink the wine today," Bradley told Lizzie quietly. "Do you think she'll be offended if I ask for coffee?"

"Of course not. You have a right to order anything you want. I'll drink the wine. Do you think we can make her understand?"

That turned out not to be a problem. Lizzie barely uttered the word and the woman rushed to the kitchen and returned with a coffee pot and cups, then stood by and watched in anticipation as they ate, eager for reaction. They tried to make it clear that they enjoyed her cooking. She brought more caponata, refilled Lizzie's wine glass from the decanter, and poured more coffee for Bradley.

The woman spoke no more than a few words of faulty English, but had little difficulty understanding their needs. She was small and wiry, very pretty, with soft brown eyes and gleaming black hair that had no trace of gray although she obviously was beyond middle-age. It occurred to Bradley that she must have been quite beautiful as a girl. I wonder if she stood out among the girls of Vizzini the way Lizzie stood out in Simpson's Ridge, he thought to himself. He was curious about her family and regretted the language barrier that kept them from learning more.

They lingered in the little restaurant as long as they dared. It was as if they had been there often, almost like they were family. In any case, they had no reason now to hurry; they'd want no dinner in Caltagirone. As they stood up and made ready to leave, they tried to express their satisfaction with the food and service but knew their words would not be understood. Lizzie put a hand on the woman's arm and smiled and the woman smiled back in a knowing way.

Back on the sidewalk, in the brilliant sunshine, Bradley shaded his eyes and looked in both directions. "I don't think I know where the car is," he said. "We came around one corner, but it looks the same both ways. Do you remember a street name?"

"I don't think there was a sign," Lizzie said. "If there was, I didn't see it."

They agreed on a direction and started walking. The stone sidewalk was rough and narrow, visibly worn by the tread of feet over hundreds of years. At the first corner, they saw the yellow Fiat parked a few yards down the hill on a side street. It looked more compact than Bradley had remembered.

"I'm beginning to feel real affection for this little car," Lizzie said. "I think we ought to give it a name."

"And I think we ought not to give it a name. You get too attached to things anyway. Start calling it by name and you won't want to give it up when it comes time to leave."

"Well, come to think of it, wouldn't you like to have it back home? You'd be a dashing figure zipping around Memphis in something like this."

Bradley opened the door for her. "Actually," he said, "I'll be kind of glad to get back to the old Buick."

As they drove back through Vizzini, it struck them as much more vibrant. More people were out, in some places crowding the sidewalks and spilling into the constricted traffic lanes. This time they backtracked, following the same streets they had traveled before but going in the opposite direction. They made slow progress. Bradley was relieved when they reached the edge of town, and reassured a short time later by a sign promising that Caltagirone was only fifteen kilometers ahead.

They soon found themselves on a better road, but there were more cars and, now, lots of heavy trucks. The mountains were more daunting. Instead of paralleling the ridgelines, this route transversed the mountain crests and valleys at a right angle like a stitch threaded across the wale of corduroy fabric. There was an endless series of long, steep climbs followed inevitably by menacing descents. High bridges crossed numerous small rivers. Most of the rivers were dry, or nearly so, and the Sicilian countryside lay parched and brown in the afternoon sun.

"This is not the way I'll remember Sicily," Lizzie said. "Out here it seems remote, but the little cities are beautiful and that's what I'll remember. And the people."

"I wish we had ignored that old woman in Gela," Bradley said, as if he hadn't heard. "I can't get her out of my head."

"Nonsense. I know you don't believe in fortune tellers, and neither do I. But she looked so poor I didn't have the heart to pass her by."

"I know, but—"

"Forget about her, Brad. Remember what we came to see. We're looking for the place where you fought, right?"

"Yes," Bradley said, "and it was somewhere over there." He pointed off to his left, to the south, where the Mediterranean lay in the distance. "We would have been fighting our way up one of these river valleys—but they all look alike, and I've no way to tell which one it was."

"Were there any landmarks you can remember?"

"None that come to mind. I don't even know if these little rivers have names. I suppose somebody higher up knew exactly where we were, but all we knew was that we were fighting our way toward Vizzini and Caltagirone. After the first two days the fighting got a lot tougher and we weren't moving much."

"And that's when you got hit," Lizzie said softly. "So it was somewhere out there."

"I got hit and Carson Streator was killed."

At the foot of the next long mountain decline the highway shoulder widened, and Bradley eased the Fiat off the road onto a rocky, relatively level area of bare ground that overlooked one of the streams. Dust swirled around them as he brought the car to a quick stop.

"Be careful," Lizzie said. "Mr. De Luca may not come along the next time we have trouble."

"I know you're joking, but don't worry—I learned my lesson!"

They got out of the car and flexed tired backs and limbs. Lizzie walked toward the bank of the river. This one had water, slow-moving and peaceful, rippling through confined channels that threaded their way among the small granite boulders that were the most prominent feature of the river bed. The water was clean and clear.

"I never see a place like this without thinking of Limestone Creek," she said as Bradley caught up. "Remember?"

"How could I ever forget Limestone Creek?"

"That was a long time ago, Brad."

"Sometimes it doesn't seem so long. Back in Simpson's Ridge, when we were young, before the war and all . . . sometimes it doesn't seem so long ago."

He reached out to her and they stood in a long embrace, after which they made their way, hand-in-hand, down to the river's edge. There was a steady drone of traffic across the bridge over their heads, but the placid stream made this a quiet and restful place that could have been miles from the rest of the world. They might have been back on Limestone Creek, back in that cherished time in Kentucky when they were carefree teenagers falling in love.

Service at the Villa San Mauro in Caltagirone was brisk and efficient. They were in their room in a matter of minutes. In the fading afternoon sun, mid-day heat had given way to cooling breezes that drew them to the balcony. The view was breathtaking. Looking down the Via Roma past the municipal plaza, they could see the fabled Santa Maria del Monte Stairway and the ancient cathedral beyond. Everything Lizzie's travel book promised, and then some. Caltagirone was a truly stunning city.

"It's beautiful!" Lizzie exclaimed. "We'll get to Chicago and Matt and Sarah will ask what we saw, and I can't begin to describe this place! Could you?"

"I don't think I could do it justice," Bradley said.

"How's your leg holding up to all this running around?"

"I'm doing pretty well," he said.

"I know you won't complain, Brad, even if the leg pain's killing you."

Bradley always walked with a pronounced limp and his step had grown more hesitant as the day wore on. Lizzie was correct, though. Pain was an element of life he had taken for granted ever since the day on the battlefield when shrapnel mangled his left leg just above the knee. Only the courageous action of a medic, who risked his life to crawl through heavy fire to reach him, and the skill of a battlefield surgeon had saved the limb from amputation. Army doctors marveled that he had not bled to death and said it was his strong will to live that saved him. In his own mind, it was his determination to get home to Lizzie.

Three operations and countless hours of physical therapy had worked wonders, but he still had the tiresome limp, a mass of ugly scars, and a level of pain that varied according to circumstances but never went away completely. He never talked about his injury. He was hurt in that final battle, yes, but Carson Streator was killed. Bradley had vowed long ago not to complain.

Lizzie seemed to understand, and quickly changed the subject. "I'm sorry you couldn't find the battlefield," she said. "Is it a big disappointment? If you want, we can spend more time looking tomorrow."

Bradley gazed off toward the cathedral, considering the full meaning of Lizzie's question. "Maybe it doesn't matter all that much," he said. "It was there, right where we were. The 45th was fighting all over the place, and our little stretch was only a tiny part of the big picture. I think we were close enough."

"Are you sure? We can ask around. Surely there are locals who still remember the war."

"I'm sure. Somehow, I thought that seeing the actual place where Carson Streator died might make a difference. It just seemed like such an awful, god-forsaken place, nothing worth a man's life. Out there in some dry river bed it still might look that way. But that ignores the people, like the old couple who were so good to us. And now I've seen Vizzini and Caltagirone, and there are good people here, too. I think seeing the people has helped."

Lizzie persisted. "Are you going to be sorry later if we don't keep trying?"

"No. I'm content with what I've seen."

"The old man, Silvestro—he still seems very bitter about the loss of his brother. And you think that could have been in the same battle?"

"Yes," Bradley said. "I really think it might have been. And he said he's never been back to the battlefield. His brother was a young man and he feels guilty because his brother died and he didn't."

"Yes, I think so."

With the sunset, the scene before them gradually underwent a series of subtle changes. The gleaming white marble, visible in every direction, first turned to soft gold and then to hues of bronze and red and finally to varied shades of gray. Struck by the sheer beauty of it all, they fell silent as the transformation took place before their eyes. Twilight came fast and lights began to show in the darker areas of the city.

They would have been content to stay on the unlit balcony for hours, but the need to make plans for the rest of their stay in Sicily eventually forced them inside. With no reason to search further for old battle sites, Bradley said, they should make the best of the time they had left. He went back to his road maps and calculated that they were little more than a hundred miles from Palermo to the northwest. If they traveled by way of Agrigento and across the interior of the island it should be an easy trip. And time for stops along the way. From Palermo, they would drive along the northern coast to Messina, and from there down to Syracuse and back to Catania for their last night in Sicily and return flight to Rome.

"We'll be coming down the Ionian coast right along here," he said, pointing out a route on the map. "We ought to have a good view of Mount Etna. Arnold Calder would never forgive me if I missed that."

Lizzie made a list of places they wanted to see, starting early in the morning with the temple ruins at Agrigento. Bradley carefully plotted routes, distances, and approximate driving times, using the motor club map. They had become ordinary tourists.

Lizzie was radiant. "We need to do some shopping," she said. "Maybe in Palermo. I'd like to get something for Anna. And the grandchildren, of course. It will have to be something small for Beth, that we can send to California."

Bradley frowned. "She ought not to be so far away," he said.

"I know. I don't want to sound selfish, but I wish Paul had never considered Los Angeles. I thought he was doing well in Memphis."

"Of course he was. A surgeon can do well anywhere. I think he wanted the glamour of California. And there are more German cars out there."

"Don't be sarcastic, Brad. You can't still hold it against Paul that he drives a Mercedes."

"I can as long as it's German."

Lizzie, he knew, would not pursue this argument. She accepted his deep-seated dislike for all things German, even automobiles. She quickly turned the subject back to their grandchildren: "It's hard to believe, but Beth's almost thirteen now. We've missed a lot of her growing-up years."

"I know. Mark's and Jeff's, too. But we lost them because Matthew's work took him to Chicago, so he didn't have a choice like Paul did. Remember when Matt came home from Vietnam? He said he'd seen as much of the world as he cared to, and he'd live the rest of his life in Memphis. And I know Sarah and the boys didn't want to go. But he had to go where the company sent him, or lose his good job."

"Maybe Paul had good reasons, too."

"If he did he sure kept them to himself."

Bradley did not mean to be cynical. He had yet to see a place that suited him better than Memphis, and until now he had always stayed pretty close to home after the war. If he could have things his way, Jennie and Matthew would still live in Memphis, where he and his father and grandfather before him were born, and keep the Morris family together for generations to come.

Lizzie's eternal optimism—it was a wonder to him how she managed it—had helped him deal with the fact that this no longer was possible. She said they had a good life, they were in good health and looked after one another, and with the children and grandchildren all gone they had nobody else to answer to. But he knew that she still missed their only granddaughter terribly.

Lizzie ignored his sarcasm. "I hope they'll bring Beth to visit again before too long," she said. "It seems so long since we've seen her."

"It's been a year. A child can change a lot in that length of time. I lost out on so much with Jennie and Matt, but by the time you realize how fast it's happening it's too late. You don't get to go back and do it over."

"But you had to work such long hours then, Brad. You had to put food on the table and clothes on our backs, and we stretched things to buy the big house and the overtime helped make the mortgage payments. You were a good father, and Matthew and Jennie would be the first to tell you so."

"I hope so. But I still feel like I missed too much. Once those years are gone, they're gone forever. It'll be good to see Mark and Jeff next week, too."

"I doubt that we'll see them much. They're older now, and have busy lives of their own. But we'd better get to bed. We've got a full day tomorrow."

Bradley Morris was almost asleep when he sensed Lizzie's emotion. Curled against her on the bed, he felt her body tremble and heard an almost inaudible sob.

"What's wrong?" he whispered.

"Yesterday on the beach," she said, her voice muted, "you said I would have found someone else if you had been killed. I can't even think like that, Brad. There never could have been anyone else. If anything had ever happened to you, I would have waited until we could be together again in heaven."

5

Their plane banked through a wide arc over Lake Michigan, which stretched blue and sparkling to the north and east. The smooth surface of the water was disturbed only by a half-dozen small sailboats visible as insignificant specks in the distance. The pilot made a sharp turn that took them over the heart of Chicago and began the final descent for a landing at O'Hare airport. Traffic below crawled sluggishly along Lakeshore Drive and a sightseers' launch that plied the Chicago River trailed a thin white wake as it disappeared under one of the city's many bridges.

Bradley was pensive. He'd been mildly apprehensive during the last leg of the flight, and now he was deeply troubled. He was still haunted by the fierce arguments he'd had with Matthew over Vietnam, and because his and Lizzie's trip to Sicily was directly related to his own war, he was worried that the old disagreements—even though years in the past—might be inadvertently reopened.

The original quarrel was his own fault. He had supported the war in Vietnam early on, but at some point become convinced that young Americans were dying for nothing. Matt also had come full circle, but in the opposite direction: He protested the war at first, but later, even as he neared draft age, came to believe that it was the right thing for his country to do. He felt duty-bound to take part. All hell broke out between them when Matt enlisted in the Marine Corps just about the time his father decided the war was wrong, and both uttered harsh words they would come to regret. Despite Lizzie's valiant efforts to make peace, Matt left for boot camp at Parris Island without so much as a simple farewell for his father.

Bradley had agonized over their relationship almost to the point of an emotional collapse. After perceiving the mortal danger his son had been in at Khe Sanh, he lay awake long hours into the night for weeks, certain that Matt would be killed in action before they had a chance at reconciliation.

Unlike his father, Matt survived his war unscathed physically. Like his father, he suffered serious emotional hurt. Return to a normal civilian life turned out to be a struggle of some proportion and Bradley, painful as it was to admit, had been of little help. The gulf between father and son, two strong-willed men, had been too wide and too deep. Even in the presence of Lizzie, their conversations were awkward and uncomfortable; they managed to get along essentially by avoiding the topic of Vietnam.

Real healing came slowly, as it always does when people are hurt by the ones they love. They rebuilt their relationship over time mainly through Lizzie's careful intervention and the reappearance of Sarah, a childhood sweetheart Matt had lost contact with over the years. Sarah had quickly captivated everyone in the family, beginning with her father-in-law, and a peaceful if superficial alliance between the two men had kept the lid on things for the next several years. The births of two grandsons helped, as well, and eventually all outward evidence of trouble between them had been erased.

Deep down, though, Bradley knew that something still was missing. There was an empty spot that needed to be filled, a dialog yet to be engaged in, a true, heart-felt understanding yet to be reached. He owed this much to Matthew and he owed it to Lizzie.

Lost in thought, he was barely aware that the plane was landing until he felt the jolt and heard the screech of tires hitting the runway. "Well, we made it," he said passively.

"Did you think we might not?" Lizzie teased. "I never knew you had any fear of flying."

"I don't. But I'd still rather take a train if I have a choice."

The plane taxied to the gate and they waited patiently for passengers in the front part of the cabin to depart. Lizzie stood motionless on the aisle and Bradley kept his seat by the window until it was their turn to shuffle ahead and make their exit. They climbed the long ramp into the crowded terminal reception area and looked about for Matthew and Sarah. Sarah saw them first and hurried their way. She was trim and attractive, still young-looking, taller than average and usually energetic. But today she looked tired.

Sarah embraced them both warmly, explaining that Matt had a conference of some sort that kept him from being there. She chattered as they walked, gestured with her hands, complained good-naturedly about how chaotic her life had become.

"I can't wait to hear all about your trip," she said. "Was Sicily all you thought it would be?"

Bradley tried hard not to show his discomfort from the pain in his leg after the long flight, and hoped to sound enthusiastic when he answered her questions. "I'd say it probably was more," he said.

Traffic around O'Hare was heavy and slow-moving, and by the time they got to the comfortable old brick house in Oak Park Matthew was waiting. He was the image of his father: hair black as coal, as Bradley's had been in younger days; deep-set gray eyes, and an expression of amusement, just below the surface, always ready to burst forth. He was beginning to show his age somewhat more than Sarah and had lost weight since they had last seen him.

The two men shook hands. Bradley had a fleeting sense of detachment on Matt's part, but maybe it was his imagination.

Sarah said the boys would be along later.

"Now that they're on their own, do they keep in touch?" Lizzie asked.

Sarah laughed. "More or less," she said. "We don't see them as often as we'd like, but I guess we're lucky they're still close."

"Do they have girlfriends?"

"We'll be the last to know. One of them probably will pop in someday and say, 'Oh, yeah, I forgot to tell you—I'm getting married tomorrow.' That'll be the first we hear of it!"

Bradley asked about Mark's long-standing interest in baseball, and did he get to lots of games?

"Actually, he's still the same rabid St. Louis Cardinals fan you remember from when he was a boy in Memphis," Matthew said. "He goes to Cubs and Sox games once in a while, but he only gets serious when the Cards come to town."

"And Jeff—does he still have his band?"

"Oh, yes. They say they're professional, but I think they play most of the time for next to nothing. Jeff says it's the only way to be discovered, so they never turn down a chance to perform. We'll all go hear them one night if you'd like."

"We'd be disappointed if we didn't," Lizzie said. "I'm happy he hasn't given up his music."

"We'll go Saturday night. Do you miss the hospital, Mother?"

"Honestly, no. But I put in almost as many hours as a volunteer as I did when I worked for pay. But now, of course, I can take time whenever I want for things like a trip to Sicily."

Matthew put a hand on Sarah's arm. "That sounds good," he said. "I think Sarah's job is getting to be less fun every day. Her bank was taken over by a bigger one, and everybody's kind of in limbo as to what may happen next."

Matt repeated many of Sarah's questions about their travels. This was the first time in months that the four of them had been together and there was much to catch up on. They stayed up and talked late into the night, even though Bradley and Lizzie were exhausted from their trip. Bradley felt a sense of relief when the conversation finally ended and they all got ready for bed. None of the old divisions between him and Matt had surfaced. Questions about Sicily were those asked of tourists, not those asked of old soldiers revisiting sites of battle. He slept peacefully.

Saturday arrived sunny and bright, with a cool breeze off Lake Michigan breaking a hot spell that had gripped the city. The Loop was alive with people as Matt and Sarah escorted their visitors on an afternoon stroll down Michigan Avenue's Magnificent Mile, window shopping and looking about more or less at random in the high-priced department stores. Sarah said the festive mood was self-feeding: "People start smiling, and just watch how quick it catches on!"

At the Sears Tower, they took a fast express elevator to the 103rd floor observation deck with its splendid view of the city. Tourists packed the area, peering out through the dark glass and scanning the horizon in all directions.

Matt pointed out prominent landmarks. "Sometimes things that are very impressive at street level don't look like much from up here," he said.

Bradley agreed. "We had the greatest view of Mount Etna you could imagine as we flew out of Catania," he said, "but from the plane it looked like the plaster scenery on a model railroad table."

"You were a bit higher than we are here, I guess. There are still a lot of things I want to ask you about Sicily, and I know the boys are eager to hear about your trip. Which reminds me, we'd better get home and get ready for a big night on the town. Jeff expects us all to be there to hear his band."

It took longer than expected to get back to the car and make the drive home to Oak Park. Mark, the older of the two grand-sons, was sitting on the porch when they arrived at the house. He was a handsome youth who bore a greater resemblance to his mother than to the Morris side of the family, and Bradley had always suspected that he was Lizzie's favorite. But Lizzie was too careful ever to let it show.

Mark had a string of rapid-fire questions.

"You've not changed a bit," his grandmother told him. "Still our curious little Mark. It will be good to see both of you together again, when we get to wherever it is Jeff's playing."

Mark said his brother's band was performing at some new and out-of-the-way club, not yet well known as best he could tell. He cautioned them not to expect too much. "I've only heard this particular combination playing together a couple of times, and it seemed to me they still had a ways to go," he said. "They did have potential, though, and they may be better now."

After dinner, Mark drove them all to a rundown part of town and led the way to a dingy old building that apparently had enjoyed a previous life as a drug store. A narrow marquee extended over the sidewalk and announced the attraction: "Live performance tonight—VANDALIA." There was a crude, hand-lettered billboard tacked to the entrance door that identified Vandalia as "one of Chicago's fastest rising new music groups" and noted a "$2 cover charge for tonight only," a clear tribute to the band's standing.

A line already had formed.

Once inside, they found the little club crowded and dimly lit, the air thick and stale with cigarette smoke and the acrid, mingled odors of beer and sweat. Most of the patrons were standing. They worked their way to a table in a dark corner, hemmed in on all sides by young bodies. Bradley felt very much out-of-place. He could tell that Lizzie was uncomfortable, too. The atmosphere here was different from that on Beale Street, where they sometimes took in the popular Saturday night blues performances. This audience was youthful and boisterous, the room too dark, too crowded. But in time, as his eyes grew accustomed to the low light and he gained a good view of the makeshift stage, he got caught up in the excitement and grew restless for the band.

With a deafening clamor from the crowd, Jeff's musicians appeared. Loud screaming and whistling, clapping, yelling, foot-stomping filled the room, along with youthful compliments in the form of shrill obscenities. This band had a following, no doubt about it.

Vandalia's lead singer commanded the greatest attention. He was brilliantly spotlighted by a thin white beam from somewhere at the back of the room, ceiling high, that followed his every move. Other musicians could be seen in the flash of red, green, and yellow strobe lights, giving their best on guitars and electric keyboard. A frenzied drummer at the back of the stage was nearly obscured by the ubiquitous electronic gear of a rock band.

Words of the singer, mouthed irregularly into a standing microphone, were unintelligible, but no one seemed to notice. The crowd moved in concert with the music. The guitars screamed their passionate message, sweet and terrible, louder and faster, amplified and projected by thrusting speakers until it physically enveloped the listeners, driving into their bodies. Mesmerized by the sound, the young fans responded only to the throbbing beat of the drums and piercing rhythm of the guitars, as if oblivious to everything else. Only the music mattered.

When the room suddenly went dark, Bradley thought there had been a power failure. But it was a ploy to highlight the lead guitarist's solo performance. When the brilliant spotlight pierced the blackness again, a lean, black-clad entertainer, perspiration glistening on his face and beginning to dampen his long straight hair, prowled the stage like a caged animal, stroking a gleaming plastic and metal guitar slung low in front. It was Jeff. His music was pure, his talent obviously several notches above that of the other band members. On this night, with this audience, he was king of the world.

Bradley realized that Matt and Sarah were watching for signs of disapproval, but they needn't have worried. Even though he felt like the most conspicuous outsider, he was enthralled by what he saw and heard, and Lizzie, across the table, looked like a young girl who belonged among those who filled this place, excited and happy.

The band's performance ended all too soon. The crowd called them back for two encores and pleaded for yet another. As Mark explained it, though, the musicians had performed every piece they knew. And anyway, Jeff had told him they believed strongly in the philosophy of always leaving an audience wanting more.

Later, back at the house, there was jubilation. Everyone talked at once, raving to Jeff about how good he was and how much they'd liked his band. Although Jeff still manifested much the same shyness he had shown as a child, there could be no doubt that he was glad for the attention from his family. Lizzie brought out the gifts from Sicily and told the grandsons that their ceramic mugs were from Caltagirone, even though they had bought them in Palermo. She told them Caltagirone was one of the places she and their grandfather had liked best.

"I'll treasure this," Jeff said. "And I'll always remember getting it the night you heard my band for the first time. Count on it—it'll still be around for *my* grandchildren."

On Sunday afternoon, Matthew proposed an outing to the lakefront yacht basin. He said the boats would be out in force on such a beautiful day. Bradley was tired and didn't especially want to go, but reluctant to decline for fear of disappointing his son. Fortunately, Sarah and Lizzie both said they would be content to stay home and enjoy some quiet conversation.

"We still have so much to catch up on," Sarah said, and Lizzie agreed.

Matt readily bowed to the women's preference.

Sarah made a pitcher of strong, sweet tea and brought out ice and glasses. "We've not seen Aunt Catherine in ages," she said, as she handed a glass to Lizzie. "Are she and Walter okay?"

"Yes, they are," Lizzie told her. "We probably will see them next week. I'll tell them you asked."

"Have you heard from Jennie lately?"

"She called just before we left. I'll call her as soon as we get home. I can't wait to tell her about Jeff's music!"

"Jeff still says his musical talent comes naturally because he's from Memphis," Matt said. "I know he's kidding, but I'm not sure there aren't people who believe it. If you're from Memphis you ought to be musically inclined!"

Bradley laughed. "Well, he certainly was surrounded by music in Memphis," he said. "It's the home of the blues, after all, not to mention Elvis."

Sarah, after serving all the others, poured herself a glass of tea. "It's hard to imagine people really thinking that way," she said. "But you never know. Since we moved to Chicago I've heard plenty of wrong-headed stereotypes of Southerners. Especially Southern women. I think our image has been affected way too much by fictional characters like Scarlet O'Hara. I went to a lecture at the University of Chicago and the speaker, a sociologist from South Carolina, I think it was, said the Southern belle has been romanticized to the extent she's more of a caricature than a true historical character. Like the cowboy."

"But there were Southern belles—still are, I suppose," Lizzie said.

"Sure there are. She said Scarlet O'Hara is an accurate depiction of a certain type of woman, not necessarily Southern. Privileged women, I guess. But she said life was hard in the early South and the women had to be strong to get by, not fragile belles like Scarlet."

"I think that's still true for most of us," Lizzie said. "Most women, I mean, Southern or not."

"So do I. And I guess if anyone ever mistook me for a Scarlet O'Hara, they found out pretty quick they were wrong. But I have to admit, when I think of strong Southern women, I think of you."

Lizzie looked embarrassed. "Oh, I'm not strong," she said. "God has been good to me, but I can't take much credit for myself."

"Well, I think you're strong," Matthew said. "And I'm sure Dad does, too, so that's something we all agree on. You're outvoted on this one, Mom."

Sarah asked more questions about Sicily. What was their favorite site, did they meet interesting people?

Bradley said the temple ruins at Agrigento probably would be the most impressive thing they saw and, yes, they met interesting people. "We met a businessman from Detroit on the way to Gela," he said, "and there was a waiter in Palermo who lived here in Chicago for thirty years. He told us he was the bookkeeper for a Ford dealer, and went back to Sicily to take care of his aging mother."

"But you owe Mr. De Luca more than that," Lizzie exclaimed. "And we can't leave out the wonderful old farm couple."

Sarah raised a hand, as if to signal a halt in the conversation. "We can't keep up with your cast of characters," she said. "Who was Mr. De Luca? And how did you happen to meet an old farm couple?"

"I may as well confess to my failings," Bradley said. "Mr. De Luca was the man from Detroit, and he helped us after I carelessly ran off the road and got our car stuck in a ditch. The old farmer had a mule and pulled us out, then we spent some time with him and his wife." He stopped short, suddenly realizing that to say more would be to bring up the war—the topic he had been careful to avoid.

Lizzie quickly bailed him out. "I'd say the most interesting people we met were a couple of young Brits," she said.

Bradley groaned. "I don't think that's a story we need to get into," he warned Lizzie.

"But you've already said too much!" Matthew declared. "Now, you *have* to tell us."

Lizzie waved a hand dismissively. "Brad's embarrassed about it," she said. "But I think it's too funny not to tell. You may find it hard to believe, though."

"Then tell us, for Pete's sake!" Sarah said.

Lizzie looked across the room, smiling at Bradley. "You don't really mind if I tell it, do you?" she asked. "Actually, I think it reflects rather well on you."

Bradley shrugged. "I won't enjoy hearing it, but if you want to tell them, go ahead."

"Well, then. They were a young married couple named Philip and Leslie. We met them in Taormina, and spent most of our last day on the island with them. They seemed like a very nice couple, but we didn't think so highly of them at the end."

"Why?" Sarah asked. "What happened?"

"Oh, your father's right: This is embarrassing. I shouldn't have mentioned them."

Matthew grimaced in exasperation. "You're the one who's always said you can't un-ring a bell," he said. "You can't not tell us now, not after you've piqued our interest like that!"

Lizzie, slightly flushed, laughed and again looked across the room to Bradley. "Help me," she said, mock pleading in her voice.

"You probably shouldn't have started it," Bradley told her. "But Matt's right: You've said too much to quit now."

"Well, okay then. Here goes. After we had played the tourists' role in Taormina, Philip took Brad aside and said they'd enjoyed our company so much they thought we might like to 'double and share' with them that night. Brad didn't know what that meant, of course, but as Philip explained it, it seems that Leslie took a fancy to older men from time to time and found Brad very attractive. And Philip felt that I mightn't object to a good frolic with a vigorous young man! Can you believe it?"

"I guess nothing surprises me any more," Sarah said. "How did you handle it, Dad?"

"I wanted to punch him in the nose once I understood what he meant. But I just told him that's not our way and he said okay, no hard feelings."

It was clear that Matthew and Sarah were trying hard not to laugh, but after a few seconds they couldn't hold back any longer. Lizzie laughed, too. She said she hadn't planned to tell about this part of their trip, but now that she had it didn't seem as embarrassing as she expected. She would not be telling anyone else, though.

They talked more about Sicily, Bradley describing as best he could the beauty of Caltagirone, the hotels and wonderful food, the drive down the Ionian coast and view of Mount Etna. And the coffee! Lizzie marveled again over the ancient ruins in Agrigento and Taormina.

When Matt suggested they all move to the den and watch football on television, Bradley readily accepted. Sarah held back, and after the men were gone said softly to Lizzie, "Do you think the trip will help Dad with his problems over the war? The nightmares and such?"

"I'm hopeful, but it's too early to tell," Lizzie said. "I think he believes it will, and that's a good start. He still feels guilty, Sarah, because he survived and other boys got killed."

"After all these years?"

"Yes. But I think the trip will help. He remembered Sicily as a wasteland, not worth losing lives over. Now he's seen it in a completely different light. Lots of beautiful places, lots of very nice people."

"Will you keep me informed if you see any difference? Matt still has such turmoil over Vietnam. I wonder if it might be good for him to go back over there."

"Of course I will. Isn't it awful what war does to our men!"

"It's terrible," Sarah said. "I just pray that Mark and Jeff never have to go. Every year I'm grateful that they're a step closer to being too old, that if we get into a war someone else's children will have to go. Is that selfish of me?"

"No, Sarah, it's not selfish. It's being a mother."

The few days in Chicago passed quickly. Bradley's feelings were somewhat ambiguous. Their visit seemed terribly short, but he was anxious to get home. Although it had been barely more than two weeks since he and Lizzie boarded a plane in Memphis and set out for Sicily, he felt as if they had been gone much longer. He wanted to get back to his ordinary daily routine, to eat breakfast at his own kitchen table and sleep in his own bed. And though he knew she would not say so, he sensed that Lizzie felt much the same way.

He also looked forward to the trip from Chicago to Memphis on the fast Amtrak *City of New Orleans* passenger train. He still believed that trains were the way to travel, his view admittedly skewed by the years he had worked for the Memphis division of the Illinois Central Railroad.

Mark and Jeff joined their mother and father to see them off. The terminal was busy, but Bradley pointed out that it was nothing like the old days. At one time there would have been a great number of trains coming and going, he said, with arrivals and departures at all hours on many different tracks.

An announcement screen proclaimed that their train would leave on schedule. They hadn't a great deal of time to get aboard. Goodbyes were hurried. There was a swirl of activity, an atmosphere of excitement appropriate to the beginning of a journey, as uniformed coachmen called passengers to their proper cars.

Bradley and Lizzie soon were settled in their seat and the train started to move. It traveled slowly as it exited the city, through what seemed to be endless miles of dirty train yards and the smoke-smudged industrial plants of Chicago's backside, then gained speed rapidly as it glided southward into the open country of the vast Illinois prairie.

6

Bradley Morris had walked the tree-lined neighborhood streets for more years than he cared to remember. Every bump and crack in the sidewalk was familiar. He had seen many of these trees planted as saplings to succeed those ravaged by storm or disease, or others that simply had lived out their life cycles. Some of the younger stock was mature now, though still poor imitations of the majestic old oaks they had replaced. But even oak trees, he had said to Lizzie just the other day, eventually must succumb to old age. Lizzie said that was nature's way.

Colorful chalk drawings on the sidewalk and abandoned toys in random driveways testified to the presence of children. He and Lizzie had watched the transition, as old couples moved on and young families moved in. All this was part of the natural cycle too, according to Lizzie, just like the changing seasons. He supposed she was right. Whatever happened, life went on.

Bradley was a big man, a bit over six feet tall. Lizzie sometimes complained that he was overweight, but he was confident that he could lose weight anytime he chose. His close-cropped gray hair still showed black around the fringes. His clean white Reebok walking shoes contrasted markedly with his otherwise drab but neat dress.

By force of habit, he walked slowly. If he walked too fast or too far his crippled leg was sure to remind him of his physical limitations. In any case, on a day like this it would be foolish to hurry. It was a pleasant time of year in Memphis, the coldest winter days long past and signs of spring all around.

September in Sicily might have been a hundred years ago. He

and Lizzie had quickly fallen back into the routines of daily life when they got home, then the weather turned cold almost overnight, the holiday season was upon them, and they had settled in for the winter. The visit he had planned to Simpson's Ridge to see Arnold Calder had been lost in the shuffle of normalcy. But there was no timetable; Simpson's Ridge was on the list of things to do whenever they got around to it.

They had remembered—or, rather, Lizzie had remembered—to send a note to Jack De Luca. She extended their greetings, thanked him again for his generous aid and hospitality in Sicily, and invited him to visit if he ever found himself in Memphis.

A block from the house Bradley met Anna Corydon, pushing Randolph in a wheelchair. Anna smiled warmly. Her husband sat helplessly, unable to speak, his eyes without expression. There was an instant in which Bradley thought he saw a slight flicker of recognition, then the empty stare returned.

The old man's mouth dropped open on one side and a thin thread of saliva ran part way down his chin. He looked to weigh no more than a hundred pounds, his skin deathly sallow and his only visible movement an uncontrolled, palsied tremor of his left hand. And although the day was warm and sunny, Randolph was covered by a heavy blanket across his lap and over his knees and legs.

Anna asked about Lizzie. What had they heard from Jennie and Matthew? Were their families well?

"I try to get Randolph out at least once a week, now that the weather's good," she said. "But it's been hard since his last stroke. He has to be strapped in the chair, and the sidewalks are so rough I'm afraid he's going to tip over and I won't be able to catch him."

Anna and Randolph Corydon had been their neighbors for as long as they had lived on the street. Lizzie and Anna were closest friends, although they had not been able to spent a great deal of time together since the commencement of Randolph's most recent physical problems. Bradley wanted to say comforting words to Anna, but he was reluctant for Randolph to hear. Whatever dignity the old man had left shouldn't be violated by their free and open discussion of his assorted physical frailties.

They had talked only briefly before the painful resignation in Anna's eyes signaled an end to the conversation. She had to get Randolph back inside. "Please bring Lizzie over and visit us," she pleaded. "It's hard for us to get out. And please remind Lizzie to call me."

Bradley promised that he would. He was about to bid farewell to Randolph, then recognized the futility and said nothing more.

As he walked on, he reflected on Randolph Corydon's condition. Surely it was a terrible injustice for a human being to have to exist in such a helpless state. If there is a god, he mused, why does he allow such misery?

He also thought back to the first time he'd seen Anna and Randolph, a recollection he had tried unsuccessfully to put out of his mind for years. A memory not altogether unpleasant, but one that still left him uncomfortable. On a Saturday afternoon shortly after he and Lizzie moved in next door to the Corydons, he had been stowing packing boxes in the attic and discovered that the attic windows offered remarkable views. From the front, he could see across the street and up and down the block for some distance, and from a single small window on the north side he could see directly down into the Corydons' upstairs bedroom.

Randolph and Anna had been standing in the middle of the room, in full view. He had not intended to spy, but found that he couldn't help but watch as Anna unbuttoned the top of her dress, slipped it down over her shoulders and let it fall to the floor. She removed the rest of her clothing piece by piece, as if by ritual, first exposing her ungirded breasts and then standing fully naked in a shaft of sunlight, facing the window. Randolph undressed too and the couple embraced passionately, stroking and petting, then climbed onto the bed and made love furiously. The passion subsided quickly. The lovers dressed and departed, leaving Bradley Morris, his mouth dry and his face flushed, feeling guilty and embarrassed for having viewed an intimate moment he had no right to see.

He had studiously avoided the new neighbors for some weeks

after that, half afraid that his feelings of guilt would give him away if he had to confront them directly. For a long time he had kept a particularly warm feeling for Anna, the only woman besides Lizzie that he ever had seen unclothed. He was surprised at how sensuous he'd found her, and ashamed of the exhilaration he had felt at the sight of her ample body.

But ironically, as he recalled the incident now, it was not Anna that he pictured in his mind's eye. It was Randolph. What a ludicrous figure Randolph had been that rainy Saturday afternoon all those years ago, a wiry little man with face and arms weathered deep bronze by the summer sun while the rest of his body was chalky white. He considered the pitiful invalid Randolph Corydon had become, and felt sad.

Lizzie was waiting at the door when Bradley got home. Her dark eyes sparkled and a bright smile lit her face. He promptly heard why: Jennie was coming, bringing Beth to Memphis for a week-long visit. All the arrangements were confirmed in a letter that had come in the morning mail.

"Paul is taking a medical team to the Philippines to work among the poor children of Manila," Lizzie explained. "Beth's spring vacation from school is coming up, and Jennie thought it would be a good time to bring her to see us."

Bradley was glad to see Lizzie more cheerful again. It wasn't in her nature to be gloomy, but she had been somewhat melancholy in recent weeks. Only yesterday she had come home from her volunteer work at the hospital questioning whether anyone really appreciated what she did. Jennie's letter had changed all that, and when Lizzie was happy he was happy.

They sat on the veranda with tall glasses of sweet iced tea and enjoyed the mid-day warmth, and even though it still was some time away Lizzie could talk of nothing but Beth's visit. "Jennie says we shouldn't plan much for them to do," she said, looking over their daughter's letter again. "They just want to spend their time at home with us."

"That suits me," Bradley told her. "Anyway, if they're only here for a week there won't be a lot of time for other things."

"We ought to call Matthew tonight, don't you think? It would be nice if he and Sarah could come down that week." Lizzie grew more animated as she talked. She hoped that Mark and Jeff could come, too, for wouldn't it be wonderful to have all of the children and grandchildren together under one roof again!

"And you should call Catherine," Bradley said. "She and Walter probably would like to come if they can."

"Yes, they would. And even if Jennie doesn't want us to make a lot of plans, I'd like to give Beth enough to do to make it a perfect and memorable week. They'll be home in no time, Brad. I can't wait!"

Lizzie was up and about early in the morning. She rarely missed a Sunday at the Park Street Baptist Church, and Bradley knew that she especially looked forward to services today. She had good news to share; her granddaughter was coming.

For his part, Bradley was not enthusiastic about Sunday rituals at Park Street or anywhere else. He hated to let Lizzie go without him, yet he often felt hypocritical in church, pretending to participate when he no longer considered himself a religious person. He would not have to go, of course. Lizzie would call around and find friends to join her, and say she didn't mind if he chose to stay home.

But he was being selfish and inconsiderate. Surely he could bear an hour or so of minor discomfort, understanding how much it meant to Lizzie.

The Park Street congregation, said to have been the largest of any church in Memphis at one time, had steadily dwindled in number through the years. No more than thirty-five or forty of his faithful charges were present when the Reverend Buford Acklin began his morning sermon. And his audience looked even more sparse than that, scattered about a sanctuary designed to hold five times their number. But Pastor Acklin had no reason to expect large crowds; he never had seen his church filled to even half its capacity, and in any event he always had professed to choose quality over quantity, dedication over padded rolls.

Buford Acklin was short and squat with thick red hair and dense eyebrows and a neatly trimmed but unbecoming moustache. To Bradley Morris, he resembled a dozen other men who had pastored the church over the years—not in physical appearance, but in demeanor. They all might have been cut from the same cloth, although those of more recent tenure had been better educated, less firebrand in nature than some of the earlier preachers who came to mind.

When he and Lizzie had first gone to Park Street, the front-row pews were filled regularly by white-haired deacons whose vigorous chorus of "Amens" encouraged the sin-and-salvation, heaven-or-hell evangelists. The old-timers were all gone now and the congregation, including a good number of aging widows, was generally subdued. The newer preachers, Buford Acklin among them, had been forced to find their inspiration within themselves or, as they might claim, from divine revelation.

Pastor Acklin preached eternal life. None would be allowed to doubt his excitement at the good news he had to share. His voice rose and his delivery quickened as he recounted a visit with an elderly woman in a nursing home: "Her doctor says she doesn't have many months to live. But she said, 'Brother Acklin, I'm not afraid to die. I'm looking forward to going home to be with Jesus.'"

He ceased speaking dramatically, clasping his hands behind his back, then turned and paced slowly to the other side of the pulpit. When he spoke again his voice thundered out over the sanctuary.

"Brothers and sisters, I rejoice with that dear woman that Jesus went on to prepare a place for her. I rejoice with her that she can look forward in the faith of her salvation to an eternal life free from all the cares and infirmities of this earthly existence. I rejoice with her that she will be reunited with her dear departed husband, and all those other loved ones who have gone on before, through the grace of Jesus Christ."

Bradley knew what was to come. There was but one way for the sinner, and that way was born-again salvation through the mercy of Jesus. Throughout his entire experience in the church, it had been a rare sermon that did not end on this same note. There would be an emotional appeal to sinners to seek redemption, and in the end the love and righteousness and the sin and hypocrisy all mattered not; the born-again would gain their reward in heaven, while those who failed to see the light were condemned to the suffering of everlasting damnation.

In his mind, Bradley drifted back to Sundays long-past, when he was a young man sitting close beside Lizzie in a little country church in Kentucky. An earlier preacher's words filtered through the layers of memory and the message was the same. He had not questioned the message then, but now there was doubt; the blind faith of the young man could not be his. But there was, also, a disquieting sense of loss, a barely perceptible longing for what used to be.

The congregation was hushed, waiting. Pastor Acklin was building to his climax. He had been true to Bradley's expectations, urging sinners to salvation through the power of the cross. Their prize would be eternal life in paradise.

"Brothers and sisters, Jesus told us we must take no thought of what we should eat or drink, or where we get the clothes on our backs," the pastor proclaimed. "These things are not important! But He said, 'Rejoice ye in that day, and leap for joy'—*leap for joy, brothers and sisters*—'for behold your reward is great in heaven.'"

Minutes later, as his congregation filed from the church, the preacher stood at the door exchanging flattery and enthusiastically pumping the hands of his followers. He greeted Bradley and Lizzie pleasantly, apparently oblivious to the fact that Bradley Morris was not among the most devoted members of his flock.

Lizzie said complimentary things about the young minister on the way home. She never had doubted the message preached by the Reverend Buford Acklin or any other pastor she could remember. For her, the riches awaiting born-again Christians in the hereafter were a matter of firm conviction.

Bradley withheld comment for some time, but finally said, "I only wish Acklin and the rest of them wouldn't be so quick to accept human suffering on earth just because they believe there will be rewards in heaven."

Lizzie did not disagree. "But a lot of people aren't as fortunate as we are, Brad," she said, "and they deserve something to look forward to. As for me, I take great comfort in my faith, and I hope you will too, someday. None of us is going to live forever."

Bradley had no response. Discussions of faith always left him ill at ease. As if sensing his discomfort, Lizzie changed the subject. "Anna wanted us to take that box of books to her sister in Bolivar," she said. "Should we do it this afternoon?"

"Yes, I guess we could. It's a nice day for a drive." He hoped she couldn't hear the relief in his voice.

Lizzie had made potato salad and coleslaw before they left for church, and soon had them on the table. Bradley filled tall glasses with ice cubes and retrieved a pitcher of sweet tea from the refrigerator. While he poured tea, she fixed ham and cheese sandwiches. Bradley remembered that he'd not told Lizzie about seeing Anna and Randolph Corydon the day before and passed along Anna's greetings.

"I'll call her when we get home this evening if it's not too late," she said.

An hour or so later, Bradley stowed the box of books in the trunk of the Buick and let Lizzie know he was ready to go. They drove east, away from the city and into the wooded Tennessee hills, where white dogwood blossoms had started to appear on the sunny southern slopes and the oak trees were beginning to display green fringes of leaves.

He followed Route 64 to Bolivar. They found Anna's sister's house easily and stopped for a short visit, dropped off the books, then drove on through the Chickasaw State Park, leisurely, in no hurry to start home. But it was later than they had expected when they reached Jackson, already past the time they should have turned back.

Bradley was annoyed with himself. "It'll be dark before we get to Memphis," he complained. "Would you mind driving? You can see at night a lot better than I can."

"Yes, if I can get off the back roads and take the interstate."

They stopped and traded places, and soon were caught up in a heavy flow of traffic heading toward the city on I-40.

"We've done our good deed for the day," Bradley said. "Does Anna see her sister often?"

Lizzie never had a chance to answer. At that instant a large buck deer with a full, proud rack of antlers, followed by two mature does and a single younger animal, rocketed from the trees to the right of the highway and ran headlong into the westbound traffic lanes a few hundred feet ahead of the car. Warning lights flashed and tires screeched as drivers braked and swerved in sudden panic. A long tractor-trailer in the outside lane bounced onto the shoulder of the highway.

A heavy station wagon in the passing lane smashed into the buck, blasting it onto the median between the eastbound and westbound lanes. One doe managed to evade the traffic, darting across the highway and disappearing over a high embankment on the south side, while the second one jerked to a stop, whirled, and bounded back toward the right-of-way fence the four animals had just cleared.

The younger animal, terrified and confused, slowed for an instant and then ran directly in front of the Morris's Buick. Lizzie had no chance to evade it. There was a slight thump as the car seemed to brush the animal aside, sending it sprawling onto the grassy median.

Then it was all over.

Five cars, including the heavily damaged station wagon, and two large trucks were halted along the roadside. Other traffic had slowed but kept moving, while people in the stopped vehicles began to alight, hesitantly, and approach one another warily. The driver of the station wagon looked back furtively at the dead buck, moved cautiously around to the front of his automobile and began to inspect the damage. Crumpled steel and broken plastic made evident the violence of the impact when the car smashed into living flesh. The windshield was shattered, apparently from having been struck directly by the big buck's antlers.

Bradley urged Lizzie to stay in the car, at least until he could see what needed to be done, but she insisted on getting out. She stayed behind, though, when he joined a group walking reluctantly back toward the animals.

The buck, strong and graceful only moments before, lay grotesquely in the tall grass. Its neck was broken and its head twisted awkwardly to one side. Both front legs had been snapped in the crash, causing the beast to collapse in a clumsy kneeling position in which it looked as though its final seconds of life had been spent in a desperate act of propitiation, beseeching a merciful divinity. Its eyes were open, staring sightlessly, and its purple-gray tongue dangled from the side of its mouth.

Something stirred near a clump of low highway landscaping shrubs, drawing the attention of the subdued human witnesses away from the dead buck. It was the younger deer, stunned by the Morris car, regaining its senses and trying to struggle to its feet.

Even from the distance of several yards, Bradley could see the terror in the animal's large brown eyes as it fought vainly to regain a standing position. He could see, too, that one front leg had been ripped almost from the shoulder and the deer was bleeding profusely. As he and two men from the other cars approached, the animal kicked frantically in its desperation, rose partly on its rear legs, then sank helplessly back to the ground. Its whole body trembled, its breath came in sporadic gasps. No longer able to control its functions, it dribbled urine from under its belly.

One of the truck drivers joined the little huddle. The men stood silently, impotent in the face of the wretched death struggle unfolding before them.

"God almighty," someone said in a hushed voice. "We ought to put it out of its misery. Has anybody got a gun in your car?"

"I've got a .38 in the cab," the trucker responded. "Reckon that'd do it?"

"Why hell yes. Put the barrel right to its head!"

The driver walked back to his truck, hauled a snub-nosed revolver from under the seat, and returned to the group posted in dismal fascination over the dying animal. He wanted to get it over with, but hesitated.

"I ain't doing nothing illegal, am I? Hell, I'm from Wyoming. I don't know nothing about Tennessee law. I sure can't afford to get into trouble over something like this."

"Shoot it, for God's sake," Bradley Morris demanded. "Don't just let it lie there. It's not against the law to destroy an injured animal to put an end to its suffering."

In truth, Bradley had no notion what the law might be, but he could not bear to see the young deer's agony prolonged. It was preposterous that the animal could still be alive, given the extent of its injuries and the amount of blood it had lost. But the badly maimed deer, certain to die in the end, looked as if it might survive for hours.

"Well, all right then," the trucker said. "I'll shoot it. You fellows are all my witnesses. It's dying sure as hell. Right?"

The trucker pointed the gun directly at the deer's head, from a distance of about a foot, aiming midway between the eyes. The animal no longer had the strength to resist. Despite its terror, it lay placidly, looking at the truck driver in dumb bewilderment. Bradley turned away, unwilling to view the brutality of the shooting—no matter how benevolent the intent. He heard one last sigh from the animal, followed by the report of the .38. Then nothing.

He saw the other travelers, clustered together several yards down the road, viewing the euthanasic slaying in rapt silence. Lizzie was among them and stood with her hand to her mouth, as if stifling a cry.

He could not resist taking one last look at the young deer. The bullet from the truck driver's revolver had killed it instantly, though blood pumped by the last few beats of its heart spurted from the wound in its head. But there was no more trembling in the animal's body; no fear in its eyes, almost closed now; no pain in its torn tissues and broken bones.

Lizzie insisted that Bradley drive the rest of the way home.

She was visibly shaken, and said she felt responsible for the deer's suffering and death. He tried to reassure her, told her over and over that there was no way she could have avoided the animal, that none of what happened was her fault, but she clearly found little solace in his words.

It was late when they got home, both of them bone-weary. Although neither had an appetite, Lizzie fixed snacks and they sat for a time in the kitchen talking about the day's events and how things could change so quickly when something unexpected happened. They went to bed knowing that sleep would not come easily.

Only after Lizzie's rhythmic breathing told him that she finally had drifted into a sound slumber did Bradley allow himself to relax. He slept fitfully for a while, but woke sometime in the middle of the night to Lizzie's restless stirring.

"Are you okay?" he asked.

"Yes, I'll be fine."

"I'm sorry you had such a rough day."

"I don't always tell you when I should, but you're a great comfort to me at times like this," Lizzie said quietly. "I feel sorry for people who have to face the world alone, Brad."

"You've said it often enough: We take care of each other."

7

Lizzie's agenda worked out as if by magic. Except for Paul, the family would be together for Jennie's visit. Matthew and Sarah would come to Memphis for four days, grateful for an occasion to see Jennie and Beth without having to make the long trip to California. The boys planned to join them for at least a couple of days. Catherine and Walter would drive down from Paducah for a weekend. Once again, the big house in Memphis would be filled with happy voices.

Lizzie called the medical center to let people know she'd be taking a break from her volunteer work at the hospital. Then she called Anna Corydon to share her good news. Their talk was happy until the conversation got around to Randolph. Anna said he seemed to be going down hill pretty fast. Lizzie listened quietly, voicing sympathetic support where she could.

After she had hung up the phone, she told Bradley, "I'm more concerned about Anna than I am about him. She's never been one to complain, but her life must be very hard. I can't tell her, but I think Randolph's death would be the best thing that could happen. For her, I mean."

"You and I know that," Bradley said, "but Anna's devoted her life to Randolph. She'll be lost without him."

"Yes, she will. There's no denying that most women outlive their husbands, but that's not easy to face up to. I don't even like to think about it."

"I'm glad it's that way instead of the other way around."

The telephone rang, cutting their conversation short. Bradley was grateful; he did not care to discuss death. He had made sure that Lizzie would be well provided for when he was gone and had no reservations about her ability to get along without him. Lizzie was a strong and capable woman who could look after herself.

He hoped fervently to avoid a lingering death like Randolph Corydon's, partly because the mere thought of not being able to exercise his own free will was intolerable and partly because he never wanted Lizzie to face what Anna was going through. Maybe a sudden illness, and go quickly. Give Lizzie just enough time to prepare for his passing, so that the shock wouldn't be too great.

"That was Lois Burgess," Lizzie said, turning again from the phone. "They're going to be a few minutes late tonight. Or had you forgotten?"

Bradley had forgotten, but wouldn't admit it. They had dinner with Russell and Lois Burgess once a month. Before his retirement, he and Russell had worked side-by-side for nearly two decades. They'd always got on well together, and Lizzie and Lois—a soft-spoken, elegant woman who always seemed an unlikely match for Russell—had become close friends as well.

Russell was in his usual good mood when they met at the inconspicuous neighborhood family restaurant that had become their favorite. He was a small, energetic man, animated in conversation. Lizzie claimed he had more different facial expressions than anybody else she knew. The others willingly let him dominate the conversation.

"Do you know why lawyers don't want to go to heaven?" Russell asked Lizzie, as they waited for their food.

"I could tell you why most of them probably won't," Lizzie said, "but not why they don't want to. So I give up, Russ. Why don't lawyers want to go to heaven?"

"Because they're used to stealing the gold out of your teeth, not having to pick it out of potholes in the street."

Lizzie and Lois both laughed, but Bradley frowned. "I don't get it," he said.

"Streets of gold, Brad, streets of gold. The streets of heaven are paved with gold," Russell Burgess explained. "Maybe you've not heard enough good preaching lately!"

"Brad has become a serious backslider," Lizzie said. "He and good preaching don't seem to be compatible."

Russell was openly amused and Bradley accepted the discussion with good humor. Among most of those in his and Lizzie's circle of friends, religion and "good preaching" were taken for granted. To be labeled a backslider carried the good-natured implication of a temporary lapse or transient juggling of priorities, but little more. Such a state required a solid religious foundation to begin with and the backslider could be expected to see the error of his ways eventually and return to the fold.

Over dinner, Russell brought up the Morris's Sicilian trip, even though it had been thoroughly reported before. "It's hard for me to think of Sicily and not think of the *Mafioso*," he said. "Were there any overt Mafia activities that you were aware of?"

"That connection must be exaggerated," Bradley said. "We heard there were roadblocks around Gela the day we were there that had something to do with the Mafia, but we didn't see anything. Nobody shot down in the streets, or anything like that."

Lois announced that she and Russell were going on a cruise to Alaska in August, escaping to a cooler climate just when the Memphis summer was at its worst. "You two ought to come with us," she said. "It would do you both good to get out of town for a couple of weeks."

"I don't think you will ever get Bradley Morris on a cruise ship," Lizzie said, laughing. "He's been there before, and didn't enjoy it all that much."

"Really? Where did you go?"

"Brad's cruise was on a troop ship," Russell Burgess told his wife. "Isn't that what you meant, Lizzie?"

Lizzie said yes, it was, and Bradley concurred that he had had enough ocean voyage on that trip to last a lifetime. Lois wanted to know more. Did he mind talking about it?

"It was not a pleasant experience," Bradley said. "Most of what I remember isn't the kind of thing you'd want to hear about at dinner. You'll have a lot more fun than I did, though that's not a high standard to meet."

On the way home, Lizzie was unusually quiet.

"Are you worried about something?" Bradley asked.

"Not worried. I was thinking about Jennie and Beth. Jennie seems happy enough in California, but I think she still misses Memphis."

"She never really wanted to move. But Paul was intent on it. Do you think she'd tell us if she really was unhappy?"

"I'm just not sure. I hate to say it but the truth is, I don't feel like I'm close enough to Jennie anymore to know."

He recognized a note of resignation in her voice. Lizzie had told him more than once that she felt alienated from their daughter. Not that there had been any sort of falling out between them. They'd never had a disagreement, as far as he could remember. The distance that separated them had developed more gradually.

In the first several months in Los Angeles, little had gone on in her family that Jennie did not report in great detail: Paul's triumphs and setbacks in his new medical center, Beth's growing pains, her own somewhat reluctant transition to the West Coast lifestyle, her fund-raising work with the American Red Cross. But once that transition was complete, she apparently had become too busy to think of them as often as she had in the past. She had seldom called during the last few years and her infrequent letters were short and impersonal.

"I guess she'll tell us whatever she wants us to know when she's here," Bradley said.

"Yes, I suppose so. She knows we won't pry. And anyway, I'm more concerned right now about keeping Beth entertained. At her age she's not likely to be content for a week just visiting with us old folks."

"But remember, Jennie said she doesn't want us to schedule a lot of things to do."

"I know. And we don't want to keep the child so busy she feels like a tourist. But I'd like some things we can all do together, maybe at the end of the week after the others are gone."

Bradley had an idea that had been running through his mind for several days. He wasn't sure how Lizzie would react to it, and had hesitated to bring it up. This might be a good time. "Why don't we drive up to Simpson's Ridge and let Beth see where her grandmother came from?" he said. "She was too little the last time she was there to remember much. We could make the trip we planned to make last fall, after Sicily."

"Yes, we could. You'd enjoy telling Arnold Calder about Sicily. We haven't been there in a long time, and we used to go so often."

He was happy that she liked his suggestion. Simpson's Ridge was filled with memories for both of them, but especially Lizzie. It was the home she had left when they married, the place where her Kraft family roots ran deep. For him, it had been home for only a few short years, but these were the most important years of his life. The little Kentucky town would always be dear to his heart.

With a visit to Simpson's Ridge added to their list of things to do, their plans were complete. Now it was only a matter of waiting. They talked about the danger of counting too much on what was to come and letting their expectations get too high. After the family had come and gone, it was inevitable that there would be a letdown. The big house would seem empty again.

But Lizzie said they shouldn't worry about that. Their lives would go on as they were, and their lives were good. There was great joy to be found in the small things, the commonplace happenings of days spent with each other. Bradley agreed. Although he could not have put his feelings into words as effectively as she did, he felt the same way. The greatest pleasure of his life was Lizzie. Time spent with Lizzie was happy time.

Lizzie checked off the days on her calendar. The weeks went by quickly and almost before they realized it the date had come. Jennie called to let them know that she and Beth would be arriving in Memphis on a late afternoon flight the next day.

Lizzie was in the kitchen rinsing supper dishes when the call came, and Bradley answered the phone. Jennie sounded excited—eager, she said, to be on her way home. She said Beth was impatient, too, and couldn't wait to see her grandmother and granddaddy. The conversation was brief, but it left him feeling good. Jennie's enthusiasm seemed genuine. In fact, she sounded much like the Jennie of old. Had they been too hard on her?

He hurried to tell Lizzie, but Lizzie was nowhere in sight. When he spied her, lying crumpled on the floor, he was struck by sudden panic.

"Lizzie, Lizzie—oh, God, what's happened?"

8

He never had thought of Lizzie as being old. She still was youthful in his eyes, so pretty and full of life, still the same girl he had fallen in love with in those carefree days in Simpson's Ridge. After all their years together, he simply could not imagine life without her. But now Lizzie lay in the medical center's grim intensive care unit, clinging precariously to life, and Bradley Morris felt all alone.

Since Lizzie's sudden collapse four days earlier, he had stayed at her bedside almost around the clock. For three seemingly endless days he had waited expectantly, confident that she would open her eyes at any minute and smile and tell him not to worry, that she was going to be all right. Those first three days were critical, the doctors said. Lizzie had suffered a massive heart attack which she was lucky to have survived. Seventy-two hours was a decisive juncture; either she would show clear signs of progress by then, or she might be in an interminable coma, kept alive only by the machines.

But Bradley knew better. When three days came and went with no apparent change in her condition, he knew the doctors were wrong. Lizzie was strong and full of life. Everyone simply must be patient and expect the best, just as Lizzie always did.

He had finally given in, reluctantly, to his family's pleas and agreed to go home and go to bed. With only a few hours of unsettled rest during the last four days, napping on a lumpy couch in the cramped ICU anteroom, he was too tired to resist their appeals any longer. He would get some sleep and be back at the hospital early in the morning, and one of the children would meet him at the door and tell him their mother was awake and eager to get home. He would have his Lizzie back in no time.

He dragged himself upstairs and undressed mechanically. After a superficial shower, he dropped onto the bed, bone-weary, without bothering to turn down the covers. He was asleep almost immediately. And then, as real and terrifying as ever, the nightmare.

German artillery shells fell like rain on the battle-ravaged hillside, where he lay surrounded by the wounded and dying. This was the dream he knew, the dream that caused him to cry out in his sleep and shake violently in the bed until Lizzie took him in her arms and soothed away his demons. It had come less frequently in recent years, and especially since the visit to Sicily, but this time it descended to its darkest level. His whole world became a continuous explosion of shellfire. He smelled the carnage. He felt the searing steel shrapnel that tore through his leg and left him dazed and semi-conscious, and heard the shrieking fragment that ripped through the heart of Carson Streator. He tried to scream but could make no sound.

At this point his subconscious mind kicked in, in that merciful way it protects us against agonies beyond our fragile endurance, and even in his fitful sleep he understood that he must end his own torment and force himself to wake. There was the inevitable episode of agitated confusion before he was fully alert, but then he remembered where he was and the terrible illusions of his nightmare were replaced by the awful reality: He was in their bed, but Lizzie was not beside him.

With no hope of getting back to sleep, Bradley got up wearily, dressed, and set out for the hospital. A powerful anxiety pulled at his senses. He must fight it, he told himself, lest it overwhelm his optimism and replace it with dreadful hopelessness. He had to believe that he would find things changed for the better since he left the medical center just a few hours earlier, that Lizzie would show visible signs of improvement.

Jennie met him at the door of the ICU, putting up a brave and positive front. How much she looked like her mother! She reacted gently when he said he couldn't sleep, as if she understood, and didn't pursue the matter.

"She seems to be comfortable," Jennie said, speaking softly. "The doctor said she doesn't feel any pain. I don't know how they can tell. I feel helpless just sitting by the bedside, but there really is nothing we can do."

He put his hand on her arm. "It's important that we be here," he said.

"I know. And we've been here all along. But I still feel helpless."

"She knows you're here. That means a lot."

The expression on Jennie's face betrayed her misgivings. "I wish I could be sure of that," she said. "And I wish Paul was here. It's a terrible time for him to be out of the country."

"He's doing good work. Your mother will be up and around soon, and Paul can come and visit when he gets back to California. Why don't you go on home now? You should be there when Beth wakes up."

"Sarah's there with Beth," Jennie said, still speaking in lowered tone. "She'll be fine. Did Aunt Catherine get to the house before you left? She didn't want to leave, but Matthew insisted that she get some rest. Uncle Walter's coming tomorrow."

"No, I didn't see her. Where is Matt?"

"He went downstairs for coffee. I think I'll go down, too, just to stretch my legs a bit. Is there anything I can do for you before I leave?"

"I don't need anything. Go on down and find your brother."

As he came to Lizzie's bedside, Bradley's heart sank. Whatever spirit he had been able to muster evaporated as he looked down on Lizzie's expressionless face. Her skin was the color of gray marble and although her eyes moved beneath their closed lids the movement was sporadic and uncontrolled, not the action of a sentient being. Her mouth was slightly open and an ugly oxygen tube was taped to her nose. He pressed his hand against her cheek. She felt cold and damp to his lingering touch. He stooped and kissed her face softly.

On previous days, he had made himself believe that Lizzie felt his kisses. She could not respond, but surely she must be aware of his presence. She would expect him to be at her side, and she knew he was there.

Today he had no such confidence. Yet he would not give up hope, and as long as there was a breath of life he would cling to it—to her. What else could he do? Lizzie had been the core of his being, the one who made him whole, for more than fifty years. Even before they were married, during the darkest weeks and months after Sicily, just knowing that Lizzie waited had kept him going. Time had not eroded her place in his heart and mind. Had strengthened it, in fact, until he truly felt as though the two of them were one.

He pulled a chair close beside his wife's bed and sat, slumped forlornly, oblivious to his surroundings in the dimly lit hospital room. His thoughts centered on Lizzie, and Lizzie alone.

Bradley Morris loved his children and grandchildren, would walk through fire or sacrifice his life for any one of them in the blink of an eye. But even though they were of his own flesh, they were not part of him the way Lizzie was. In recent years, particularly after Jennie and Matthew had moved away, he had come to recognize that a parent's love is sacrificial, destined to end in preordained fashion: In whatever scheme there is to the human universe, it is given that the children endure, charting their own course and leaving the elder generation to fade into its own sunset, the flow of life continuing uninterrupted. This is the way one generation succeeds another. As Lizzie would say, "the natural order of things."

He and Lizzie were content to be a part of that elder generation. Their years had been abundant and they had led good lives, and he had believed for some while that they would be ready when it came time to hand over their torch to those next in line. They would go without regret or whimper.

But now, with Lizzie lying near death, he had an overwhelming sense that the time should not have come so suddenly. They deserved a warning, more time to prepare. Surely the fullness of their decades together had earned them the right to fade into their sunset as one, side by side. And if not side by side, then let him lead the way. It would be easier for Lizzie to live without him; she would await her time patiently, comforted by the family and trusting herself to God's hands. Not once had he considered the possibility of Lizzie going first.

Bradley Morris never had been one to express his emotions outwardly. Could he make the children understand his feelings? How he wished now that he had tried harder, and more often, to let Lizzie know how deeply he loved her. He longed to hold her in his arms and tell her one more time and see the light in her eyes and hear in her soft and gentle voice that she returned his utter devotion. Overcome by his sense of helplessness, he pressed his face into the sheet that covered her and sobbed quietly. Monitors over her bed recorded and displayed by rude and jagged electronic impulse every heartbeat of this woman he loved so very much.

Moments later, Matt put a hand gently on his father's shoulder. "I thought you were going to go home and get some sleep," he said. "You need some rest, Dad. Jennie and I are here. Mother won't be alone."

"I tried to sleep. I did sleep a little. But I wanted to be here when she wakes up."

"You know we'll call you the minute anything changes," Matt said. "Let me take you home. Aunt Catherine's there. Did you have dinner?"

"I'm not hungry. Have you talked to Dr. Garvey tonight?"

"Yes. He was in about ten o'clock. He'd been seeing patients in his office all day."

"What did he say? About your mother, I mean."

"He said nothing has changed. But, Dad, I think she has deteriorated some."

"But your mother's strong, Matthew. Always has been. She'll pull through this. I'm going to stay the rest of the night. You and Jennie go home and go to bed. Maybe I'll lie on the couch a little while, but I'll be here in case she wakes up. When will you come back?"

Matt seemed to know that his father's mind was made up and it would be pointless to try to persuade him to leave. "I'll be back by early afternoon," he said. "You know Aunt Catherine will be here by mid-morning or so, and Jennie is going to stay. I have to make some calls before noon, but I'll come back as early as I can."

Jennie had been waiting in the anteroom. Matt spoke with her momentarily and then left, and she came and stood by her father's side. Neither of them spoke. Jennie smoothed the hair away from her mother's colorless face and pulled a second chair close by the bed, next to her father. She took his hand and the two kept vigil through the remainder of the night. Only occasional visits by the nurses, gentle but efficient, violated the solitude of the room.

Bradley had no sense of time. The first few hours after Lizzie's attack had been desperate ones, with her survival a matter of touch and go. After that, he had been acutely conscious of the seventy-two-hour turning point cited by the doctors. Now that this mark had come and gone with no conspicuous change in Lizzie's condition, the hours had passed without notice. He felt compelled to look ahead, to think about the days to come.

Whatever happened, it was his responsibility to take care of Lizzie. The two of them always had cared for each other, leaning on one another to get through hard times. He could not let her down now.

Lizzie always had been much better at dealing with their problems than he had. He'd learned early, during rounds of surgery and rehabilitation on his war-mangled leg, just how strong she really was. If he were the one lying there on the hospital bed Lizzie would know what to do. But this was not the way things were. Lizzie was the one who needed help, and Bradley was afraid.

Jennie stood, yawning and stretching. "It's morning," she said. "We should get some breakfast."

"I don't really want anything but coffee."

"Daddy, you've got to eat. You've hardly been eating at all."

"Well, I'll try," her father said, "but I'm not hungry, and I have an awful headache. Please give me a minute."

Bradley entered a small washroom off the hall and splashed cold water on his face and pressed fingertips hard against throbbing temples. He stared at himself in the mirror, seeing a man he hardly recognized—an old man, tired and pale, despair in his eyes. There was another mirror on the opposite wall and as he started to turn away, he saw in it a reflection of the mirror in front of him. One reflection repeated the other, so that there was an endless chain of images of his own face, each a little smaller, until at last he disappeared into infinity.

The visual impact paralleled his feeling. *I'm nothing without Lizzie at my side. If I could just fade away . . . but I have to be there for her when she wakes up . . .* He forced himself to put on a more pleasant countenance and rejoined Jennie in the hallway.

They made their way on to the cafeteria and soon were joined by Walter, who had just arrived at the medical center. Walter had shown great concern for his sister-in-law from the minute he and Catherine received word of her illness, but it had been difficult for him to get away from his business in Paducah and come to Memphis. He was a slender man, almost as tall as Bradley, with angular features and kind eyes and prematurely white hair that made him look older than he was. "I'm sorry I couldn't get here sooner," Walter said. "How is she doing?"

"There hasn't been any change," Jennie told him. "The situation looks pretty hopeless."

"We can't give up hope," Bradley said, his voice rising. "Lizzie is strong. She's going to pull through this. We just have to be patient."

"I guess I'll go on up and see her," Walter said. "You two stay here and finish your breakfast. They probably don't want too many of us in her room at once, anyway. Is Paul here, Jennie?"

"He's in the Philippines. Otherwise he'd be here."

"The Philippines? What's going on there?"

"Oh, it's kind of a mission of mercy. Every year, he takes a team of doctors and nurses someplace where medical care is scarce or people just can't afford it. And this year it's the Philippines. Local agencies there have tons of children lined up for surgery. Cleft palate, facial deformities, that sort of thing."

"And they do this for free?"

"Yes," Jennie said. "The doctors and nurses all donate their time. Corporate sponsors help pay their expenses."

"Lizzie will be interested in hearing all about his trip," Bradley said. "I hope Paul can come and visit soon after he gets back."

Although he hated to leave the medical center, Bradley went home at mid-afternoon. He could no longer bear the tension of the ICU. His headache had become almost unbearable and the pain in his leg was worse from long stretches without rest. The others would watch over Lizzie in his absence and call him the instant her condition changed.

He looked back over the Memphis skyline once outside the hospital and felt as if he were viewing it for the first time in months. Lizzie's illness had dominated his consciousness so completely that everyday events were remote and insignificant. In the distance, the giant stylized M formed by the steelwork of the interstate highway bridge that crossed the Mississippi into Arkansas offered a familiar backdrop. The wide, shimmering ribbon of river was visible for miles in each direction.

He left the parking garage and drove slowly, reflecting on changes in the Memphis landscape since he and Lizzie arrived as young and hopeful newlyweds eager to find their place. For him, it had been a return to familiar streets; for Lizzie, a new world. Memphis then was a modest country town compared to Memphis now, but still crowded and noisy measured against the open spaces of Lizzie's western Kentucky girlhood. She hated the city in the beginning, but adapted remarkably well and quickly came to feel at home.

The neighborhood where they lived wasn't much different, but the old Cotton Row business district on the bluffs along the river bore little resemblance to the way it looked then. As it is with people, Bradley thought, the changes had been gradual and often barely noticed. *Change is a fact of life . . . I know we'll get through this . . . Lizzie will be well again.* But at this moment, he would have given anything to go back to that earlier time when they were young and Lizzie was vital and healthy and the most daunting threats he faced were the pitfalls of earning a decent living and taking care of his family.

When he turned into the driveway at the big house, his arrival felt the same as it had on countless homecomings through the years; he might have forgotten that Lizzie was not there to greet him. But he faced no such illusions once inside. Sarah urged him to eat something. He tried because he wanted to please her, but he had little appetite. A hot shower helped ease his physical discomfort but brought no reprieve from the apprehensions that tortured his mind and spirit.

In the bedroom, he took Lizzie's photograph from the dresser. He held it lovingly and with fresh gratitude for its presence. The picture was nearly twenty years old, and although time had taken some toll he recognized that Lizzie really had not aged all that much. Her dark eyes still sparkled and her radiant smile was still there, her pretty brown hair grayed but not faded.

Bradley often had trouble recalling recent events—a source of great and growing agitation—but memories from the old days were still sharp in his mind. He remembered distinctly the very instant he first saw Lizzie, sitting in a classroom where he had been assigned to a history course that he didn't want and was sure that he didn't need. His family had just moved to Simpson's Ridge; Elizabeth Kraft was a farm girl who had lived there all her young existence. He had been stricken the moment he saw her.

As a newcomer, accustomed to city life in Memphis, he had been lonely and depressed—until that day. Lizzie liked him, too, and soon they became sweethearts.

Even now, Bradley felt a sense of wonder that Lizzie had chosen him. She was outgoing and popular and could easily claim the friendship of every student in school. But from that day forward she ignored all others and devoted her time to him. She even paid less attention to Danny Boy, the big sorrel gelding that was her passion, and the old collie dog, Butterball, a primary object of her affection for a decade.

Young Bradley Morris had become as familiar as a member of the family at the Kraft house for Sunday dinner. He regularly and proudly escorted Lizzie to services at the nearby Shiloh Missionary Baptist Church, her family's place of worship for three generations. Shiloh Church was the place where her mother and father and one set of grandparents had said their wedding vows. Old-timers in the congregation liked to recount the romances they had watched blossom in the little church's pews, and Bradley and Lizzie quickly won both their approval and their prayers. Prayers and sermons notwithstanding, though, the thrill he experienced on those sultry Sunday evenings came from the beautiful girl beside him and not from any strong religious conviction.

During the tranquil summer that followed their first school year together, they found ways to be with other almost every day. They could not have imagined it then, but it would be their last truly lighthearted summer for years to come. The Japanese bombed Pearl Harbor in December of their senior year, after which Bradley Morris and most of the other boys in their class vowed to join the armed forces as soon as they graduated.

Sitting alone in an upstairs bedroom of the big house with Lizzie's picture in his hands, Bradley remembered the unrest and anxiety of that time. He remembered his father and mother and some of their neighbors huddled around the big radio console in the Morris living room as President Franklin D. Roosevelt addressed the nation in what they all knew was a call to arms. He remembered being stirred, himself, by the words of the president. He remembered the words of his father.

"I hate to see you go, son, but I know you feel it's what you have to do," his father told him. "God knows, if I were younger I'd do the same thing."

He remembered the tears that flooded his mother's eyes the day he boarded a bus that carried him away from Simpson's Ridge for good. It was two weeks after he finished high school and one day after he turned eighteen. He remembered the bus ride to the army induction station, during which he vowed to himself his undying love for Lizzie, his parents, and his country and viewed the passing landscape with new appreciation. He might be seeing it for the last time.

He remembered best of all how Lizzie clung to him, finally releasing all her pent-up distress in a single flood of emotion and whispers of "I love you."

For a fleeting moment, Bradley Morris forgot the circumstances under which he had commenced his reverie—Lizzie lying comatose in the medical center and the terrible apprehension with which he faced the future. He was a soldier again, young and strong and believing fervently in his mission, never wavering in doing his duty as he saw it, determined to do his job to the best of his ability and come home to Lizzie sound in mind and body—or, should it fall his lot, sacrifice himself for all that he held dear.

All this replayed in his mind like recent history.

The two young lovers wrote one another every day, so that their letters often arrived in bundles. Every day they promised to spend the rest of their lives together. "My darling Bradley," Lizzie always wrote. And she concluded every letter, "Yours eternally, Elizabeth."

He never told her how the other men in his company came to hoot and yell at mail call when the clerk shouted his name. It was good-natured ribbing; they were happy for him, or for any other soldier who received regular mail—especially letters like hers, in their soft pastel envelopes with dainty feminine handwriting.

He saved Lizzie's letters, though some got lost as the army shuffled him helplessly between hospitals, and she saved his. The treasured collection was in a cedar chest in the attic, tied in separate packets with faded blue ribbons. It had been years since the letters saw the light of day.

Bradley carefully placed Lizzie's photograph face down on the bed, close at his side, and turned to other things. There were pictures of Jennie and Matthew, much younger, and an album of snapshots from family vacations when the children were little. He carefully thumbed through the old album. Every page told its own story, with pictures from Biloxi and Charleston and Myrtle Beach. He loved the ocean, in spite of his dreadful days aboard a troop ship, and used to tell Lizzie he wanted to move to the coast somewhere farther south when they retired. But Lizzie wanted to stay in Memphis. "Our house is filled with memories," she said, "and I'd hate to give up all that for a few more days of sunshine."

Hers was always the wiser head, Bradley reflected. *She is such a good mother, and God knows she's held us together.*

Lizzie had been a buffer between him and Matt, especially, because Matthew was strong-willed like his father and without her the friction might have been more than their relationship could bear. But their disagreements had been over minor things, except for Vietnam, and Lizzie always had been able to patch things up between them before their wrangling got out of hand.

And it was Lizzie who soothed a broken-hearted Jennie and helped her rebuild her life after the first man their daughter loved asked her to marry him and then changed his mind. Jennie always had been a near-perfect likeness of her mother in both physical appearance and temperament and until she moved to California she and Lizzie had been as close as a mother and child possibly could be.

She was a rock for Matt and Jennie, always there when they needed her. I could make a long list of the hard times when Lizzie was the one they came to. Although he always had tried to be a good father, he was certain that it was Lizzie who deserved the greatest credit for molding them into the noble man and woman they had become. Perhaps he was being selfish in his grief. The children and grand-children would be lost without her, too. *But they would go on, and I don't think I could live without her . . .* He broke down in sobs, and fell asleep lying across the bed, clutching Lizzie's photograph to his breast.

Dr. Witte Garvey had lived up to his reputation of being altogether dedicated to the welfare of his patients and had shown Lizzie's family inordinate consideration. He was a large man, pink-faced and flabby, always with an air of being rushed. This morning he looked somewhat drawn and haggard. He introduced himself to Walter, seeing him for the first time, then walked to Bradley Morris and gently placed a hand on his shoulder.

"I wish I had better news for you, Mr. Morris," the doctor said softly.

"Do you think she knows we're here?" Bradley asked.

"No, I'm afraid she doesn't. There is a minimum of brain activity and it's highly unlikely that any of her senses are functioning. She's not aware of anything that goes on around her."

"But she's still breathing regularly," Bradley protested. "And there must be a strong heartbeat. Lizzie's strong, doctor. She always has been."

"We're maintaining life artificially, Mr. Morris. We might do that for some time, but we know now that any prospect for recovery is extremely small. Her attack did too much damage and her brain was oxygen-starved for too long. I'm terribly sorry, but we've done everything we can. I have to be candid with you. I can't in good conscience offer any hope that your wife is going to recover."

Bradley Morris slumped, as if a heavy weight had just been dropped on his shoulders. Matthew and Jennie, one on each side, took him by the arms and guided him to a chair. He sat down heavily.

"We can't give up hope," he murmured. "We just can't give up hope. Lizzie is a strong woman. She always has been. She'll wake up. We just can't give up hope."

Dr. Garvey stood mutely for a moment. "We will do whatever you want," he said then. "We can keep her alive indefinitely in a comatose state. If you decide to let her go, we will remove the respirator and let nature take its course."

"Would she be in any pain?" Matthew asked.

"Oh, no. We'll keep her free of pain, either way. And again, I'm very sorry."

The doctor quietly left the room and the small family huddled in silence. Walter put his arm around Catherine. The two of them, along with Jennie and Matthew, formed a crescent around

Bradley's chair. Walter spoke: "What would Lizzie want?"

"She wouldn't want to go on this way," Jennie said.

Matthew nodded agreement. "There's no question about it. She would want us to let her go."

"No," his father said. "I won't give up. We can't talk this way. Lizzie's still alive. She's a strong woman, she's going to get well. We just have to be patient. I'll stay here by her side, and be here when she wakes up."

9

Two days had passed since the family's meeting with Dr. Garvey, and Lizzie's condition had not changed. She still lay motionless and silent in the ICU, attached to machines that regulated her breathing and monitored every pulse and heartbeat, and tubes that carried nutrients into her body and waste out. For all practical purposes, her care was now in the hands of medical technicians. Her nurses systematically checked and regulated the apparatus and watched over their patient by way of a video monitor which was fed by a wall-mounted camera in her room.

The nurses were no less compassionate, but there was no communication between them and Lizzie. They assumed that she could neither see nor hear them, that she was not aware of their presence.

Jennie and her aunt Catherine and Sarah had worked out a schedule so that one of them always was at Lizzie's bedside. Matthew was trying to keep up with his work by phone and computer connections with his Chicago office, but spent several hours a day at the hospital. Walter had gone home to look after his business in Paducah, and Paul had been informed of Lizzie's condition and was having surgeries in Los Angeles rescheduled so that he could fly to Memphis as soon as he returned from the Philippines, should that prove useful.

The grandsons, Jeff and Mark, had driven down from Chicago. They had stopped by the hospital several times for brief visits, standing somberly beside their grandmother's bed and saying little.

Beth had been to the hospital only twice. Both times, she had been overcome with emotion almost immediately at the sight of her comatose grandmother. Jennie insisted that she not visit again, to spare herself and the rest of the family the trauma of her distress. Beth had accepted her mother's dictum reluctantly.

The support of his family had been of immense benefit to Bradley, who finally had come to grips with the fact that he could not be at the hospital every hour; he was physically and emotionally drained. This was easier to accept after he conceded at last that Lizzie's coma might go on indefinitely, and no longer expected her to regain consciousness at any minute.

He faced his visits to the hospital with a mixture of hope and dread. Every hour away from Lizzie was an empty hour and he couldn't wait to be with her again, but he hated seeing her the way she was and always feared she might be worse.

Jennie and Sarah were with Lizzie this morning. Bradley had promised to sleep late and come to the hospital in the afternoon, but he was awakened at an early hour by the euphony of songbirds outside his window and a shaft of sunlight streaming in through a partially open shade. His first impulse, as it was every day, was to rush to Lizzie's bedside.

Matthew was in the kitchen when his father came downstairs. "Did you get some sleep?" he asked, skipping the formalities of morning greetings.

"I slept pretty well," Bradley said. "Jennie and Sarah wanted me to stay away this morning, but I think it was just so I'd get more rest. But I feel pretty good. Since I'm up, I'll probably go on to the hospital."

"You don't need to go yet, Dad. Sarah and Jennie will look after Mother. Why don't you stay home this morning, and I'll take you over to the medical center later?"

Bradley felt strongly that he should go to the hospital right away, but he did not want to offend Jennie and Sarah or quarrel with Matthew. And besides, there was something else he wanted to do. He promised Matthew he would wait at home.

The concern apparent in Matt's face seemed to dissolve. "I

have to take care of a few things, but I'll be back before noon," he said. "Will you be okay?"

"Of course I will. Don't worry about me."

Matthew left his father alone in the kitchen. As soon as Bradley heard his son's car leave, he trudged up the narrow stairs to the attic. He waited a moment for his eyes to become accustomed to the dim light, then made his way to the old cedar chest and dug out the packets of letters he and Lizzie had written during the war. He carried them downstairs, fumbled in eager anticipation as he untied the faded blue ribbons, opened the bundles carefully and spread the letters on the kitchen table in small, neat stacks.

Lizzie's very first letter was there. The envelope was worn and discolored. He had packed this letter and carried it with him, and now he was especially grateful that his first mail from Lizzie was not among the letters he had lost. He handled it lovingly, overtaken by the same feelings he had back then, when her letters were the chain that linked them. It was almost as if the girlish Lizzie were there beside him, her soft, happy voice speaking in his ear:

> July 15, 1942
> My darling Brad,
>
> What are you doing at this very minute? I hope that your training is not too rough! I cannot believe that you are gone. It has only been three weeks since you left, but it seems like an eternity. I thought I would die before I heard from you.
>
> Butterball misses you too. You don't know how much he really likes you. I would have a hard time getting along without you if I didn't have him.
>
> I will only write a short letter now. It sounded like your address was temporary and I don't know for sure when this will catch up with you. I will write every day—I have so much to tell you—and I will wait impatiently for every day's return mail.

We pray that this war will be short, and that
you will soon be home again. But if it takes forever,
Brad, you know that I will be waiting. I love you, I
love you, I love you. Sweetest dreams.

Yours eternally,
Elizabeth

Bradley recalled the day he received this letter, along with
half a dozen others. How it lifted his spirits! And he remembered
how he messed up in his response, writing back that "Butterball"
was a funny name for a collie dog. He meant it light-heartedly,
but Lizzie was miffed. She'd named the dog when she was a little
girl and it was a puppy, she declared, and "Butterball" was an appropriate name at the time. He also remembered her grief when,
some months later, Butterball died of old age.

Lizzie's letters were slow to arrive in the beginning, while he
endured a hectic progression of processing, assignment, and re-
assignment. His received his first mail soon after he started basic
training at Fort Gordon, Georgia, then a new post that was mostly
mud. The heavy red clay clung to and discolored everything that
touched it, sentencing timorous young recruits to endless hours
of cleaning and polishing on boots and barracks floors alike. More
than one night he was so tired by the time their floor sergeant
called "lights out" that he collapsed into instant sleep clutching
Lizzie's letters in his hands.

Recalling Fort Gordon brought an impulsive smile to Bradley's face. *McCorkle! I wonder how many other old vets still remember
Sergeant McCorkle's rifle instruction.*

Sergeant McCorkle was a pudgy, red-faced Irishman, foul-
mouthed and foul-tempered, who brought sheer agony to his
young charges. He was a sadistic bully who always left the im-
pression that he'd crack your head with a rifle butt in the blink of
an eye if you gave him trouble. But because of a slight speech
impediment, he couldn't pronounce the "th" sound and his dire
warning in the rifle pit to "Keep your t'umb out of da way" left
the recruits struggling painfully to hold back their snickers. His

training sessions were nothing short of unrelieved torture.

As he remembered McCorkle, Bradley's smile grew into a short outburst of quiet laughter. It was the first time in many days that he had been able to laugh.

Long after leaving Fort Gordon, he actually gained some respect for McCorkle. It was the chubby little Irishman who told his naive charges, "Don't make real close friends wit' other guys in your outfit. When somebody gets blown to bits by a mortar round, you ain't got time to lay around and cry about it." Carson Streator's death would have been easier had Bradley heeded that advice, but who could have imagined during those weeks of drill in Georgia what hell real combat would turn out to be?

Mail from home, especially the letters from Lizzie, had helped Bradley through the tough days and weeks of boot camp. He had found the physical demands of infantry training easy enough to meet, being young and accustomed to hard work, and he had readily accommodated the emotional impact of learning to fight and kill, which after all was what he had enlisted for. But he had found the dehumanizing regimentation of army life much more difficult.

Boot camp was designed to keep the recruits on a training schedule so demanding that they did not have time to get homesick, but for Bradley it never worked. He would think about Lizzie, and long for her, many times a day. During the night he sometimes woke suddenly from his dreams, his mind's eye still filled with vivid images of Lizzie's face and his body still sensing her tender caresses, the ache in his heart almost unbearable.

As his squad marched to breakfast, he would wonder if Lizzie was up and having breakfast, too. He would imagine her riding Danny Boy along the tree-lined lane in front of the Kraft house, with Butterball loping behind, and miss her so much that it was a struggle just to make it through the day.

A letter from Lizzie had been worth more than all the gold in the world. He had read each letter over and over, and even after receiving a dozen more he often pulled out favorites days later to read again. He counted on Lizzie's letters to help maintain some connection with the world he had left behind. He wanted to hear all about her daily life, their families, her animals—everything about the common, ordinary goings on back home in Simpson's Ridge. Home had come to seem a million miles away.

Lizzie never let him down:

Aug. 3, 1942
My darling Brad,

I had a letter from you today, the first one in a week. I hope my letters to you have been arriving regularly. I promised to write every day. So far, I've managed to keep my word!

Last night I made a wish on our star. I wished that you would be safe, and that you would be home to me soon. I know my wish will come true!

My momma and daddy and yours are getting to be good friends. They visit a lot. That makes me feel even closer to you, my dearest Brad. Catherine and your daddy have a great time together. (I might get a little bit jealous!) I love your momma and daddy. I already feel like part of the family. Aren't you glad?

Rev. Watterson told me to tell you how much everybody misses you at church. He prays for you and all the other soldiers every service. I'm so glad you got saved before you left. There was a baptizing in Limestone Creek last week. I wish you could have been there. I know God will look after you and bring you back to me safe.

I think I've not been riding Danny Boy often enough. He gets real petty sometimes. Yesterday he actually walked under a limb and tried to drag me off. I get pretty mad at him when he does things like that. But you know me—I never stay mad for very long. Danny Boy is still the greatest horse in the world. While you're gone, I don't know how I'd get along without him.

Butterball is lame. I'm afraid he's getting old. He has problems getting around.

I can't even begin to tell you how much I miss you. I can't hardly sleep at night, I miss you so. There isn't anything I want to do and nothing that I'm interested in, as long as you're gone. Momma says she worries about me sometimes, but I tell her I just miss my Bradley. And I do. I miss you, miss you, miss you.

You haven't told me much about your training. How long will it be before you get to come home on leave? Not long, I hope. I can't wait to see you. Did I tell you I miss you???

And while I'm at it, I may as well tell you something else. I love you, Brad Morris, and I always will. (And I hope you can stay off "KP" if it's really as bad as you say!) All the family sends their love. I'll still be missing you tomorrow, and loving you just as much as today. Sweetest dreams.

> Yours eternally,
> Elizabeth

Sitting alone at the kitchen table, Bradley fought back tears. This was the spirited girl he left behind in Kentucky when he went off to war—could it really have been that long ago?—and the woman he loved today with all his heart. He had missed her so much then that he thought he would die, and now, overwhelmed by the fear that Lizzie might be taken from him, he felt much the same.

This letter would have brightened his day immensely when it arrived at Fort Gordon. As he reread it now it reminded him of Lizzie's elation the night he went to the front of Shiloh Church to seek salvation, dropping to his knees to pray for forgiveness for his sins. The congregation softly sang "Just as I Am" while Pastor Watterson knelt beside him and beseeched the Almighty to redeem him through the blood of Jesus Christ. That night, Bradley had faith. And when it was all over and Lizzie came down to the front of the church and stood beside him, holding his hand so tightly, he was truly jubilant.

Looking back, he had to admit that his new-found religious convictions stood him in good stead for a time and helped him through some of his darkest days. His budding faith held an exaggerated importance for him partly because it was new, and even more so because he had been led to it through his devotion to Lizzie. Later, when he met Carson Streator, he found that Streator knew a great deal more about such matters than he did. Streator professed a degree of faith that Bradley admired, and his earnest confidence that God would look after him would later magnify Bradley's bitterness over his young friend's death.

Carefully untying more of the ribbon-bound packets and sorting Lizzie's letters neatly on the kitchen table, Bradley Morris treasured them now more than ever. Each letter was as precious to him as it had been the moment he first touched it, after some company mail clerk tossed it rudely in his direction and allowed it to pass through the hands of any number of men on its way.

He was content to lose himself in the delicate pages, to go back in time and relive every word and sentence as if seeing it for the first time.

He had little desire to see what he had written to Lizzie. He never had had her way with words and, unlike her delicate and flowing hand, his writing was an awkward scrawl. During his time overseas, everything he wrote was passed through the hands of military censors and reproduced as microfilm for faster transport back to the states, and delivered as V-mail. His letters were short and mechanical, though certainly there were times when he was able to pour out his heart.

Without enthusiasm, he opened an early one and read:

Aug. 10, 1942
Dear Elizabeth,
    We had a pretty hard day today, on the range all day. I'm writing this after lights out, and I hope

I can mail it tomorrow. I got two letters from you today—what a lucky mail call!

I hope that everyone there is well. How are Danny Boy and Butterball? I know Butterball misses me. As for Danny Boy, when I get home I'll go riding with you as often as you want, and Danny Boy will get to know me too.

We hardly get a break here. There's physical training before breakfast, then today we marched out five or six miles to the range and back again at the end. After supper, we have to clean weapons and spiff up our areas and you're in big trouble if you're not done by lights out.

But I think we're getting tough and ready, and when they send us over there, we will be ready to do our job. The sooner the better, as far as I'm concerned. I'd give anything to see you right now. I miss you more than I can tell you. I love you, my darling Elizabeth. Sweetest dreams. (I know I will see you in mine.)

Always, Bradley

p.s. If you happen to see my mother or dad, please tell them hi for me. I will write them soon.

How young and foolish he'd been! Not for loving and missing Lizzie, but for his eagerness to get into the war. He had felt then that it might take forever to get his overseas orders, but eleven months after writing that letter he was aboard a landing craft churning toward a Sicilian beach and an unseen enemy, about to face his personal introduction to perdition.

Lizzie showed no sign of change; she still lay motionless and unresponsive, exactly as she had been when he left her the night before. Sarah had been at her bedside for the last three hours, and looked worn. "I think you're the one who needs sleep now," Bradley said. "Go home and rest. We'll be fine."

"I am tired," Sarah said. "But I always hate to leave her."

She stooped and kissed her mother-in-law tenderly on the forehead. Bradley took the chair beside the bed and, after Sarah was gone, moved closer and took Lizzie's hand, caressing it softly.

"How are you doing today?" he asked, speaking barely above a whisper. "I've missed you so much. We need you—all of us. I've been reading our letters, Lizzie. Do you remember how we promised to be together forever? That kept me going during the war, even when I thought I wasn't going to make it. But I had to come back, because you were here."

A nurse entered the room and quietly changed a pouch connected to a tube feeding fluids into Lizzie's arm. No one had told Bradley what the fluids were and it had not occurred to him to ask.

"How are you today, Mr. Morris?" the nurse asked.

He told her that he was well, and thanked her as she left the room.

"Well, Lizzie, we've had a good life." He spoke now in a normal voice, as if he expected his wife to hear and understand. "I've been thinking about the years we've been together, and back to Kentucky and the days before we got married. Do you remember Danny Boy? I never told you, but I was scared to death of that horse! You rode him so easy, but I never knew what he was going to do next. He didn't like me, you know. Actually, I think he was kind of jealous.

"I know you always wanted a horse after we moved to Memphis. I'm sorry that didn't work out, Lizzie. You didn't complain, but I know there must have been a stable around somewhere, close enough where we could have boarded one . . . I'm sorry, Lizzie . . . We should have got you a horse."

The sudden awareness that he had not been attentive to Lizzie's wishes, even though it was long ago, made him despondent. He had been thoughtless not to get her a horse, and now he might never have a chance to make up for it. He was about to apologize again when a new nurse came into the room and chased him out. They had to change the bed and do other things

102

for Lizzie, the nurse said, and he would just be in the way.

"You can come back in about twenty minutes," she added. And then, more sympathetically, "Don't worry, Mr. Morris, We take good care of her."

He met Catherine in the hall, on her way to join him in the ICU. While Lizzie was the image of their mother, Catherine favored the Kraft side of the family and bore little resemblance to her sister. But like Lizzie, she was petite and pretty, and always energetic.

"Has anything changed?" Catherine asked.

"No, she seems to be about the same. It's discouraging, Catherine. It's just so hard to see her this way."

They went to the cafeteria and got coffee, and Catherine tried for awhile to make small talk, as if reluctant to acknowledge what was on both their minds. Then she reached across the table and put her hand on his, as tears began to well up in her eyes.

"Brad," she said, "I really think it's time for us to let her go. I love my sister, and I know how much you love her. But I don't think there's any hope. It's for you to decide, of course, and none of us would go against your wishes. But I just think the last good thing we can do for Lizzie is to let her go peacefully, and not prolong things any longer."

"You mean pull the plug."

"Yes."

Bradley hesitated a moment, considering his answer carefully, then breathed out in a long, slow sigh. "In my mind I know you may be right," he said. "But in my heart, I just don't know how I can do it. Catherine, I can't imagine being without her. I can't bear even to think about it."

"I know, I know," she said, patting his hand lightly. "It's been the hardest thing for us all to deal with. And I don't know if I'm right, Brad. We can't know for certain what's the best thing to do. You have to do what's in your heart, I think, and whatever you decide, the rest of us will go along with. I know that Jennie and Matt have struggled with it. Walter's been a great help to me, otherwise this would have been a lot more difficult."

"Both of you have been good to Lizzie all these years, Catherine. She's always been proud of her little sister, and I always felt like she was lucky to have a sister who was so close."

"And I've felt lucky, too."

The question of Lizzie's care hadn't been resolved, but Bradley knew that Catherine was too considerate to push it further and he still lacked the courage to face what he knew might be true about Lizzie's condition. He felt helpless and confused and alone, even with Catherine's reassurances. He was grateful for his family's understanding, though; Catherine and the others obviously had discussed it, and they would leave the decision in his hands.

They went back to the ICU after the nurses had finished attending to Lizzie. Only the bedding had changed.

"It's still painful to see her lying there that way," Catherine said. "I just wish there was something I could do for her."

"Just being here means a lot," Bradley answered, stroking Lizzie's hair. "I still believe that she knows we're here. She just can't show it."

As his hand touched her face, there was a slight tremor in Lizzie's fingers and he was certain that he saw a flicker of eye movement beneath her closed lids. "She felt my hand!" he exclaimed. "She moved, Catherine!"

"I saw it, too," Catherine said.

Their elation was short-lived. The attending floor nurse said the movement was meaningless and offered a technical medical explanation that came down to nerve endings artificially stimulated. She said they mustn't get their hopes up. Lizzie's condition had not changed.

Bradley Morris refused to accept it. Lizzie's movement, even if involuntary, signified life. As long as there was life in her body he would not give up.

10

Matthew and Jennie met with Dr. Witte Garvey late in the afternoon. They admitted, reluctantly, that they had given up all hope of their mother's survival. It had been two weeks since her attack, and every passing hour solidified their conviction that the family was maintaining a futile vigil. The doctor was sympathetic. If their father shared this view, he said, the artificial support system that kept her alive would be removed.

"He won't agree to it," Matthew said. "I wish he would, but I don't feel like trying to push him on it."

"Daddy has more courage than anybody else I know," Jennie said. "God knows he's had more than his share of problems to deal with and he's managed to get through them. He has always been able to see things rationally and do what had to be done. He has amazing willpower. But this is beyond his control, and I'm afraid he's being ruled by his heart and not his head."

Dr. Garvey nodded. "I know, I know," he said. "This isn't unusual, and I understand. And medicine isn't a perfect science, not by a long shot. But everything I know tells me the situation isn't going to change—unless you believe in miracles."

Lizzie had been moved from the hospital's intensive care unit to a room more in keeping with her needs, subtle acknowledgment that the medical staff no longer expected to save her life. She lay comatose and ashen, her small and wasting body exhibiting only those mechanical vital signs mandated and driven by the life support system. The doctor looked down on her lifeless face and shook his head sadly as he left the room.

"Daddy should be here in an hour or so," Jennie said. "Maybe he's beginning to see things more realistically."

Matt smiled. "You don't really believe that," he said.

"No. But it would make things a lot easier if he would."

Bradley joined them shortly afterward, well before the time he had told them he would come. "Have you seen the doctor?" he asked, as he entered the room. "I was hoping there would be some good news."

"No, Daddy, there isn't any good news," Jennie said. "We met with Dr. Garvey, and he says nothing has changed. He's not at all optimistic."

"Dad, you already look tired," Matt said. "Jennie's going to go on home now, and I'm going to go down and get some coffee. If I stay a while longer, won't you come home with me? Somebody doesn't have to be here all the time."

But Bradley insisted on staying through the night. "I've had a good rest," he said. "You can go on with your sister, Matthew. I'll be fine. Sarah's coming in the morning."

Jennie said goodbye and Matthew promised to be back soon. After they were gone, Bradley readied himself for a long vigil. He tried to read, but every few minutes cast aside his magazine and tended to Lizzie. He stroked her hair, adjusted her pillow, went through the motions of small but intimate acts of caretaking. At length he gave up all pretense of reading, pulled a straight-backed chair close beside her bed and cradled her hand in his.

"My dear, dear Lizzie," he said softly. "When am I going to get you back? I wish I could pick you up and take you home, and we could lie together in our own bed and I could feel your body warm against me. I don't sleep well without you, you know that. Sometimes I wake up in the night, and I forget you're not there. Then when I reach for you and the bed is empty . . ." His voice trailed off to silence. Tears streamed down his face.

It was several minutes before he regained his composure.

"Do you remember when we moved to the big house?" he asked. He spoke matter-of-factly, as if he expected her to answer. "You thought it was ugly the first time we saw it, and we knew we couldn't afford it. But you made it a wonderful home, Lizzie, a wonderful home."

Acquiring the old Moseley mansion was one of the best things he and Lizzie ever had done, and to this day Bradley marveled that they had pulled it off. They got it only because the heirs to Judge Duncan Moseley's estate were rich and willing to sell "cheap" to settle things quickly and because the judge had thought highly of Randall Morris, Bradley's father, and once said he wanted young Bradley and Lizzie to have his house when he died. They had calculated that mortgage payments would take every dollar they could scrape up, but they nervously took the risk and it was a gamble they'd never regretted.

"After those shabby apartments we started out in, and even our first little house, wasn't it grand!" Bradley said, again stroking Lizzie's hand and still talking as if she was a partner in his conversation. "I was trying to remember how long we've been there. But you know my memory's not what it used to be. I guess I could count it up, because we'd been there two years—hadn't we?—before Jennie was born. Do you remember how you put up old sheets over those big bedroom windows in place of curtains? But we were happy, Lizzie. We were always happy there. The azaleas will be blooming soon. You've always tended them with such care."

Matthew slipped into the room, quietly, and overheard the end of his father's monologue. "Are you all right, Dad?" he asked.

"Yes. I was talking with your mother about the big house. You know, I can't remember how long we've lived there. I think it was two years before Jennie was born, but I'm not sure."

"You still call it the 'big house.' That makes it sound like a prison."

"I know. We just started calling it that. It seemed like such a big place, after where we'd lived before. You couldn't believe some of our early places, Matthew. It was hard to find a place to live when we got married, with the war still going on."

"Yes, you showed us one of them once, but I don't remember where it was. Don't you want a more comfortable chair, Dad?

Would you like for me to get you some coffee?"

His father seemed at first not to have heard. Then he looked up as if startled, got up slowly and moved to one of the cushioned chairs beside the door. He eased himself down into the pillowed seat, his weariness apparent in every move. "I was just telling your mother how much we miss her at home," he said. "The big house seems empty without her."

The two men maintained their solemn watch for a long while without talking. Lizzie's electronic monitors registered and displayed a steady chronicle of the shallow breathing and fragile heartbeat coerced by other machines. Matt had promised Jennie that at the first appropriate time he would ask their father to let their mother go. But he searched for the right words now, and came up empty.

Bradley's thoughts went back to those early days in the big house. They moved in during the hottest part of the summer, late August, and settling into the mansion and trying to fill its spacious rooms with their meager belongings was an adventure in itself. They possessed only a little furniture, mostly second-hand odds and ends, and barely enough bedding and kitchen paraphernalia to get by, but Lizzie had made a cozy home in no time. All those who came to call had been awed by the house's grandeur.

"Remember how much your Grandfather Morris liked the big house?" he said to Matthew. "I think he was prouder of it than we were."

"I barely remember him," Matt said. "I'm sure he liked our house, though."

Bradley wouldn't attempt to explain to Matt why his grandfather took great satisfaction in the Moseley mansion, though the reason had been unmistakable at the time. The elder Morris saw his and Lizzie's move to the big house as partial reclamation of the family's heritage.

The Morris family never had been socially prominent, but had been moderately wealthy during a brief span of years when Randall Morris enjoyed success as a merchant and prospered on the cotton exchange. Bradley's mother was a Kelleher, the youngest daughter in a "black Irish" family that was said to have lost a fortune a generation or so earlier in the depressed Civil War economy. He never knew if that was true, but he did know that while many of the Irish and German families left Memphis after the war, and especially during the 1870s yellow fever epidemics, the Kellehers stuck it out and learned to make do with pride instead of money.

His father and mother loved Memphis, and it was one of the darkest days in his own life when he first heard that they were moving to Kentucky. Bradley was only a teenager at the time. He had been shielded from the most unpleasant details, but he knew that his father came out of the Great Depression in dire financial straits and, after a long struggle, finally lost both his business and the family home. They moved to Simpson's Ridge because his father found a job there, and his parents lived out their later years in modest surroundings.

How different his life would have been except for that turn of events! I never would have met Lizzie if it hadn't been for their misfortune, he thought to himself. But life without Lizzie was a circumstance he hardly could contemplate, and when he recalled life in the big house Lizzie was always at its center.

"Our first party in the big house was a birthday party for Jennie. Remember? We never were much inclined toward big social events." This was addressed again to Matthew, who had sat stoically during the long silence, as if his thoughts were on something far removed from the hospital room that demanded their presence and the old Moseley mansion that was on his father's mind.

"I don't think so, Dad. Are you still thinking about the big house?"

"I was thinking about all the things you're mother did. She planned the party and did all the work. It was supposed to be a surprise. I think Jennie knew, but she tried not to let it show."

"Was I there? If I was I don't remember." "You probably went off somewhere else. The house was full of teenagers, and you would have been a little too young."

As far as Bradley himself was concerned, the thing he recalled most clearly from the event was Jennie's embarrassment over a giddy verse the kids chanted when they thought no adults were within earshot:

> Dancing in the dining room,
> Necking in the parlor,
> Kissing in the kitchen,
> Oh, what will cool our ardor?

Jennie recognized that it was supposed to be naughty, and worried that her mother and father would be angry, but they'd carefully pretended not to hear.

Lizzie always said the Baptist influence had kept her from learning to dance when she was young, something she had come to regret. She had done her best to encourage Jennie and Matt to develop more social graces than she and their father had. Yes, they could dance in the dining room if they wanted to. Neither of the children had been particularly outgoing, though, and while Jennie did host a modest Cotton Carnival ball during her senior year in high school, Matt worked hard through his teen years to develop an image as something of a social outcast.

"I wasn't much for parties then, as you may recall," Matthew said, standing and stretching. "I think I'll go walk out the kinks. Do you want to come?"

"No, you go ahead, and take your time. I'll be here with your mother."

After his son had left the room, Bradley moved back close to Lizzie's bedside. He took her hand again and looked down on her colorless face. "Thank you for making the big house the wonderful home it is," he whispered. "Don't worry. I'll take care of it until you get well."

Walter returned on Saturday to pick up Catherine. She needed to attend to a few pressing concerns at home, but vowed to be back in Memphis at a minute's notice if anything changed. She had stayed at the hospital with Bradley, along with Matt and Sarah, late Friday night. Jennie relieved her early Saturday morning.

Bradley and Walter sat on the big house veranda, while Catherine fixed a late lunch.

"We've had an early spring," Walter said, as if determined to make casual conversation. "Looks like the rivers are up already. The Ohio's near flood stage at Paducah."

"I didn't know we'd had that much rain."

"The rain's all been up north, Illinois and Indiana and Ohio. It all gets down here sooner or later, though. Not much river-boat traffic anymore. Nothing like it used to be when you and I were young. I can remember when you'd always see at least one string of barges on the Ohio, headed one way or the other."

"Oh, yes. Same on the Mississippi. When I was a boy, before we moved to Kentucky, my dad and I spent lots of Sunday afternoons sitting along the bluffs watching the river traffic. There were still a good many steamboats then, too, before the diesel tugs took over. I never thought we'd see the day when traffic was down as much as it is now."

"What's your take on the railroads?" Walter asked.

"Rail traffic is down, too. Trucks haul so much of the freight today. And not nearly the passengers we used to get on the rails."

It seemed that Walter had chosen his topics carefully, and Bradley suspected that his brother-in-law might be operating under strict orders from Catherine to steer the conversation to subjects other than Lizzie. That was all right with him; he needed emotional relief, and this could happen only if he got his mind on other things.

The Mississippi River always was a promising subject in Memphis, and Bradley's personal connection with the railroad went back to a time when the rail yards bustled with freight cars and long passenger trains sped through town on the Illinois Central's Main Line between Chicago and New Orleans many times a day. With millions of other men still in uniform and workers hard to come by, the Illinois Central had been eager to hire young Bradley Morris when he got home from the war—his physical limitations and all. Over a period of years he had worked his way up to the IC Memphis Division management offices. He still displayed his old-fashioned, white and blue striped denim trainman's cap on a coat rack in the hallway.

"I just don't notice what's happening on the railroad the way I watch the river," Walter said. "I know it's important, though, and I know you still watch the railroads pretty close."

"It's sad to see the changes on both of them."

Catherine stepped quietly onto the veranda and interrupted their conversation to announce a visitor, the Reverend Buford Acklin. Bradley introduced Walter, who stood and greeted the young preacher formally and politely.

"I wanted to tell you how sorry I am about Mrs. Morris," the minister said. "She has been in our prayers. If there's anything in the world I can do, please call on me."

"Thank you," Bradley replied, "but I'm afraid there's nothing anybody can do."

"How are you holding up, Mr. Morris?"

"I'm doing all right. She's going to come through this, and be home before we know it."

"If it's God's will, she will be."

When it became obvious that the pastor intended to stay and visit, Bradley directed him to a chair and pointed out that Walter was the son of a minister, which he supposed would give them something in common. It turned out that Pastor Acklin had roots in Paducah and still had family there. Even so, the conversation was somewhat awkward, and talk soon got around again to the rising waters of the Mississippi. Walter repeated his observation that the Ohio River was nearing flood stage.

"God has in his hands some powerful natural forces," the minister said, "but He knows what He's doing. The Bible tells us 'All the rivers run into the sea, yet the sea is not full.'"

"Yes, the rivers can be very powerful," Bradley said.

Catherine returned and said lunch was ready. She would bring it outdoors, and would the minister stay and join them?

Pastor Acklin thanked her, but said he needed to move along. He promised to continue to pray for Lizzie, and offered his quick farewell.

"I don't know if he realizes that we're not all as religious as he'd like to think we are," Bradley said, after the minister was safely out of hearing distance. "I'm not, anyway. I guess you're more religious than I am, Walter."

"No, I'm not a particularly religious man, not if you're talking about organized religion. I guess we all have some kind of religion, though."

"Do you believe in God?"

"I believe in an ordered universe. I don't know if that means God or not. Maybe it just means natural forces . . ."

"The preacher said God holds those natural forces in His hands."

"That's what he said. I don't agree with him, but I wasn't going to get into an argument with him here on your veranda!"

"I know what the preacher would say," Catherine said. "The hand of God controls the natural forces that give us life. Otherwise, we wouldn't be here."

"Look," Walter answered, sounding a bit exasperated. "The earth rotates on its axis at a speed of a thousand miles an hour, more or less. If it turned at half that speed our days and nights would be twice as long. Or if it turned at, say, a hundred miles an hour, the temperature extremes would be so great during the long days and nights that we probably wouldn't survive. But that doesn't prove that God controls the speed of the earth to give us life, it just proves that life as we know it developed because the earth turns at the speed it does. If it turned at a different speed, different forms of life might have developed, that's all."

"Well don't fuss at *me*," Catherine said. "I'm just speculating on what the preacher would say."

"You'll get no argument from me," Bradley told them. "I don't know if your facts are correct, Walter, but I agree with your point."

"Actually," Walter replied, "the Bible explains the laws of

nature pretty well sometimes. Acklin didn't quote the rest of that verse from Ecclesiastes: 'Unto the place from whence the rivers come, thither they return again.' The rivers run into the ocean, the water evaporates and falls again as rain, and the whole cycle repeats itself. That's all there is to it."

"I'll leave all that to you Bible scholars," Bradley said.

"I never claimed to be a Bible scholar. I heard it quoted often enough to remember a lot of it, though."

Over lunch Walter began to tell preacher stories. He had a wealth of experience to draw on, being the eldest child of an oft-moving evangelist. Catherine, in turn, recalled ministers at the little Shiloh Baptist Church, many of whom had stayed on for no more than a year or two before receiving the "call" to larg-er and more rewarding pastorates.

"I'm not sure how sincere some of them were," she told Wal-ter, "but I know your daddy was sincere in his beliefs. And he was such a moving speaker he was very convincing."

"The most convincing preacher I ever heard was a chaplain on our ship," Bradley said. "When he prayed before they put us in the landing boats, he made us think God really would look after us. Carson Streator believed all that. He said he was in God's hands and nothing would happen to him."

Neither Catherine nor Walter responded. They knew who Carson Streator was, and what happened to him. They knew, also, that Bradley Morris's religious faith had been sorely tested in Sicily, and had failed.

Years later, Lizzie had confided to Catherine her great dis-appointment when Bradley came home from the war doubting the beliefs she took for granted—beliefs he once had held, also. The mere fact that he had survived strengthened her own con-viction. She was happy to have him back alive and his loss of faith seemed much less important than it might have under other circumstances. He was wounded and depressed and still had months of painful surgery and rehabilitation to endure. She expected that with time his skepticism would pass, but it never did.

Catherine changed the subject. With the unusually warm spring, she said, the azaleas should be lovely.

Catherine and Walter wanted to visit Lizzie again before they left for Paducah, and they and Bradley went to the hospital and relieved Jennie in her bedside watch. Jennie said Dr. Garvey had stopped by only a short time earlier and told her nothing had changed.

Jennie no longer tried to talk to her mother. She had whiled away the morning reading and talking occasionally with the nurses. Except for Anna Corydon, non-family visitors had not been permitted to see Lizzie from the outset, though Dr. Garvey said they might want to consider letting a few of her friends from church visit for short periods now that she was out of the ICU. Jennie thought it was a good idea, but Bradley said Lizzie would not want others to see her like this. They could wait until she was better.

"She's my only sister," Catherine said after a few minutes in Lizzie's room, "and I can't bear the thought of losing her, but Bradley, I have to tell you, I just don't think there's any hope."

"You mustn't say that," Bradley told her. "You mustn't. Lizzie's still alive. She's going to get well."

Catherine and Walter didn't stay long. They stood silently at Lizzie's bedside for only a moment longer, looking down on her as if they assumed it was the last time they would see her alive. Catherine stroked her sister's arm. Then they bid soft goodbyes and left the room, facing a long drive home.

Bradley sat in Lizzie's room for the rest of the afternoon, and long into the night. How long had she been this way? Two weeks? Three weeks? Somewhere along the way he had lost track of time, but it seemed like forever.

He couldn't admit it, even to himself, but he was slowly beginning to accept the fact that Lizzie might not recover. He had fought that notion tenaciously, but the obvious realities were about to overtake his deepest sentiments. Still, he conceded only the possibility of a fate he was not prepared for. He and Lizzie had been together all these years, loving and caring, husband and wife. They were a couple, a team; there was no one without the other, no separating the dancer from the dance. When he tried to think of life without her, there were no positive images to summon. He was determined to hold on to Lizzie as long as there was breath in her body and red blood in her veins.

Simpson's Ridge was only yesterday. When did they get old? He recalled something his mother had told him years before, when he was a young man and didn't understand: "Old people are invisible to those who don't care about them as individuals."

In recent years he had come to comprehend. *Old people like me.* But as long as he and Lizzie were together, neither could ever be invisible. They were there for each other and put each other first. Their love and companionship had no age. *The most important person in the world loves me. To her, I'll always count.*

But he did care. Simple justice was at stake. A man who had risked his life for his country and suffered the wounds of war, a man who was a good husband and father and a loving grandfather, a man who was a solid citizen who had worked hard and paid his taxes for more than fifty years—well, such a man should not be cast aside so easily.

Anyway, he did not feel like an old man. He was mentally and physically fit and confident he still could do a good day's work. If being old meant being spent, he had not yet reached that point.

And there still was much to do. They had been talking about redecorating the big house. He would do most of the work himself, and Lizzie had been looking at color charts from the paint and fabric stores for weeks. Lizzie was happy in the big house; he would make it sparkle like new.

They would go back to Sicily, revisit Ragusa and Caltagirone and spend more time in Palermo and take all day at the temple ruins at Agrigento. And travel to Minnesota and look up Carson Streator's family. Lizzie had urged that for years. Now they would do it. And they should go to Simpson's Ridge again soon and drive by Shiloh Church, where he had dragged himself down the aisle on one good leg and unsteady crutches for their wedding, and stop and see Arnold and Glory Calder at the old Kraft home and sit on the porch and look out over the meadow where Lizzie rode Danny Boy and played with Butterball while she waited for him to come back from the war.

There would be sunny afternoons to spend on the Chickasaw Bluffs, watching the river. They would see steamboats again. Maybe ride a steamboat to New Orleans—maybe go to Mardi Gras once more. And go back to Graceland, like tourists, and remember how Lizzie had come to love Elvis at a time when she said she was "old enough to know better" and Jennie always said "Sure, Mom, and too young to care" and Lizzie always laughed, as if she'd never heard that before. And they needed to see what was new on Beale Street, and was there still a restaurant high atop the Union Planters building, where Lizzie had loved the view of miles and miles of the sparkling Mississippi?

And yes, they would take endless walks along the quiet, tree-lined streets around the big house, the neighborhood that had become a refuge during Memphis's dark days of strife in the troubled '60s, their neighborhood, where Lizzie still felt a closeness rooted in hushed conversations over backyard fences after Dr. King's assassination. There should be a dozen more spring seasons when they could stroll among the azaleas and savor the beauty of the dogwood trees and the redbuds and, after them, the crape myrtle.

More than anything else, he wanted to make love to this woman countless times more—on a thousand winter afternoons in front of the fireplace, on a thousand spring and summer nights cooled by fragrant breezes, on a thousand romantic trips to secluded hideaways. In all eternity he would not get his fill of loving and being loved by Lizzie Morris.

But then Bradley remembered where he was. He looked about the bleak and cheerless room and settled his gaze on the monotonous monitors above Lizzie's bed. Lizzie was still alive, but who could say for how long? He had no dreams without her, no wish to go on living.

11

In the war, powerless as he had been to alter the hand he was dealt, his youthful idealism had made it easy for Bradley to meet thoughts of his own death philosophically. He had accepted peril as part of his mission. Danger clearly was an integral element in the life of a soldier in combat.

In the beginning, he actually had romanticized the risk and engaged in bitter-sweet fantasies about how Lizzie and his family would mourn if something happened to him. And he was certain that others in Simpson's Ridge would join in paying homage to his memory.

These illusions were nurtured by his generous reception when he came home on his first leave from the army, after boot camp and advanced infantry training, and went around town in his crisply starched new uniform, proud and naive, talking about the soldier's hard life as though he already had experienced war. The townspeople, if they could have, would have pinned medals on his chest.

"They treated me like a hero, Lizzie, even before I went off to the war. They treated me like a hero."

Sitting alone in the big house, he held Lizzie's picture and talked to her as if she were there beside him. But he didn't need to explain; Lizzie would remember. And he felt foolish now when he remembered how cocky he had been then.

"But I learned my lesson fast enough when I got back to duty. They really put us through it, and there wasn't much glory in it. And I had to leave you again, and that was real hard."

Bradley studied the photograph. Lizzie seemed to look back

at him just the way she did in life. He pulled a tissue from a box on the dresser and carefully wiped at the glass covering Lizzie's face and then inspected the glass closely. He would not allow a smudge, not permit her image to be dimmed.

He remembered distinctly the day he received his orders to the 45th Division and knew for the first time that he was about to be thrown full-force into combat, ready or not. Then the division's embarkation orders came, and he barely had forty-eight hours for a quick visit home and last-minute farewells. He and Lizzie accepted their time together as a priceless gift and treasured every minute as if it were their last.

In his reminiscing, Bradley found temporary refuge from the mental agitation that had led to his reverie in the first place. He summoned beautiful memories of those precious hours, and once again he was a young soldier deeply in love, about to go off to war and determined to live for the present, not knowing whether he would have a tomorrow.

On his final night at home, they had consummated their love. They lay on a blanket on a grassy hillside under a luminous Kentucky moon that tipped the treetops with silver. Neither had experienced love-making before and they should have been shy and awkward, but they were driven by love and not lust and they melded bodies as they already had melded minds and spirits. If they had not been certain before, they were certain now that they were joined forever.

In the weeks to come, sailing the turbulent Atlantic and facing the uncertainties that lay ahead, Bradley Morris relived that night over and over in his mind. He remembered Lizzie's white breasts in the moonlight, the way she clung to him, how he felt the beat of her heart.

He laughed at Raynor's predictions that they were headed for France, always followed by a gleeful vow to "fuck all the French girls in Paris." Then he considered the apparent emptiness of Raynor's pledge—no hint of intimacy or caring. Had Raynor ever been in love? Sympathy supplanted his amusement. Raynor had no one waiting for him back home in Louisiana.

The memory of making love to Lizzie was one so sweet and precious he was forced at times to reassure himself that it really happened. But he knew it did, and the effect had been profound, though paradoxical: On the one hand he felt that his life was complete and could hardly be diminished, even by death in battle; on the other, he was more determined than ever to come home to Lizzie, to cherish and embrace her for unnumbered years to come. And even though he was surrounded by men who were closer to him than family, without her at his side he might as well have been alone.

"I guess the hardest part was that span when we were on the ship and couldn't get any mail, Lizzie. I read your old letters over and over. I'd begin with the very first, and read them all, and every night I'd pretend that one of the old ones had just come that day. I knew them all by heart, but that didn't matter."

She wrote every day and her letters accumulated, to be delivered as soon as his ship was in port. There was an impressive bundle of new mail when he landed in Africa, mostly letters from Lizzie.

"I got a whole bunch all at once, all tied up in post office string. That was a glorious mail call, Lizzie. Of course, I had to wait all day before I could read them. They had other things for us to do. Nothing important—just something to keep us busy."

But he recalled how nightfall finally had brought freedom from the make-work duties imposed by the army, and how he lay in his cramped bunk and opened each letter in the order of its postmark and savored it like a man about to die of thirst getting his first few drops of water. Lizzie never mentioned that night in the moonlight, but he discerned right away that her letters had a more serious tone. Her writing no longer conveyed the juvenile emotion of a teenager; instead, it transmitted a mature voice, that of a woman whose seasoned love was strong enough to endure the separation of war. Her expressions of love were no less fervent, but more matter-of-fact. She understood that Bradley was likely to be away for many months and she was prepared to wait, no matter how long her wait might be.

Although she never conceded it in her letters, he could sense her worry. The happy reports of riding hillside paths on Danny Boy and romping in the fields with Butterball gave way to more tedious accounts of the War Bond drives and meatless Thursdays that let the people of Simpson's Ridge demonstrate their support for the war effort. Lizzie took comfort in playing some role, no matter how small, and he was very proud of her.

"But I'd grown up a lot, too, Lizzie," he said audibly, as if he had been sharing his thoughts. "I was just a boy when I climbed on that Greyhound bus and left Simpson's Ridge for the army, and I know the training was part of it, but you were the main reason. For the first time in my life I felt responsible for somebody besides myself. When we got to Africa I didn't have any more silly ideas about dying a hero's death."

When his division made ready for contact with the enemy, his logical mind told him that he might be killed and he accepted that notion calmly and without remorse. But it was no longer because he had dreams of being a hero. Instead, it was because he had come to feel that if it should be his destiny to die in combat—well, his life would have amounted to something good, even in his few short years, because a man who had loved and been loved by Elizabeth Kraft had been privileged as few men are.

"But I knew my odds were good, Lizzie. You were waiting for me back in Kentucky, and no man had more to live for than I did. And that's still true, Lizzie . . . but now you're . . ."

Sitting alone in the big house, still clutching Lizzie's photograph, he had come full circle. Sweet memories could no longer cover the dismal reality; he had faced his own death with equanimity, but a lifetime of challenges had not prepared him for the loss of Lizzie. He always had drawn his strength from her. She always could point to a brighter day ahead, no matter how bleak the circumstances and life's disappointments were insignificant compared to her love and devotion.

But now, with Lizzie lying helpless and unresponsive, he felt as if his anchor chain had been cut, leaving him adrift. He felt helpless and hopeless. He put Lizzie's picture aside and buried his face deeply in his hands, a figure of utter despair.

I have to talk to Jennie, the way I would to her mother. Why had it taken him so long to think of it? He had been keenly aware of the need to discuss their mother's situation more fully with the children, and fought it, but it had not occurred to him that he might lean on Jennie for the counsel he could no longer gain from Lizzie. And it should have been obvious, Jennie's nature was so like her mother's.

When Jennie got home from a long morning at the hospital, he was waiting. He sat at the kitchen table, weary and discouraged, lack of sleep and the demands of long hours at Lizzie's bedside beginning to take their heavy toll. "Has her condition changed any?" he asked.

"No, Daddy. She doesn't seem any different."

"Tell me what to do, Jennie," he said abruptly, his voice anguished. "Please tell me what to do."

Jennie seemed taken aback by her father's sudden and direct plea for help. It took a moment for her to gather her thoughts and find words to respond. Then she said softly, "I can't tell you what to do, Daddy. I think it's best that we let Mother go, but we want you to be sure it's what you want."

"I could never be sure. Jennie, as long as she is alive, I could never be sure that taking her off life support is the right thing to do. As long as there is any hope at all . . ."

"Oh, Daddy, we know how you feel. We all feel the same way. Matt and I have discussed it with Aunt Catherine, and Sarah and Uncle Walter have agonized over this, too. I wish Paul was here, but I know he'd say there is no easy answer. Dr. Garvey has told us for some days now that he sees no hope, that Mother is not going to recover. Matt asked if he ever knew of a single instance where someone in Mother's condition did recover, and he said he didn't. He seems certain that it's futile to keep her alive."

"I've shed so many tears, I don't cry much anymore," Bradley said. "But I still can't bring myself to accept the fact that she's not going to pull out of this. And I know she's not conscious, but I just can't help thinking that maybe she knows I'm there. And Jennie, I don't think I could live with the fact that we might have given up too soon."

Jennie put her arms around her father and clung to him tightly. "The strain of all this is wearing you out," she said. "Feel how thin you're getting!"

"I'm tired, but I have to be there for your mother as long as there's any hope."

"I've been thinking about something one of Mother's nurses told me. I know it's a long shot, but maybe it's something we could consider."

"I'd go along with anything. Just tell me what."

"She said they use music with patients like Mother sometimes. They're not sure why, but they think music may stimulate the brain if there's any awareness at all, and sometimes it causes the patient to respond. I think we should try it."

"If you think it's a good idea," her father replied, "then we should do it."

"We mustn't expect too much, but we don't have anything to lose. We have to use Elvis, don't you think? That's the music Mother has come to love. I know she used to laugh about Elvis, but I believe she got to be as much of an Elvis fan as anybody in the world."

"Your mother and I fell in love to the music of Glenn Miller, and she always liked Frank Sinatra and Perry Como. I suppose we liked a little of this and a little of that through the years—Neil Diamond certainly—but once your mother began to listen to Elvis she was greatly taken by him. She always said he had a wonderful way with ballads."

"I remember you still listening to Perry Como when I was listening to Bob Dylan," Jennie said, managing a quick smile.

"When we were in Sicily, we heard this great singer—I don't remember the name—and Lizzie talked later about how beautiful music can be. She said it's wonderful that you can like every kind of music, from this great Italian singer to Elvis."

"That would have been Bocelli. Such a magnificent voice. But we need one of Elvis's ballads. Something she would have listened to many times over. Do you know her favorite?"

"I know there was one she liked more than all the others, but I can't think what it was," Bradley said.

"We'll find it."

For the next half-hour, they looked though old record albums. Bradley was surprised at the extent of Lizzie's collection. She had persuaded him years back that they should get modern stereo equipment to replace the old Philco hi-fidelity record player, and she kept buying music as long as it came on vinyl. She gave up when compact disks came along; the old music was better, she said, and she still played her vinyl albums.

Bradley's spirits rose as they looked through Lizzie's recordings. He'd felt as if he was failing her completely at the very time she needed him most, but now he was among her things, holding in his hands something dear to her, and now there was something he could do. He saw familiar lyrics on a jacket liner and knew he had found the song Lizzie loved best.

"This one," he told Jennie. "This one is her favorite: 'I'll Remember You.'"

"We need to record it onto a tape so we can play it to Mother in the hospital," Jennie said. "Can we do that here?"

"Yes. She has a tape deck, if we can figure out how it works."

Lizzie always kept blank tapes in a drawer, he recalled, and they soon had one in the tape deck, recording her favorite Elvis love song directly from the album. The words were painful for Bradley to hear. Every line of the song reminded him of Lizzie. The ballad's soft, longing lyrics—beautiful and romantic words about warm summer breezes, sweet laughter, love remembered—reduced him to uncontrollable sobs.

Jennie stood by helplessly, as if she too felt a great sense of sadness, listening to the song and understanding why it affected her father the way it did. She sat down beside him and put her arm around him, and let him cry until his emotional outpouring was spent.

"We can play it for Mother tonight," she said. "I'll ask Matt and Sarah to come to the hospital. Daddy, I know we must not expect too much."

"I know, Jennie. But we have to try. And thank you for telling me about he music."

At Lizzie's bedside, the family waited expectantly as Matthew set up a small cassette tape player and put in the recording that his father and his sister had made just a few hours earlier. He also had brought headphones, but they decided to play the music aloud, to fill the room with soft lyrics familiar to Lizzie—music she loved. The speakers were mere inches from her head as the music began to play.

There was no reaction. Lizzie lay motionless, unhearing.

Around the bed, her family slowly gave in to their disappointment. Sarah, holding her mother-in-law's hand, breathed a long sigh of resignation and quietly stroked Lizzie's hair. Jennie placed a hand on her father's shoulder.

"I don't think there's any use," Matthew said. "I don't think she hears it."

"We should let it play," Jennie said. "The nurses said the effect of this kind of stimulus doesn't always show immediately. Set it to play over and over, Matt."

"It won't work that way," her brother said. "You only have a short segment of music on a forty-five-minute tape. I'll rewind it and play it again."

He replayed the song at a slightly higher volume, but Lizzie's response was the same. She lay lifeless, with no more sign of awareness than she had offered at the familiar sounds of her family's voices. Matthew rewound the tape and played it a third time, then a fourth and a fifth.

"You needn't play it again, Matthew," Bradley said. "She doesn't hear it."

"We could record more music and let it play for a long time," Matthew said. "If you think it might help, I'll go record a full tape and then we could just let it run."

"There isn't any need," his father said. "Your mother won't

hear it, Matthew. She wouldn't know it was there."

Bradley had seen the music as a desperate but final ray of hope, and now that hope was lost. He must face the awful reality at last and accept the fact that Lizzie was gone. Dr. Garvey had made clear that her survival was artificial, commanded by the life support system, but Bradley had refused to believe it. He had not been able to let go, to accept the loss he felt he could not bear. Lizzie was the center of his being, and surely life without her could hold no meaning. But he knew now that, even though there still might be breath in her mortal body, her soul and spirit had fled.

"Please call Dr. Garvey," he told Jennie. "Please tell him we want to take her off the machines."

Twenty-four hours after the respirator was removed, Lizzie still clung to life. The inevitable end sometimes comes slowly, Dr. Garvey explained, and might take several days, but it would come and the family should prepare for Lizzie's passing.

"She's waged a courageous battle," the doctor said, "but she just didn't have anything to fight with. There was too much damage from the beginning. You should take comfort in knowing that she didn't suffer, that she's had the best care she could have and that her loved ones have been here at her side."

"Yes," Bradley told him, "we're grateful for that."

But gratitude was not the feeling that pervaded Bradley Morris's senses. His heart was breaking and the perception of utter loss was beginning to set in. He doubted that he had the strength to deal with it, but of course he had no choice. His mind was numb, his spirits shattered. He felt tired beyond endurance. Yet he had an obligation to make plans. There would be decisions to make, if only he knew where to begin.

To his surprise, he slept well that night. There was no longer the tension of hoping but not believing that Lizzie would be better the next time he saw her. Now there was no uncertainty as to the outcome. It was merely a matter of waiting.

But the next day he found himself capable of only the most

routine activities essential to his own survival, the things he did mechanically, things that took no will to do. It was as if he were detached from reality, living in a dimension apart from the world with which he was familiar and oblivious to that world. Matthew and Jennie took care to see to his needs, comforting him as best they could, persuading him to eat and rest, then at mid-morning he went back to Lizzie's bedside.

If Lizzie's condition had changed, the change was not visible. The electronic monitors still presented a pattern of vital signs he had become accustomed to, indicating life. He felt deceived. The machines lied, promising continuation when there would be none. Why would the machines not tell the truth: that Lizzie Morris was dead and life no longer mattered? Yet how could he face the truth, if the truth meant they would put Lizzie in a box and bury her in the ground?

Assailed by his own bitterness, he fled the room and walked out into the streets of Memphis.

12

An anemic yellow sun pierced the light overcast. Bradley shielded his eyes with a hand to his forehead as he walked, with little regard for where he was or where he was going. He had no plan except to distance himself from the dismal hospital room where Lizzie lay dying.

Generally oblivious to his surroundings, he was several blocks from the medical center before he became aware of others on the street, and then only because of some commotion ahead. A small knot of people, including a half-dozen teenagers, clustered around an animated little figure of a man who held a Bible aloft in his left hand and gestured wildly with his free right hand, pointing and thrusting, jabbing the air, demanding and threatening. The bystanders apparently were more curious than interested in what the man had to say; their number swelled and shrank in a random sort of way as newcomers joined the fringes and others, their curiosity satisfied, moved on.

"Jesus shed His precious blood for you, that even the vilest sinner may be redeemed," the little man shouted. "Is there one among you who can say he has not sinned? Search your hearts, my friends. I come in the name of Jesus, crucified on the dark cross of Calvary, because all have sinned and fallen short of the glory of God."

The little preacher's voice rose. He spread his arms wide, imploring his listeners and waving his Bible.

"My friends, listen to Brother Percy! God will enrich your lives. Just give Him a chance. God loves you. Jesus loves you. Only in the light of Jesus will you find what you seek. Only through His blood will you find the way to salvation and eternal life. Only in accepting the will of God will you find comfort in this world."

His speech was rapid, like the chant of an auctioneer: "When you hear the voice of God and listen to His voice, and accept the love of Jesus, God will give you the strength to stand up against the wicked powers of darkness. He'll cloak you in the breastplate of His righteousness."

A teenager at the front of the circle, nearest Brother Percy, began to mimic the preacher's movements, bobbing and weaving like a boxer in the ring, pawing and jabbing with his right hand as if striking out at an imagined adversary.

"Breastplate?" mocked another. "Did he say breast? Hey, Brother Percy, does your old lady know you come down here on the street corner and talk to young chicks about breasts? Watch your language, man, Erika here has sensitive ears!"

A teenaged girl, hanging onto the arm of the youth who was verbally taunting the sidewalk preacher, screeched gleefully. "Don't give him too much credit, Rudy," she said loudly. "You know he ain't got no old lady. He probably likes little boys."

"Listen to them," parried the little preacher shrilly. "Hear the voices of evil! Young women, don't sacrifice your spirits to these idolaters, these hypocrites. They don't respect your womanhood. The Bible says the hypocrite will destroy with his mouth. But he can't touch you if you walk in the light of Jesus . . ."

Bradley Morris moved on. He had witnessed the scene before, as street-corner preachers were common in this part of Memphis. Today it was Brother Percy, another time it would be someone else, but the pattern would be the same and he knew the pattern well. The little preacher would grow more agitated, his voice rising to an ever sharper pitch in his fervor. His crowd of listeners would grow. Some would revel in his message, while others listened in embarrassed silence. A few of those who took him seriously would seek to debate his logic, or his interpretation of the Scripture. The mimic, buoyed by the swelling audience, would join forces with the teenager who had begun to mock the preacher with words. Others in the crowd would pick up the cue and challenge the self-appointed messenger of God, deriding him openly.

Bradley also knew that their insults would not deter the preacher—would invigorate him, in fact, paying him the high tribute of persecution. For it was persecution that elevated this obscure little man to the ranks of the blessed, carrying him a step closer to the Kingdom of God.

Blessed are ye, when men shall revile you, and persecute you and say all manner of evil against you . . . Memory failed. How many years ago had he heard those words, sitting at Lizzie's side in Shiloh Church? They were elusive to his own mind now, but surely must be the source of Brother Percy's determination to take up his pulpit on the street corner and suffer the certain insults and hostility.

Bradley looked about, seeking his bearings. The pain in his leg was intense and he needed a place to rest.

Across the street, on one of the somber red-brick buildings, he spied a row of pigeons lined up body against body and clinging to the false storefront crown, dipping and swaying in the spring wind gusts. They seemed to form a solid living wall, a staunch cooperative line of defense against nature's spasms. It struck him as both fascinating and absurd that some of the birds faced in one direction, some in another, so that from either front or back the view would be head, tail, tail, head, head, tail. Did the birds know this and was it intentional, or were they like people, too often joined in what they hoped was a common effort but were in fact headed in different directions?

He tried to force his mind to dwell on such insignificant questions. A moment of consciousness devoted to the pigeons was a moment in which his brain might be relieved of the stress that came with thoughts about Lizzie.

Distracted as he was by the pigeons, he carelessly bumped into a young man coming toward him on the sidewalk. He started to apologize, but the youth cut him off, demanding angrily, "Watch where you're fuckin' going, old man!" He stepped aside to accommodate an old woman clad in a heavy, dark-colored coat and wearing a green transparent sun visor on her head, walking slowly with the aid of a cane. She carried a large purse over her free arm, clutched close to her body as though she feared there might be thieves lurking nearby.

He sought refuge in a small café at the corner, and even though it was poorly lit and dingy he felt more comfortable once he had stepped inside. A few small tables covered with red-checked oil cloth lined the walls and sat at random in the middle of the room. He ignored the tables and shuffled to the back, slid onto one of the half-dozen or so padded bar stools that stood along a short counter, and asked the lone waitress for coffee.

Something about the unpretentious little café was familiar. It reminded him of the intimate *trattoria* where he and Lizzie had stopped for lunch in Vizzini, where the pretty waitress had made him think back to Lizzie as a young girl in Simpson's ridge. This was a memory he could not elude; any escape from the image of Lizzie lying comatose in the hospital room he had just left would be short-lived.

"How 'bout setting me up to a cup of that, buddy?"

Bradley was startled by the voice of a man he hadn't noticed, approaching from the side of the room. The man was young, probably in his mid-twenties. He was missing a hand, his left arm having been severed just above the wrist, and looked unbalanced when he walked. His jeans and heavy plaid shirt were frayed but reasonably clean, his hair long and unkempt and his face covered with scruffy beard.

"Damn you, John Henry," the waitress scolded, "I told you not to bother the customers. Now get the hell out of here."

"No, no, that's all right," Bradley Morris said. "Get him the coffee. I'll pay for it."

"I told him he couldn't stay around here if he bothered the customers," the woman protested, nonetheless pouring another cup. She shoved it rudely across the counter, in the general direction of the young man. "Here. Now drink this and go."

"He can say if he don't want to talk to me," the young man whined. "I don't bother nobody that don't want me." He turned to Bradley. "Thanks, man. I appreciate this. I don't go around panhandling, just been down on my luck a little lately. You know what I mean?"

"Sure. I know what you mean."

John Henry, taking his benefactor's response as a cue, slid onto the next stool. He carefully poured a generous measure of sugar from a metal-domed glass container on the counter and stirred his coffee vigorously. When he spoke again, it was almost as if he were speaking to himself: "It's hard for a guy like me to get work, you know what I mean?" He sipped the hot coffee, then turned and looked at Bradley intently. "Man, you look like shit. You sick or what?"

The woman, whose back had been turned, whirled and glared at John Henry. He ducked, as if expecting to be hit. The woman turned her back again and John Henry gestured obscenely in her direction.

"I'm okay," Bradley said. "I'm just tired."

He had an impulse to pour out his feelings to the young stranger, to tell him about Lizzie and recount their happy years together. He wanted to speak of the emptiness of life without her and describe his overwhelming sense of loss and despair. He couldn't expect the young man to understand, but he needed to tell someone his story, to let his heartache gush forth. He said nothing, however, and the two men drank their coffee in silence, staring straight ahead.

The waitress came and refilled their cups. John Henry again poured a generous if imprecise amount of sugar and stirred with a loud clatter of spoon and cup, and drank half the coffee before speaking again: "My old man died. He didn't look no worse than you, but there was something wrong with his heart. They put him in the hospital and said he was doing okay. He was s'posed to come home next day, but he was up setting on the pot and went out like a light. Just like my old man . . . shot hisself off to the pearly gates trying to take a crap."

John Henry's voice quivered. "It's hard when you ain't got no job," he said. "You know what I mean?" He scowled at the woman, daring her to challenge his discourse with the customer, but she pretended not to hear.

"Yes, I understand," Bradley replied. At another time, he might have responded to the emotional turmoil evident in the young vagabond's manner, but now he was too encumbered with his own pain to be concerned.

The young man scooted off the stool and walked away, muttering to himself as he went out the door.

"I'm sorry about him," the waitress said. "I chase him out all the time, but he always comes back. I keep hoping he'll take his business somewhere else. I do kinda feel sorry for him sometimes, though. Like my grandma used to say, his brain's like two grains of wheat hid in two barrels of chaff."

"He didn't bother me, really."

"Don't you want some pie or something, hon? You look like you could use something to eat."

"No. I'm fine. I'd just been walking a bit too long. I've got a bad leg, and sometimes it gives out on me. But I'm all right now. I need to be moving along."

"Stay and visit," the waitress said. "I'm good to talk to, and there won't be many people in here today. I'm just like a bartender back here. You can tell me your troubles, or practice your bad jokes on me, whatever . . ."

"Thanks, but I need to go."

The waitress looked disappointed, but said nothing more.

Bradley paid for the coffee and left his change on the counter, then limped out of the café and walked west, toward the Mississippi. A few blocks farther on he came to the riverfront, where there was a modest-sized public park atop the bluff and a long, dilapidated concrete stairway that led down to the river's edge. Two solitary figures sat on park benches and looked out over the river. Overhead, a large flock of Canada geese winged its way northward, the birds' rude and incessant honking countering dramatically the graceful beauty of their flight and intricate pattern of their formation.

The wind off the river was cool. Bradley's thin cotton jacket was too light for long periods outdoors, but he gave no thought to the cold. He wanted to feel the ever-present and enduring river, to dip his hands in the murky water and tromp along the river's edge as far as he could go, to keep walking until he had lost track of time and place and no longer had to confront his mental image of Lizzie, pale and dying in her bed. He leaned heavily on the rusted iron railing and dragged his aching leg down the broken, uneven steps. The descent was longer than he thought and it took several minutes, but at last he felt the wet sand under his feet.

He walked for perhaps a hundred yards along the edge of the water, limping badly, then paused and looked back. His tracks stretched behind him like a dotted line on some giant parchment. When a man dies, he reflected, he leaves no tracks. *A life is like my tracks in the sand. The river will wash them away.*

The flat and smooth river's edge soon gave way to a ragged, muddy embankment and he was forced to turn back. He mounted the steps slowly, the arduous climb back to the top of the bluff sapping what little strength he had left, and lowered himself onto a cold wooden bench, forgetting the city at his back. All the other benches were empty now; he was alone.

From this high vantage point, Bradley could see for miles up and down the Mississippi. He studied the river as if seeing it for the first time, awed by its paradoxical power and tranquility. Rivers were created to keep pace with eons, not the infinitesimal lifespan of mortal beings. The Mississippi had churned its way toward the Gulf of Mexico for countless centuries, and who knew how many mortals had sat where he sat now, atop this bluff, looking down upon the river, astonished by its splendor.

Far downriver, a tugboat pushed a string of barges in his direction, butting stubbornly against the strong current as it made its way upstream. The throb of the tug's powerful diesel engines was barely perceptible to his ears. He could make out a lone deckhand, busy on one of the front barges, as the tug churned the water into a white wake that stretched out behind for a great distance and, measured against the flowing river, looked to be moving rapidly. In reality, though, it was making slow progress,

more accurately measured against markers along the riverbank—
the bushy willows and towering cottonwood trees.

What did the barges carry? That question occupied Bradley's
mind and helped him escape, for the moment, the mental torment that was his affliction. He wondered about the crew of the
tug. How many were there? Where was their home port? Did they
have wives and children who waited while they plied the river
with their string of barges? Were there women among them?
Who was their captain?

He watched the tug for some time before it drew close and
began to edge toward the near shore, herding its barges in the
direction of the Memphis riverfront docks. Rivers were not for
hurried people. Rivermen must be patient, their tugboats moved
so slowly. *Maybe I should have chosen life on the river instead of the
railroad. But then I would have had to be away from Lizzie, and I could
never have done that.* His anguish returned.

Bradley struggled up from the bench, uncertain at first, then
limped slowly to the lone structure at the edge of the deserted
park and entered the dimly lit men's room. He began to retch.
The heaving pulled at his stomach and strained his chest. He
pushed into a toilet stall, eyes running and throat inflamed from
the exertion, and stood over the bowl expectantly until the retching subsided. Insensible to his filthy surroundings, he felt better
inside the tiny cubicle, its walls pressing closely on three sides
and a steel door securely latched at his back. Here, no one could
invade his tranquil solitude. This was a place where he could re-
main, alone in his grief, for as long as he felt the need.

Vulgarities scrawled in ink and pencil on the cubicle walls
drew his attention: "Bash a queer for Christ," "faggot ass," then
something that must have been a racial epithet but was no longer
legible, followed by "dumb nigger" and "Save this land, join the
Klan."

Other inscriptions had been scratched into the paint, then
scratched out, as the compartment endured long seasons without
new finish. What appeared to be the most recent addition, on the
side wall at Bradley's elbow and initiated with green felt marker,

had begun as an obscene drawing of hairy testicles and a fat, dangling penis. A later artist had added to the sketch, penciling in eyes and mouth so that the scrotum became a puffy human face and the penis a bulbous nose. Below the crude drawing was scrawled "A HEBREW," and after that, "stupid jew."

The opposite wall of the cubicle, as if through some unstated but universally understood agreement, had been spared the worst obscenities. It offered an absurd collection of what its contributors must have considered contemplative discourse: "Jesus loves those who love themselves." "Those who truly love themselves do not fall into the false consciousness created by belief in religion." One writer, perhaps agitated by the coarseness of what he saw or perhaps merely eager to demonstrate a brush with intellect, had added an indictment: *Voice écrit le mots de sots.* Bradley concentrated briefly on this simple epigram. He recalled little of his high school French, but decided that it said something about the words of fools.

At another time, he would have been repulsed by the bigotry and ignorance displayed by the ugly graffiti and embarrassed that it was here in a public place in Memphis, for all the world to see. But on this day, his disgust was tempered by an inescapable sense of resignation. What did it matter?

After several minutes, although he was reluctant to surrender the haven offered by the protective walls, he left the toilet stall and moved with purpose across the room to a dirty sink. He cupped his hands under the dripping faucet, filled them with cold water and splashed it on his face. He looked about for paper towels, but the metal rack on the wall was empty. He wiped his palms on his trousers, rubbing them quickly over his thighs. He was about to turn toward the door when some subtle hint of motion in a solitary, gurgling urinal caught his eye.

A narrow shaft of fading afternoon sunlight angled across the room from a single small window near the ceiling. Like a theater spotlight, it illuminated the performer: a large cockroach trying to climb the face of the urinal, struggling against a continuously flowing sheet of water. Bradley watched, appalled yet fascinated, as the insect clawed its way torturously up the stained porcelain surface almost to the top, then finally lost its grip and slid back. At the bottom, saved by a foul wire screen in the drain, it kicked frantically until at last it gained enough traction to begin the ascent again. This time it got half way up before being washed down. But again it persisted, found treacherous footing, and began once more its hopeless climb.

What might the insect gain even if it succeeded in its heroic effort to reach the top of the urinal? There was no way for it to escape. It was fighting a battle it could not win.

Bradley Morris was a gentle man; he felt pity for all living things. Even this loathsome cockroach deserved better than the torment it must be suffering. He found a small bit of pine branch on the ground just outside the door and, returning to the urinal, raked the insect out onto the concrete floor and watched it drag itself toward a corner of the room.

It was as if he had been God for that brief instant, he thought to himself, exercising the power of life and death. *And I gave it a chance at life . . .*

But God would not favor Lizzie with new life. She would be taken from him and there was nothing he could do. He still felt intently the bitter distress that had driven him from her bedside earlier in the day, but knew that there was no eluding the awful reality. He would no longer try to run away. He went to a telephone sheltered on an outside wall of the building and, with a trembling finger, dialed the number he and Lizzie had shared for more years than he could remember. When Sarah answered on the second ring he told her, in a plaintive whisper, "I need help. Can someone come and pick me up?"

Bradley did not go back to the hospital that night. Matthew and Jennie had been there all day, and Sarah went to relieve them after dinner. She promised to call home at once should there be any change in Lizzie's condition.

Now it was a waiting game. Dr. Garvey had told them that it was only a matter of time, and that the time must come soon.

Lizzie's frail body could not sustain life for much longer.

What the doctor did not mention—and what none of them wanted to contemplate—was the fact that it would be want of food and fluids that eventually took Lizzie's life. Even though she lacked normal brain activity, her body had temporarily regained the rhythm of breathing and circulation from the impetus of the life-support system and might maintain those functions for an unpredictable period. But there was no sustenance now. The medical enterprise that had kept her alive was not divine and would not permit the mercy of an easy exit. Unless her body gave out sooner, she would be left to die by dehydration.

Russell Burgess stopped by in the evening. Although he had called several times to ask about Lizzie, this was the first time he had come to the house since her collapse. "I'm sorry I haven't come sooner," he said. "I just didn't know when was a good time."

Bradley was happy to see his old friend from the railroad. He said, "I'm glad to see you, Russ. This is a good time for me, and I hope you can stay for a while."

"Is there anything new on Lizzie?"

"No. There's no longer any hope." The admission came easily this time, a simple statement of fact.

"I can't tell you how sorry we are. You know that if there's anything Lois and I can do, just call us. Will you be all right?"

"Russ, I just don't know how I can make it. She's been so much to me for so long. You know how it is—you and Lois have been married for a long time. Can you imagine trying to get along without her?"

"No, and I've never expected to have to face that, Brad. I just assume that I'll go first."

"So did I. Men are supposed to die first. All I'd ever worried about was whether she'd have enough to live on when I died. And then after I felt she was secure, I knew she'd have the children to look after her and take care of things for her, and I didn't have to worry about that any more. I seem to be in good health, so I just thought we'd still have a good many years together."

"Are the children here?"

"Yes, and that's helped more than I can tell you. I don't think I could get through this without them. Matt and Jennie have propped me up a lot, Russ. I feel like a burden to them. They're grieving, too, and then they have to worry about me."

"Oh, I'm sure that's not true. You've always been a strong man. You're not a burden to anyone, Brad."

"I can't help but feel like it."

"Well, you're not. The children would be the first to tell you that. It's hard for all of you, but you just have to keep doing the best you can."

"There's something else that's been bothering me, Russ. I need you to tell me something, if you will."

"Of course I will. What is it?"

"I keep worrying that I may have said things about Lizzie that I didn't mean. You know, when the men at work start talking about things at home, and then one thing leads to another . . . I keep thinking I might have said something negative about Lizzie. She's a wonderful woman, Russ, and I'd never intend to say anything that might lead anybody to think different."

Russell Burgess smiled, then laughed aloud. "Brad, every man who ever worked with you knows how much you love Lizzie," he said. "Anytime there was talk like that, you made it clear how lucky you felt. If there was ever a negative word about Lizzie Morris, it sure didn't come from you."

They talked about lighter topics—the old days on the Illinois Central, fishing trips they had taken together down in Mississippi, comparative notes on the grandchildren. Then Russell had to go, slowly stretching out his departure with promises to keep in touch and extracting in turn Bradley's pledge to let him know the instant there was any change in Lizzie's condition.

After he was gone, Bradley got into Lizzie's things, fumbling through drawers and boxes, little hoards she'd put away in the top of her closet. He recalled her saying she wanted to sort all this out before the end of summer and get some of it to the attic. But she never would have parted with these things handily, for here were her true treasures: photographs, notes, clippings, letters, , small remembrances from Jennie's and Matthew's child-hoods, an odd and touching collection of precious mementos gathered over a lifetime.

He was familiar with most of the things he found, but others were altogether new discoveries. Pictures of Beth were every-where. After Jeff and Mark, Lizzie had once worried that all of their grandchildren might be boys, "and I want a granddaughter to buy pink dresses for!" But there were ample reflections of the grandsons' lives, as well, and even a casual observer couldn't miss the evidence of Mark's baseball talent and Jeff's love of music.

Matthew's letters from Vietnam were there, tucked away in a lower drawer. Matt had addressed his correspondence to both of them, but it was clear that he was writing to his mother. These would be difficult for Bradley; he could not forget the strained relationship he'd had with Matt then, any more than he could forget how hard Lizzie had worked to hold things together, and he felt guilty. I have to talk to Matt about Vietnam, he mused. *Lizzie wants us to put all that behind us.*

There were keepsakes from Lizzie's girlhood in Simpson's Ridge and things that had been her mother's or father's, includ-ing a letter that a teenaged Matthew had written to his grandfa-ther Kraft. Bradley felt guilty again, sensing that he was invading his son's privacy, but the letter was so sweetly light-hearted and naive that he couldn't stop reading. "You told me to make sure any girl I like has a warm heart and warm feet," young Matt had written. "Well, I like this girl a lot and I believe she has a warm heart. I don't know about her feet." The girl's name, he said, was Sarah.

He carefully folded the letter and replaced it, considering whether he should reveal it to the children. Sarah would love it, of course, and there was no reason that it should embarrass Matthew. He decided to put it aside and slip it to Sarah the first thing in the morning.

In a small box, carefully wrapped in yellowed tissue paper, was Bradley's Purple Heart. Lizzie had been the one to care for the medal, preserving it conscientiously and treating it with greatest respect. He was proud when he received it. But later, during the period of his worst pain, resentful of his wounds and his slow progress in healing and bitter over Carson Streator's death, he threw it away. He was grateful that others had retrieved it and got it into Lizzie's hands, for now it meant a great deal.

There was an old program from the Sunset Symphony. The popular outdoor concert had always been a favorite of Lizzie's, and she had saved this memento of the first one, more than twenty years past.

He remembered that evening. He knew exactly how Lizzie looked, how happy she was, on their first outing with a new baby grandson. Thousands of people had congregated on the bank of the Mississippi in the grand finale of the month-long "Memphis in May" celebration, to watch the sunset and listen to the music. The concert ended with fireworks and Lizzie had insisted that Sarah wake Mark, sleeping soundly in a picnic basket, "so he won't miss anything."

There was a front page from the August 17, 1977, *Commercial Appeal*, fragile and carefully folded. "Death Captures Crown Of Rock and Roll—Elvis Dies Apparently After Heart Attack," proclaimed its double-decked banner headline. Lizzie was never one to idolize superstars, and he was surprised that she'd kept the newspaper. But he recalled her saying once that "Elvis is just a local boy, and we should be proud of him." That was before she had come to like his music, grudgingly at first but then without reservation. He remembered that she was visibly upset when Elvis died, and he understood now that she had been more deeply affected than she'd let on.

Bradley's mind flashed back to the recording that he and Jennie had made for the hospital. The soft, sweet lyrics ran through his mind, over and over. He imagined himself singing the words to Lizzie, holding her softly in his arms, dancing slowly across the room. It was as if the words and music were theirs, meant for them alone.

If passion is for the young, perfect devotion knows no boundaries of age or circumstance. His devotion to Lizzie was beyond measure; surely there was nothing more perfect in all the realm of earth or heaven. As in the words of the song, he would remember his dearest Lizzie, so gently and so sweetly. But in his longing, he knew that memories could never be enough.

13

Bradley waited in an austere examining room on the fifth floor of the medical center. Reluctantly, he had conceded to Jennie's insistence that he see a doctor. A nasty rash on his back and chest, a mere nuisance to him, was still there after four days and Jennie urged him not to ignore it. She said the rash might be a symptom of something more serious.

He hoped this session would go quickly. He was eager to get to Lizzie's room in the adjacent hospital. If he had to wait too long, he had promised himself earlier, he simply would leave whether he'd been seen by a doctor or not, and get on to Lizzie's bedside. Any little problem he might have surely wasn't enough to keep him away from Lizzie.

There was a soft knock at the door. A young man rushed in, greeted Bradley perfunctorily, and said his name was Scott. He needed to check temperature and blood pressure.

"What brings you to us this morning, Mr. Morris?" Scott asked, hastily making notes on Bradley's medical chart.

"I have a rash."

"Where is it?"

"Mostly on my back, but some on my chest."

"How long have you had it?"

"Four days, I think. Maybe five."

"Take your shirt off and have a seat up here on the examining table," Scott said, completing his notes and laying the chart, opened to his entry, on the desk. "The doctor will be in to see you in a few minutes."

Bradley followed Scott's instructions. He barely had seated

himself on the table when there was a rustle outside the door, followed by another soft knock. A very tall man whose appearance was dominated by a garish red bow tie and long, pastel blue lab coat entered the room. He extended his hand to Bradley.

"I'm Dr. Christman," he said. "So you have a rash? Let's take a look."

The doctor studied Bradley's back for a couple of minutes, then looked quickly at his chest.

"Anything else going on? Any unusual pain?" Dr. Christman asked.

"Nothing much. I've had some shooting pains down the side of my back, kind of under the shoulder, but nothing too serious."

"Not much doubt about this one. You have a classic case of *herpes zoster*, young man—shingles."

"So it's nothing serious, then?"

"It can be very serious. How long have you had the rash?"

"Four days, I think. Maybe five."

"I wish you'd come to see me about three days sooner. I can give you some medicine, but it won't do too much good at this late date. It works a lot better if we can start it earlier, say in the first two days."

"I've heard of shingles, but I never knew what it was," Bradley said. "Where did I get it?"

"You gave it to yourself. Shingles comes from the chicken pox virus that's been lying dormant in your body all these years, just waiting for a chance. Have you been ill, or under a lot of stress recently?"

"Yes. My wife's very ill."

"I'm sorry. A stressful situation like that can slow you down just enough to give this vicious little bug an opening. The rash will go away in a few weeks, and if we're lucky the pain in your back will go with it."

"What if I'm not lucky? What's the worst that can happen?"

"The worst that can happen is you'll have pain the rest of your life. That's not too likely, but if often lasts several weeks or even months. The virus damages the nerves. Sometimes it can get pretty bad. Now, I'm going to give you a prescription for an antiviral agent that may help some. Be sure and follow the directions. It would help more if I'd seen you earlier, I'm afraid. And I'll also give you Darvocet for the pain. Do you have any other questions?"

"Just one. Is this something I can give to other people, something I can spread around?"

"That's extremely unlikely. They'd have to come in direct contact with your rash, so keep yourself covered. This antiviral medicine will last ten days. Be sure and take it all. Then I'd like to see you back here in two weeks."

Dr. Christman exited the room just as he'd entered: in a sudden rush. Bradley barely had time for a hasty "thank you."

When the doctor was gone, Bradley dressed hurriedly. He stopped at the outer desk and made a return appointment, then went to the clinic pharmacy and had his prescriptions filled. He went straight to Lizzie's room from there and was at her bedside when Jennie and Beth arrived.

Jennie had expressed confidence a day earlier that Beth finally had come to accept her grandmother's illness without being overwrought, and Jennie felt that it was time for her to visit the hospital again and see her grandmother for what might be the last time. Beth was subdued as she and her mother entered the room, obviously determined to stifle any show of emotion. "Hi, Granddaddy," she said. "I'm not going to be disruptive today."

"Oh, dear child, you've never been disruptive," Bradley answered. "We've all found this really hard to handle."

"Did you see a doctor?" Jennie asked.

"Yes. It's nothing serious. I'll tell you about it later. I see that Beth brought flowers."

"It's a silk azalea," Beth said proudly. "Grandmama's missing the azaleas this year and I know how she loves them."

"It's very pretty, Beth. I thought it was real."

Beth looked about the room for a place to put her offering. The cramped, barren chamber had little space for such niceties, though the family had brought fresh flowers almost every day. Beth settled on the window ledge, placing her azalea carefully. Then she returned to the bedside and gingerly touched her grandmother's hand, but looked uncertain as to what she should do next. "I wish she could talk to me," she said. "I've missed our talks more than anything."

"She loves talking with you, too," Bradley told her. "I believe the weeks you've spent with her at the big house have meant more to her than anything else in the world."

"She looks peaceful now," Beth said. "Don't you think so, Granddaddy?"

"Yes, I think she does."

Jennie had stayed back, leaving the space nearest Lizzie's bed to Beth and her grandfather. She stepped forward, moving close behind her daughter and putting her hands on Beth's shoulders. Beth reached up and placed a hand over her mother's, gripping tightly, and the two stood frozen in place, looking down upon the frail, still woman in the bed.

"She knows so much about everything," Beth said. "I think I drive her crazy with all my questions, but she can always explain things so I can understand. And she knows when something's bothering me before I even tell her."

"She's always been that way," Jennie said. "She did the same thing for me when I was your age. And a long time after your age, for that matter. I think she should have been a diplomat."

They stood beside the bed as Jennie told stories from her own childhood, stories of her mother that were the stories she wanted Beth to know and remember about her grandmother. Her stories held no surprises for Bradley, who had long since ceased to be astonished at how wise Lizzie could be when life got too complicated for those she loved.

"Daddy, do you remember the old Sears catalogs Mama saved way back when I was little?" Jennie asked. "She said they would be interesting in years to come, when we could look back and see how things have changed. Do you know if they're still around? I'd like to show Beth sometime."

"They're probably in the attic," Bradley said. "Your mother has a sentimental attachment to mail-order catalogs, because when she was a girl in Kentucky they used to order things through the mail. Your Grandfather Kraft used to say that if you couldn't find it in the Sears catalog you didn't need it in the first place."

"I remember she used to check things out in the Sears catalog before we went shopping," Jennie said. "She wanted to know what was available and what it cost before she went looking for it in the store."

Beth said she'd like to see the old catalogs, and her grandfather made a mental note to get into the attic one day soon and try to find them, thinking even as he spoke that this might not be an easy task. For years, the big house attic had been a repository for everything the family no longer needed but believed still might prove useful. He had little sense of just what might be there, because from the day they moved in they'd thrown away very little that wasn't worn out or broken beyond repair. He viewed the attic holdings differently now, though, for what he might have criticized a month ago as an accumulation of junk had become a priceless treasure; the attic contained timeless memories of Lizzie.

Jennie asked her father to take Beth somewhere for an early dinner and then home. Matthew and Sarah were coming soon, and the three of them would sit with her mother. She would be home before Beth's bedtime.

"Of course I will," he said. "The company of this young lady is always a pleasure!"

Beth giggled, and said it would be a pleasure for her, too.

As they left the hospital, Bradley was struck by the great number of old people in and around the complex of buildings that made up the medical center. There were couples who walked together slowly, hand in hand, and somber-faced, solitary men and women who appeared to be lost and uncertain. A feeble, emaciated woman was being hurried along by an impatient young couple who addressed her rudely and seemed to feel that they had more important things to do. Even though she was not alone, she looked lonely and despondent. The scene was depressing, and he was happy to get to the car and drive away from it all.

He found an affable restaurant only a few blocks away that was quiet and uncrowded, ahead of the dinner rush. It had a "Please Seat Yourself" sign and Beth led the way to a booth by a front window. The lone waitress brought tall glasses of water and menus and promised to be right back.

"I don't remember the last time you and I were out together, just the two of us," Bradley told his granddaughter.

"We went to the Dairy Queen. Does that count?"

"Sure it does. How long ago was it?"

"I'm not sure. Maybe a year ago," Beth said.

"Well, I've kind of lost track of time since your grandmother's illness. It would be fun if we could do this more often, don't you think?"

"I'd like that, Granddaddy."

The waitress, with few other diners to occupy her time, returned promptly for their order and soon had food on their table. Bradley Morris would not have believed he could be hungry, but the chicken tasted very good and he ate heartily. Beth dug into her plate of spaghetti and meatballs like a ravenous workman who had missed his lunch, and had finished half her food before pausing to make conversation.

"Granddaddy," she said then, "can I ask you some things about Grandmama?"

"Of course you can, Beth."

"Did you know her when she was a girl my age."

"Not quite that young, but just a few years older than you. We were both in high school when we met."

"So you're the same age?"

"Just about. I am a few weeks older."

"What was she like when you first met her?"

"Oh, child, she was the brightest and happiest girl I'd ever seen. And the prettiest. Every bit as pretty as you are. You look a lot like her, but you don't have her dark hair and eyes. Your mother looks like her, even more than you. But I'll bet you don't remember what your mother looked like when she was sixteen."

Beth looked perplexed for an instant, then quickly picked up on her grandfather's jest and laughed. "So you met her when she was sixteen?" she asked, serious again.

"Yes. And I left for the war just before she turned eighteen, and we were married when she was twenty."

"World War II, right? We've been studying it in school."

"Really? So you know all about it."

"I wouldn't say I know all about it, but we've learned a lot. I like General MacArthur and General Patton."

"You don't say! I served under General Patton."

"Did you really? General George S. Patton Jr.?"

"I did, really. General George S. Patton Jr. He was in charge of the invasion of Sicily. That's where I got wounded."

Beth's eyes were alight with interest. She had known since she was little that her grandfather was hurt in a war, and had asked lots of questions about his injuries and how much pain he'd been in and whether his leg still hurt all the time. Although these were topics Bradley usually avoided, he had been candid with her and answered her questions patiently and fully. But this was the first time she had been able to fit his personal experience into a context she had learned about in school, and she seemed excited to know that he had a connection with one of the war's great heroes.

"Did you ever see him?" she asked. "General Patton, I mean."

"Yes, I did. Believe it or not, he visited me one day in the hospital after I was wounded. Not just me, of course, but everybody. He pinned a medal on me, but I'd been given so much morphine I hardly knew what was going on. But I do remember seeing him."

"I'm proud of you, Granddaddy. Our teacher says all the soldiers who fought in World War II were heroes."

"Well, I wasn't a hero. I just did my job like everybody else. Lots of people who didn't even go into the service helped win the war just as much as those of us who did."

"Well, I still think you're a hero," Beth said.

Her bright smile made him feel good. If he was to be applauded for his role as a soldier simply doing what he had joined up to do, there was no source from which he would rather hear the praise than this granddaughter he treasured. He was proud that she understood something about the war—his war—and happy to have her link him with one of its eminent and truly heroic figures. Although he had not been a great Patton fan at the time he was wounded, he eventually came to see the fiery general as a brilliant military mind and exceptional leader and he suspected that his old commander's tough reputation had led lots of aging veterans to claim they had served under General Patton even if they hadn't. But he still was not comfortable with the "hero" talk.

"How is your dinner," he asked. "Ready to order dessert?"

"It's very good. But I think I've had enough."

"Whatever you say."

"Can I ask you something, Granddaddy?"

"Of course you can. You know you've always been able to ask me anything, don't you? What do you want to know?"

"Well . . . I may be all wrong about something," the girl said. She suddenly appeared to be uneasy.

Beth was rarely hesitant. Bradley had carried on mature conversations with her from the time she was four years old and could never remember seeing her reluctant to speak her mind. He was afraid to push her, afraid he might cause her to say things she would be sorry for later, but if his granddaughter was bothered by something he wanted her to feel free to talk about it. Lizzie would know what to do, he thought. *She would find out what the problem is and make everything all right in no time.* But he decided it was better not to press the child too hard. Beth would talk whenever she felt the time was right.

"Let's have some ice cream, and then you can decide whether you want to ask me," he said.

"I really don't care for anything more," Beth answered, sounding very mature. "We can talk in the car, though. But you do get ice cream if you'd like it."

He told her he didn't have much room for dessert, either.

The waitress brought the check, saying what a pretty girl Beth was and how honored he must be to keep such company. Beth beamed with pride.

They left the restaurant and drove toward the big house, soft music playing on the car radio. Beth rode along for several minutes pretending to listen to the music, not speaking. Her grandfather asked about school and got an unenthusiastic reply. He asked about her friends. She said her best friend had moved away during the winter, to Oregon, but she had lots more.

They were a few blocks from the big house when she blurted out her question: "I heard my mother and Uncle Matthew talking, and I think they said you might come to California and live with us. Is that true, Granddaddy?"

Bradley was stunned. Now he was the one who was hesitant, astonished by his granddaughter's question and uncertain how to respond. "Maybe you misunderstood, Beth," he said. "I'd love to visit you in California, but I don't have any plans to move. Are you sure they weren't talking about a visit?"

"No, I'm sure they said you might come and live with us. And Uncle Matthew said maybe you'd like Chicago better. I hoped it was true, Granddaddy. I wish you were coming to live in California."

Much as he wanted to believe that Beth had misunderstood some conversation between her mother and Matt, he could tell that she was confident about what she heard. He wanted to confront his children. And he would.

Late that night, long after Beth was in bed and sound asleep, he faced Jennie and Matthew with what his granddaughter had told him. They were taken by surprise, and obviously embarrassed, unaware that Beth had overheard the quiet conversation in which they shared their mutual concern about their father's future. Matt was defensive, and said there must be some misunderstanding, but Jennie chose to drop the secrecy: "We weren't scheming behind your back, Daddy. We were just talking about what would be best for you."

"I'll decide what's best for me," he said, his voice rising. "This is my home. Your mother and I have lived here—here in this house—since before either of you was born. I don't plan to leave it."

"Dad, you can't live here by yourself," Matthew said. "What happens if you have a problem? We'd like for you to be close to one of us, in Chicago or Los Angeles."

"We have lots of space," Jennie said. "You could move into the apartment over our garage and be totally self-sufficient. Beth would love to have you, and so would Paul and I. But we didn't intend to make that decision for you. We just want you to think about it. Will you do that, Daddy?"

"I don't have to think about it," Bradley said brusquely. "I have no plans to leave here. Not now and not ever. There's no reason to talk about it." He pulled himself up from his chair and limped from the room. Jennie and Matthew looked at one another dejectedly, but neither made an effort to stop him.

Jeff and Mark left Memphis early the next morning, after apologizing almost timidly for the fact that they had to go. Reluctant as they were to leave, Jeff said, they felt that there was nothing more they could do for their grandmother and they were afraid to be away from work much longer. Mark also was worried that he would be seriously behind in an evening MBA class he was taking at the University of Chicago if he missed another session. They extended their sympathies again and said goodbye to their grandfather and drove out ahead of the rush-hour traffic.

Bradley understood. The situation was getting difficult for all of them. Beth was missing school and Jennie would have to get her back to California soon, although she planned to return to Memphis alone once Paul got home from the Philippines. Matt and Sarah undoubtedly needed to get home, as well. He wished Walter and Catherine were there, though he wouldn't ask them to come. He felt great resentment toward Matt and Jennie since last night's confrontation, and Catherine's presence, especially, would make things less tense.

The children meant well, of course, but he was annoyed that

they had gone behind his back to plan his future, particularly given that their plans were not acceptable to him and never would be. And more than that, he was indignant that they were discussing life without Lizzie while Lizzie was still here. If the children loved her as he did, how could they talk as if she were gone?

Even as he considered what to do next, Catherine phoned. She and Walter were planning to leave for Memphis early in the afternoon.

"I'll be glad to see you," Bradley told her. "Don't worry about what time you get here. We'll wait up if it's late."

Her call was reassuring.

Although he wouldn't mention it, his irritation with the children was magnified by intense physical distress from his shingles. He had been awakened early in the morning by sharp nerve pain, almost like intermittent electrical shocks, in an area deep under his left shoulder blade. The pain medicine had brought little relief.

Jennie and Matthew came to breakfast and treated their father as though nothing had happened. Their immediate concern was to work out the day's schedule, and it was decided that Jennie would stay with Beth this morning while Matt and Sarah went with Bradley to the hospital, then Sarah would come back to the big house in the afternoon and Jennie would take her place at Lizzie's bedside.

"Won't you come back with Sarah, Daddy?" Jennie asked. "There's nothing you can do there. We're worried about you wearing yourself out. Why don't you come home and rest?"

"I'll think about it," Bradley told her. That was the only commitment he was willing to make.

They left for the hospital as soon as they finished breakfast, but the parking garage was crowded when they arrived and it took more time than usual to park the car and make their way through busy corridors to Lizzie's room. Medical technicians waited at elevators with patients on gurneys, off to x-ray or wherever, and doctors making their morning rounds hurried from room to room. Nurses at their stations pored over charts and briefed their replacements in preparation for a change of shifts.

The quiet of Lizzie's little chamber contrasted starkly to the commotion elsewhere in the building. The room was dark and cool, the only activity evident in the monitors over Lizzie's bed. It struck Bradley that this patient no longer seemed to matter to the medical establishment; it was as if she had been cast aside and forgotten.

Sarah apparently sensed his discouragement. She promptly turned on lights, made a great fuss over moving flowers from the window sill to the bedside table, fluffed and smoothed the pillows under Lizzie's head. "Let's make ourselves comfortable," she said. "We're going to be here for a long while this morning. Matt, we need another chair. Just tell them at the nurses' station. I don't know why they're always taking one away."

"They probably don't want more than two people at a time to be here," Bradley said. "But they never told us any rules about that."

"There aren't any rules," Matthew said. "They don't care how many of us visit, as long as we can all fit into the room. Make yourselves comfortable. I'll go find another chair."

But Bradley stood over Lizzie and tried to sort out his emotions. Although her condition surely must be deteriorating a little every day, no further change was evident and the monitors still flaunted the same deceitful signs of life. Electronic gadgetry might delude the uninformed into a false sense of hope, but he would not be duped again. He no longer had any illusion that his presence at Lizzie's side mattered. The ashen face was no longer hers; it was that of an apparition, a mere specter of the mortal being to whom he was unfailingly devoted. Love for her still filled his heart and gave him his reason for living, but now, to what end? She would never again be aware of his company.

Sarah urged him to take a chair. She told him she understood his feelings and how sorry they all were and how she loved Lizzie like her own mother, and he found comfort in her words.

"The boys hated to leave," Sarah said. "If they were better situated—more secure in their jobs—they could have stayed longer."

"It's hard to find a job today where there's any consideration of personal needs," he answered, grateful for ordinary conversation. "I mean consideration by the people you work for, the way it used to be."

"Yes, it is. It seems like everyone has to answer to some higher level management that doesn't know or care who you are."

There was a note of bitterness in her voice that was unusual for Sarah, but then he remembered that she lost her job at the bank not long after he and Lizzie were in Chicago. It obviously was a sensitive issue, because she had kept it from them for several weeks. Sarah had always liked her work, and since she and Matt arrived in Memphis he had heard enough of the details to know that she'd been treated rather shabbily.

"They weren't fair with you," he said.

Matthew returned with a third chair. "I'm sorry it took me so long," he said. "What have I missed? Who wasn't fair?"

"The bank wasn't fair with Sarah. She's more accepting than I would be. I'm afraid I might have wanted to go down there and blow the place up!"

"I think she may have felt like that when it happened," Matt said. "Fortunately, though, she doesn't have our hot Morris temper, Dad. And it's a good thing, I suppose. We'd have a hard time living together if she didn't have a cooler head than I do."

"How about the boys? It seems to me they take more after you, Sarah."

"They're as different as night and day," Sarah said. "Jeff has the patience of a saint, but Mark's just like his father. I think Jeff's music has had a lot to do with that, though."

"I'm glad we got to hear him play when we were there in September," Bradley said. "We knew he was good, but when we heard his band play that night we were really overwhelmed. Lizzie raved about Jeff's music for weeks."

"He was impressed that she liked his music," Matt said. "He

still tells people his grandmother is his biggest fan."

"But she doesn't hear the music anymore," Bradley said, once again conscious of Lizzie, lying comatose only a few feet away. "She didn't hear Elvis, she wouldn't hear Jeff. I wish she'd been able to hear Jeff's band more than that one time. She really did like it. I should have brought her to Chicago more often."

"You can't dwell on things like that now," Sarah said. "We all could spend our lives looking back at the things we might have done, but where does that get us?"

Bradley barely heard what Sarah was saying. His mind had wondered back to that amazing night in September, to the dingy little club where Jeff had held the spotlight and mesmerized the crowd. In recent days, he had come to understand better why the young listeners reacted the way they did. The music had carried them away from their worries, offered them a respite from their cares. How much he had needed such relief, himself, since Lizzie was stricken! Lizzie had said later that hearing Jeff's band that night was the most fun she'd had in ages, and Lizzie's pleasure was what he remembered best.

Bradley agreed to go with Sarah back to the big house as Jennie had asked him to. He wanted to be home when Catherine and Walter arrived, and he also remembered his promise to Jennie to look in the attic for Lizzie's old mail-order catalogs. He intended to keep his word, despite his falling out with the children the night before. He could go home with Sarah, and then spend the afternoon in the attic. That should make everyone happy.

They were about to leave when the Reverend Buford Acklin appeared at the door of Lizzie's room.

"I don't want to intrude," Pastor Acklin said. "I just wanted to look in for a minute. We all miss her so at the church." He stepped close to Lizzie's bedside and asked if he might say a prayer. No one objected, of course.

"Please join me," the minister said, as he bowed his head and placed a hand on Lizzie's arm.

Deep down, Bradley Morris wanted to pray, as he once might

have, and believe in his heart and mind that a benevolent God would hear and answer. He wanted to believe that he could commit Lizzie to God's care and take comfort that he'd done the right thing, that he'd done his best and God would look after the soulmate who meant more to him than all the world, the one whose love and companionship he could never live without.

He envied those who had faith in an Almighty who controlled human destiny. But such conviction was not within him. It had been years since he last believed in a God who involved Himself in human endeavor, or perhaps in any God at all. While the others prayed, he gazed at Lizzie's colorless face and silently wept.

14

T he spot where he sat was warm and cozy. He leaned back against a post, rough-hewn and darkened with age, and studied the particles of dust that swam before his eyes, suspended in mid-air and glowing like tiny golden flakes of neon in a shaft of bright sunlight that streamed in through the west window. He imagined Lizzie visiting the attic to put away things she wanted to save, and wondered how many cool spring or autumn afternoons the children had spent here, playing in sunny comfort. Were these very same particles of dust present then, these wee bits of matter that hung like Lilliputian planets in their own miniature universe? Were they disturbed by Lizzie's passing? Had they been dislodged and set afloat by the feet of happy children?

He exhaled a puff of breath and watched in fascination as the movement of air caused the dust specks to dance and swirl, the intensity of their motion diminishing as the distance from him increased. Then the heavier particles sank gradually toward the floor, as if to await new stirring in another season.

Bradley had no idea where to begin his search. The accumulation in the attic had grown by substantial portions over the years, and boxes and cartons, broken furniture, old appliances, all the things he and Lizzie had been reluctant to throw away were crammed into the single large room under the sloping roof. The only clear areas were a narrow pathway that ran haphazardly down the middle of the floor and constricted tributary aisles that gave access to the windows. Memories of Lizzie were everywhere.

With no conspicuous starting point, he began to rummage

through boxes at random. At first there was nothing of particular interest, but then he found old high school yearbooks, both his and Lizzie's, musty after having sat untouched for years. He was caught up at once in the thin books with the Simpson's Ridge "Racers" logo marking their gaudy covers, amused by images of long-forgotten classmates and fascinated by scenes around the little school rendered in simple black and white photographs. These were the hallways once trod by Elizabeth Kraft, the sweet and pretty schoolgirl who had enchanted him from the very first. He studied the books page by page, searching for any glimpse or mention of Lizzie, all the while rebuking himself for not getting into the old books earlier.

Inscriptions written by other students filled virtually all the otherwise-empty space in Lizzie's books. *I'd forgotten how popular she was. Maybe I didn't even realize it at the time.* There were autographs and greetings, elaborate paragraphs of verse, and simple signatures. Mundane and plain, creative, pretentious. It didn't matter. He was intrigued by the writing of Lizzie's friends.

"Dear Liz, you're a nut but I'm a squirrel. You know the connection."

Bradley smiled. *Were we really like this when I first met you? Such an innocent world. They were happy days, Lizzie, and we had such fun.*

He found a page where Catherine had been at work. A childish scrawl and drawing stood out in contrast to the writing of the older students. "My big sister is cute, and the boys all like her," Catherine had scribbled. Then she'd added a cartoon-like drawing of a girl with a wide-mouthed smile and ringleted hair labeled "Elizabeth" and credited her work, "Your sister, Catherine Kraft."

In Lizzie's 1941 book, he found an entry that surprised and annoyed him. It was much too suggestive. Owen Rhodes wrote that he had enjoyed knowing Lizzie in Miss Munson's English class and added a rhyme he had composed "in memory of that scintillating educational experience":

> Her belly was smooth and hot from her navel
> to her twat

and her breasts stood out like granite
  under the moon.
But the action ended there, though to
  pause for him was rare,
for he knew old Munson's paper was due
  soon.

He did not remember Owen Rhodes. Would Lizzie remember him? He wished he could ask. And had her father seen what Owen Rhodes wrote? He could readily imagine stern old Roscoe Kraft's outrage!

Bradley had written poetry, too, in Lizzie's senior book, a fact that he recalled after finding Owen Rhodes's offensive effort from the year before. In his case, though, he'd not tried to be clever or creative, but had drawn on Emily Dickinson for lines he thought were especially fitting to their time and circumstance. As he read his awkward script now, and remembered how impressed Lizzie had been, he felt proud of his effort:

The face we choose to miss,
Be it but for a day—
As absent as a hundred years
When it has rode away.

He'd had in mind the separation they both knew was coming, with him about to go off to war, a fact that Lizzie had understood and appreciated.

And now her face will be absent for as long as I live.

But he was determined not to give in to the morose emotions that were sure to drag him down. He forced himself to concentrate on the school yearbooks, and found Lizzie's simple message inside the front cover of his 1942 book. "To my special Bradley," she'd written. "Didn't we have a wonderful year! I know this isn't the end. Whatever the world holds for us now, we'll face it together. Sweetest dreams. Yours eternally, Elizabeth." Simple and direct. That had always been Lizzie's way.

He spent another hour reading the things other Simpson's Ridge students had written to Elizabeth Kraft, temporarily lost in a happier time that spared him from the pain of his present world. Then he turned to a collection of yellowed and brittle old newspaper clippings that yielded death notices for Lizzie's parents and his, from the Simpson's Ridge *Press-Record*. There also were recipes that had been cut out but never used and an old crime story that had no relevance he could recall, lacking a single familiar name.

His pulse quickened when he came across a long-forgotten article from July 1938 that reported on the price of local black-berries. It quoted "13-year-old Elizabeth Kraft of the Shiloh Church neighborhood," who told the writer that she was "tickled with the 10 cents a gallon she'd received for her berries." Oh, if they only had taken her picture!

Commercial-Appeal articles from the 1950s and 1960s were mixed in with the old Simpson's Ridge clippings. Bradley didn't remember saving them; Lizzie apparently had. An undated news story analyzed "Memphis's spectacular economic development" in the years following World War II. There was a long piece on Chucalissa, the prehistoric Indian village south of the city, and another on W. C. Handy, identified by the writer as "the immortal blues composer who put Memphis on the music map."

So much we should have talked about . . . She was interested in all these things, but I don't remember that we ever discussed them.

He looked through a series of articles on the sanitation workers' strike in 1968 that brought Dr. King to Memphis. He'd almost forgotten how the riots had left Main and Beale streets blood-stained and littered with bricks and broken glass, how the National Guard had been called in to preserve order—helmeted soldiers escorting the strikers in armored troop carriers equipped with heavy machine guns. There was a large front-page photo of sanitation workers, almost all of them black, carrying protest signs proclaiming "I am a man." It all came back readily as he read the newspaper clippings Lizzie had saved.

There were stories about Dr. King's assassination.

Bradley recalled how Lizzie had spent hours in quiet discussions in the neighborhood after that terrible event, sorting out her own feelings and helping others deal with their anger and resentment and understand better their attitudes about race and class in Memphis. He hated to admit it to himself now, but at the time he had not fully comprehended how important all this was to her. Only after she managed to push the women of Park Street Baptist Church to launch an adult literacy project had he begun to understand. This proved a formidable task, but Lizzie was undaunted and simply refused to give up until she won. "This is my contribution," she explained. "It doesn't seem like much, but it's what I can do."

She made them face things they didn't want to think about. You've done so much good, Lizzie. So much good . . .

He found Lizzie's first Bible, carefully wrapped in tissue paper. Her mother and father gave it to her when she was a little girl and it had her name, ELIZABETH KRAFT, printed on the cover in gold letters.

The name had been smudged. He remembered Lizzie's explanation: Catherine had painted over her name with pink nail polish. Lizzie had been furious at her little sister and demanded that she be punished, but Papa Kraft and her mother, to Lizzie's dismay, took it in good humor and Catherine escaped with only a mild reprimand.

Bradley thumbed through the pages. He found pressed wildflowers that Lizzie had preserved—violets and spring beauties, fragile to the touch and crumbling, their images indelibly stained onto the thin paper. He caught his breath at the sight of a four-leaf clover, deteriorated almost into dust. It would be the one that he and Lizzie found under the ancient elm tree in front of Shiloh Church. They made secret wishes on it, then told them and found they were the same. Both wished to be together until the end of time.

There were handmade bookmarks, probably Sunday school projects, though he couldn't tell whether these were intended to mark particular locations or simply had been stuck in at random.

The first opened a passage in Psalms and his eye fell on a verse in the middle of the page: "My heart is smitten, and withered like grass; so that I forget to eat my bread." *That's the way I feel now, Lizzie. My heart breaks more every minute.* There was no escaping reality.

He had no sense of how long he had been in the attic, but he had spent too much time kneeling and stooping and his back and knees were beginning to ache. He stood up straight and flexed painful joints, then made his way to a side window and stared down into the Corydon house next door. It was from here that he had inadvertently spied on Anna and Randolph Corydon years earlier.

The old couple no longer used the upper story, Anna had told them. The climb had become difficult for Randolph even before he was confined to the wheelchair and she'd also come to find the stairs extremely challenging of late. Fortunately, with only the two of them in the large house, they had ample room to arrange all the living area they needed on the first floor. He considered the irony of his and Lizzie's situation in comparison; both of them had been in apparent good health, and not put off by stair-climbing, up to the instant that Lizzie collapsed.

What would Randolph do if something happened to Anna? And if Randolph lingered much longer, would Anna at some point soon be as lost as Bradley felt now?

But such thoughts, again, were depressing. He must push them aside and make himself get back to his exploration. The touching memories brought on by some of the things he'd found also had been dispiriting at times, but he vowed that everything he came across from this point on would be deemed Morris family treasures—collectively a fitting, intimate tribute to their long life together—and went back to his search.

He discovered drawings by Jennie and Matt, beginning as mere doodles in crayon, and articles they'd made in school with paper and paste; hand-lettered greeting cards for birthdays, holidays, school events, just ordinary days; crude handicrafts from summer camp and vacation Bible school. There were little

Christmas stockings of red and white felt, lettered with the children's names. One was labeled "Nap." That would have been for Napoleon, the cat that had shared their lives for a dozen years.

Here and there were old pieces of baby furniture and old chests filled mostly with baby and children's clothing, even some old clothes of his that should have been thrown out years ago. He rummaged through these hurriedly, then turned to a cavernous wood and leather steamer trunk that had been in the family for three generations.

The old trunk yielded an astonishing array of odds and ends. He found the cast that Matthew had worn on his left arm, broken when he fell out of the wild cherry tree in the back yard—the tree Bradley had planted a decade earlier, carrying out his father's dictum that a man should plant trees everywhere he goes to make the earth a better place. Matt hadn't considered the tree a particularly worthwhile addition after his fall, and lost his enthusiasm for tree-climbing. The cast bore the signatures of Jennie, five of Matt's boyhood friends, and Dr. Asa Bonner, the orthopedic specialist who set the arm and put on the cast.

Lizzie's baseball glove! She got it for a single reason: to play in the back yard with Mark. Even as a six-year-old, Mark had a consuming interest in baseball, determined to be a player, and Lizzie never failed to encourage him. Mark would plead with her to play ball the minute he set foot in the big house and she almost always obliged. He soon outgrew her in talent, but up to the day he left for Chicago Mark credited his grandmother with helping his game. The whole family believed Mark was good enough to make it to the pros if he chose to, particularly after he excelled as a player in high school. Lizzie had always believed passionately that he should one day wear a St. Louis Cardinals uniform.

At the bottom of the trunk Bradley found a small box of baby things, never used. These were to have been for the child they lost. The tiny baby girl, stillborn weeks before the expected delivery date, would have been their first. Lizzie had been devastated. There had been some question whether she could conceive again

167

and she agonized over the prospect of going childless. She would say later that only her faith in God got her through that disheartening period, along with the love and support of Bradley and her friends. One of those friends was Anna Corydon, who persuaded her that she still would bear children no matter what the doctors said.

"Doctors don't know lots of things," Anna told her, "and the biggest thing they don't know is what they don't know."

Anna's way of putting things always cheered up Lizzie. For years to come, Lizzie had applied appropriately modified versions of Anna's declaration to any situation she encountered that involved a level of uncertainty. These eventually evolved into what Matthew had labeled The Morris Family Proverb: "Most people would be better off if they worried less about what they think they know and more about what they don't know."

Besides bringing Lizzie and Anna closer, losing the baby had given Bradley the impetus he needed to win the battle against an oppressive personal problem of his own.

Though he never had been a social drinker—drinking alcohol was frowned on in both the Morris and Kraft families—he'd taken his doctor's advice and turned to hot toddies to ease the pain of his war wounds and help him sleep at night. He made the drinks stronger and stronger, rationalizing that the pain was worse and relief was harder to come by, and in time he found himself taking an occasional drink during the day. He came to need the alcohol more and more often, until eventually his bottle became his crutch.

He already was well aware that his drinking was out of control by the time Lizzie demanded that he take a hard look at what he was doing to himself. A younger Bradley Morris never would have doubted his ability to master a challenge as uncomplicated as this one. It was only a matter of self-control, after all. Until that dismal day in Sicily when the German shell fragment ripped through his leg, he'd had absolute faith in his own willpower.

But such over-confidence had not rendered fate its due. After Sicily he had been far less optimistic that he could deal with whatever troubles life had in store. Was he strong enough to overcome his drinking problem? He'd had serious misgivings. Nonetheless, he resisted Lizzie's plea that he turn to Alcoholics Anonymous and promised to beat the problem himself, with her support. During the next year, he was able to get by for several weeks at a time without drinking, only to slide back into his old dependence. He lost confidence every time he failed, and grew more apprehensive, and became even more distressed once they knew that Lizzie was expecting.

Lizzie's support never wavered. She applauded his successes and lamented his failures and made clear that this was a battle they shared. She wanted and expected to know, every hour of every day, exactly where the fight stood, whether he was hopeful or discouraged, what she could do to help. Then she lost the baby, and he felt terribly guilty for adding to her grief. He vowed never to drink again and summoned the fortitude to make his vow stick.

Bradley dug deeper in the old trunk. Among an assortment of children's clothing he found Jennie's ballet dress, still like new but so tiny! Could she ever have been that small? Jennie had shown real talent, her teacher said, but she soon discovered other pursuits and dropped her interest in ballet as suddenly as she'd found it. He and Lizzie had been disappointed, but Jennie, in her usual fashion, never looked back.

Reminders of things Jennie and Matthew had been involved in through the years were abundant. Recital programs, kindergarten open house invitations, a paper on Matt's senior high school science project. Lizzie had kept them all.

Then, flat against the bottom of the trunk, he saw a small and simple booklet that brought a rush of new and different emotions. It had black print on a yellowed white paper cover, with the title superimposed over the outline of an island: *This is Sicily*.

He opened the thin military manual carefully and began to thumb through the pages methodically. The contents were familiar. There was a concise pre-war history of Sicily followed by a section on local customs and advice on how soldiers were to conduct themselves when dealing with civilians. It concluded with a brief dictionary of the most common Italian words and phrases, complete with phonetic pronunciations—words and phrases he'd never had occasion to use.

In his mind's eye he saw Carson Streator and the other men in his squad nervously studying the handbook and trying out Italian expressions on one another. They were aboard ship, just out of the Algiers harbor, about to launch an invasion. This little handbook was the first clue they had had that Sicily was their destination.

His meditation was interrupted by the sound of someone climbing the attic stairs.

"Bradley? Are you up here?"

"I'm here, Catherine."

Catherine's face showed at the undersized attic door, and she paused to get accustomed to the dim light before making her way to where he sat beside the battered steamer trunk, the old army booklet in his hand. He waited for her without speaking.

"What in the world are you doing?" she asked, coming to him.

"I was looking for Lizzie's old Sears catalogs for Jennie and Beth. She used to save them."

"I remember that," Catherine said. "She always said they'd be interesting to look back on in years to come. Did you find them?"

"Not yet."

"What's that you have in your hand?"

"It's what the army gave us to get us ready for Sicily. I saw this little book the first time in July 1943 on a troop ship ready for the invasion. Until we got this, we didn't know where we were going."

"May I see it?" Catherine asked.

Struggling up from the floor, he handed her the booklet.

"It must bring back lots of memories," she said.

"I remember Sykes saying 'Where the hell is Sicily?' And he wasn't alone. Most of us didn't know much about Mediterranean geography, I'm afraid."

"I think it's ironic that you find it now, after your trip to Sicily in September."

"I wish I'd found it before we went," Bradley said. "It might have made a difference in how I looked at things. Back then, I didn't get to see much of Sicily. I wasn't there long enough."

"Well, what you lacked in time you made up in action, I suppose. You probably saw as much of it as you wanted to, under the circumstances."

"That's true. The war left me with such a black picture of Sicily in my mind all these years, and it's really a beautiful place. Lizzie loved it. She wanted to go back and spend more time. There were lots of places we didn't get to see. I guess we should have—"

Catherine apparently saw the tears in his eyes. "It's nearly dinner time," she interrupted softly. "Let's go downstairs, and we can come back another day and look for the catalogs."

Bradley closed the trunk.

"I found other things," he said. "Lots of Lizzie's things."

15

The ban on non-family visitors to Lizzie's bedside never had applied to Anna Corydon, as Bradley had made clear from the outset. Anna inquired about Lizzie often. She seemed desperate to see her dear friend one more time, before it was too late, and Walter agreed to stay with her invalid husband so that she could.

"I miss her so," Anna said tearfully, as Catherine drove her and Bradley to the medical center. "It seems like forever since I've seen her. We had such great plans for the summer."

She said Lizzie had insisted that she get out of the house more, perhaps find a caretaker who would look after Randolph for two or three afternoons a week. Anna resisted the idea at first, but Lizzie told her there were agencies that would help find good people to take care of her husband while she took some time for herself.

"I hate to sound selfish," Anna said, "but I do feel awfully much tied to that house. I can barely remember when I was out last without Randolph."

"That's not selfish," Catherine assured her. "Everyone needs some time of their own. Walter and I once got so tired of each other we took separate vacations."

Anna seemed oblivious to Catherine's efforts to downplay her admission of remorse. "I shouldn't complain," she said. "Randolph is the one who's suffered and I have no right to whine. But I had been looking forward to getting out more, and Lizzie and I had talked about all the things we were going to do together, just like in years past."

"Lizzie enjoys your company," Bradley said. "She's always been happy to have you next door."

The truth was, he envied Lizzie's and Anna's closeness. It always had been something of a frustration for him, given that he and Randolph had so little in common. Lizzie and Anna could spend hours together and never run out of things to talk about, while he and Randolph often reached that point in fifteen minutes. Lizzie said they didn't try hard enough to find things of mutual interest, but he had long since decided that there was little of mutual interest for them to find. Randolph's background was much different from his.

Several generations of Corydons had been wealthy Mississippi planters, but Randolph, with his father's blessing, chose to break with tradition and become a lawyer. He'd been half-way through law school when his father died. Inheriting a modest fortune, he promptly dropped his studies and vowed to spend the rest of his life living off his investments. So far as Bradley could tell, Randolph had never in his life done an honest day's work.

He suspected that Lizzie didn't like Randolph any more than he did, though she would never admit it. It was not Lizzie's way to speak ill of others. The closest she ever had come to saying something disparaging about Randolph was an off-hand comment that applied an old Kraft family adage to the Corydons: "If Anna can live with him, I can live beside him."

Anna was much more interesting than her husband. Lizzie said this was merely the norm, not unique to Anna and Randolph, because women in general were more interesting than men. The Corydons simply fit the usual mold.

"If you ask a man to talk about himself," Lizzie explained to Bradley once, "he'll tell you about the twenty years he's driven a bus or whatever. Ask a woman, and she'll talk about the things that matter to her—her husband, her children, her grandchildren, the people she loves. It's the difference in the way men and women look at the world, I think, but whatever the reason, it makes women more interesting."

He supposed Lizzie was right. Applied to Randolph Corydon,

her rule surely helped explain his and Randolph's lack of cama-raderie. They certainly would have had things to talk about if his neighbor had spent forty years working on the railroad, as he had, but the only thing that ever seemed to interest Randolph was the stock market and that subject was as foreign to Bradley as life on Mars.

Lizzie's theory also proved true when it came to the story of how Randolph and Anna got together in the first place. He had asked Randolph once, early in their acquaintance, but Randolph was evasive. Anna responded readily when Lizzie asked her the same question. She'd been a secretary in an investment firm that Randolph patronized, she explained. Both were well beyond their youthful years and Anna had given up on prospects for marriage. She said Randolph was shy and reclusive, and Anna believed—though Randolph would not acknowledge the fact—that he'd never had a date before he met her.

"Actually," Anna told Lizzie, "you couldn't really say we dat-ed. Randolph found out where I went to lunch and started showing up there. He tried to make it look like coincidence, but I knew better. He'd ask, very politely, if we might share a table."

After only a few such luncheon meetings, Randolph asked Anna to marry him and she quickly accepted. They had been married only a year when the Morrises moved in next door.

Bradley had never told Lizzie about spying on Anna and Ran-dolph from the attic window, embarrassed by what he had done even though it was unintentional. Besides, he knew it would make Lizzie uncomfortable to know that he had seen Anna naked. Anna's friendship had meant a great deal to Lizzie, virtually from the day they moved into the big house, and he hadn't wanted to do anything to impair it. If only he could have found something in common with Randolph, the four of them might have done things together that Lizzie would have enjoyed. He felt guilty for not trying harder.

At the hospital, Jennie and Catherine waited in a small family lounge down the hall while Bradley and Anna visited at Lizzie's bedside. Anna clearly was shaken by what she saw and, unable to conceal her emotion, clung to Lizzie's hand and wept openly. "Lizzie, Lizzie," she sobbed, "I've missed you so much."

Anna's grief touched Bradley deeply. Although he never had questioned the compassion family members had for Lizzie, he'd been struck by the fact that neither of the children seemed to grieve the way he did. Even Catherine, whose level of distress had come closest to his own, had accepted Lizzie's condition as hopeless, her loss inevitable, at a time when he still believed Lizzie would recover. He had not seen Catherine shed tears over her sister the way Anna was now.

He wanted to comfort Anna, but what could he say?

When her tears finally had subsided, Anna still held Lizzie's hand tightly, leaning close as she talked. "We had such great plans for the summer, Lizzie," she said softly. "What am I to do without you?"

Catherine and Jennie slipped quietly into the small and crowded room, but stood back from Lizzie's bedside so as not to interfere with Anna's communion. Matthew had arrived at the hospital, also, but waited outside. Anna suddenly straightened up and stepped back, away from the bed. "I'm sorry," she said. "I didn't mean to be in the way."

"Nonsense," Catherine told her. "We wanted you to have as much time with her as you like. Please don't let us interfere with your visit."

"I think I've said my piece," Anna said. "I know there's nothing I can do for her. I should be getting back to Randolph."

She clasped Lizzie's lifeless hand once more and stroked her arm gently. Her heartache was evident as she looked down on her dearest friend for what she supposed would be the last time. Then she asked Catherine to take her home, and Bradley Morris and his children were left to resume the vigil that had come to dominate their lives.

"I didn't realize Mother and Anna were so close," Jennie said. "Anna seems terribly upset."

"They have been friends for as long as we've lived in the big house," her father answered, "but they've become even closer in recent years. Before you and Matt moved away, so much of your mother's time was taken up with family that she didn't see Anna as often. But since the family's been gone—"

Matt interrupted. "You're her most important family, and you were still here," he said.

"Yes, of course. But you remember how much time she used to spend with Jeff and Mark when they were little, and then Beth. She had a lot more time with Anna after that."

"I doubt that I have a friend who cares as much for me as Anna seems to care for Mother," Jennie said.

Anna's visit had cast a melancholy atmosphere over the room. Matt and Jennie were plainly despondent and their father showed the strain of his long ordeal. They sat solemnly at Lizzie's bedside with no purpose except to wait. Unless there should be a miracle, only Lizzie's passing could bring respite.

From the time he had abandoned hope for Lizzie's recovery, Bradley had grown steadily more morose. Yet he had refused to plan for Lizzie's death, and when Jennie and Matt had tried to talk with him about funeral arrangements and burial plans they had been met with a stone wall of resistance. Lizzie was not gone yet. He would not presume to treat her as though she were.

His spirit broken, he went from hour to hour merely doing the things he had to do. He waited for direction from the children, coming and going between the medical center and the big house on whatever schedule they suggested and filling his time in between with whatever activity he could accomplish mechanically, with little thought or planning. He could not concentrate on the future when his mind was on the past. The past was where his heart lay, in memories of Lizzie whole and well, the two of them always together, loving and caring for one another.

But Lizzie needed him now, and there was nothing he could do. His hurt was deep and unending.

The room was quiet. Except for the low, monotonous hum of the electronic monitoring equipment, there was no sound. Lizzie may as well have been alone. Her three callers, each isolated by his or her own thoughts, were barely aware of her presence.

Bradley fell into a restless slumber. The nerve pain from his shingles, acute for much of the day, finally surrendered to the heavy dose of pain-killer he'd taken just before leaving the big house. Fleeting visions filled his dreams, commencing with an image of Lizzie as a girl of seventeen. Her vivid dark eyes danced playfully as she ran toward him, her hair flying and her soft linen dress flowing in the summer breeze. But just as she reached his outstretched arms, the scene shifted and the lovely, comforting sight of Lizzie was supplanted by a terrible view of the battlefield on which he and Carson Streator fought and Carson Streator died. This time, Bradley was prescient. He knew the artillery shell was coming and tried to warn his comrade, but his scream came too late. The shell exploded and the hot steel tore into Carson Streator's chest and everything was chaos.

"Daddy, wake up! You're having a nightmare."

Jennie tugged gently at his arm.

"You were making desperate sounds and beginning to thrash about with your hands," she said. "I know you're awfully tired, Daddy. Don't you think I should take you home now?"

"I'm sorry," her father answered. "I was having a bad dream, but I'm all right now. I hope I didn't disturb anyone."

"Of course you didn't. I just woke you up to protect you from the demons."

"You know I still have war dreams sometimes," her father told her. "I'll bet Matthew does, too. War does awful things to people."

Matthew had stood when Jennie began to arouse their father. He stretched his arms over his head, forcefully, in an effort to combat his own drowsiness. "Unfortunately, I do," he said, "but not as often as I used to. If you're still having them after all these years, though, there probably isn't much hope that mine will go away any time soon."

"My war didn't last long, so my nightmares are always pretty much the same. You were in the thick of things a lot longer than I was."

Matthew appeared to be hesitant. "Mine usually go back to one especially bad day," he said. "But I know you don't want to get into old war stories, Dad. And anyway, I came out of it pretty good compared to what happened to you."

"I'm sure you saw a lot of bad days."

Jennie put a hand of Matthew's arm. "I'm going to get us some coffee," she said. "Why don't you sit back down and tell Daddy about your nightmares? I won't be gone long."

Matthew took his chair again. He waited for Bradley to speak.

"You were at Khe Sanh," his father said. "Given what went on there it's hard to imagine one day being bad enough to stand out."

"It was the day our ammo dump got hit. I know I've told you about it."

"Not really. Not in any detail, anyway."

"Well, if there really is a fire-and-brimstone hell like the preachers used to tell us, I already know what it's like. Of all the days I spent at Khe Sanh, this was by far the worst. They came very near to annihilating us that day. A shell hit an ammunition dump and thousands of rounds of our own artillery and mortar shells were ignited. So I can say I've actually seen it rain fire."

"I can't even imagine what that was like. Plain enemy shelling is bad enough."

"You'd think so. But some of our ammo was anti-personnel stuff, and when one of those blew we'd be hit by shrapnel that tore through everything but flak jackets and helmets. Sergeant Cross took one in the neck and went around holding a vein shut with his fingers to keep from bleeding to death. But he stayed right with us."

The stress of reliving his ordeal was beginning to show in Matthew's eyes. His voice quavered.

"You don't have to talk about this any more," his father said. "I know it's awful hard."

"No, I'd rather talk about it. It's better to talk about it than just to replay it over and over in my mind like I do. I can still see those Marines walking straight into the fire and fighting it with nothing but hand extinguishers and shovels. Lieutenant Scull started picking up shells that hadn't exploded and carrying them over to a safety pit, away from the men. He was the bravest man I ever saw."

"Nobody knows what they'll do at a time like that until it happens to them, Matt."

"I guess. Heroes were a dime a dozen that day."

"It's hard to see how anybody could live through something like that and not have nightmares about it," Bradley said, his voice subdued.

"Sometimes it's so clear in my dreams it's like I'm really there. I can even hear it and smell it. But there are always different faces, different men around me. There's always one big explosion, at my feet . . . in my face, wherever. The one that would have blown me all to hell. That's when I wake up. Sometimes I wake up so scared I'm shaking."

Jennie entered the room carrying hot coffee. "Don't let me interrupt," she said. "Old soldiers need to tell their war stories. I'll be a willing audience."

"I think I've talked enough," Matthew said. There was a note of finality in his tone that Bradley and Jennie understood. They would respect his wishes.

There was a visitor who wanted very much to see Mrs. Morris, the nurse said. He was not family and she knew the family's wishes, but he had been very polite and she tended to be sympathetic. What should she do?

Matthew went with her to find out who it was, and he and the visitor returned together. The visitor was a man who looked to be in his mid-sixties, dressed in a somewhat crumpled black suit. His white shirt had a stiffly starched collar and his blue tie was faded almost to gray.

"Mr. Morris," the man said to Bradley, "you don't know me, but Mrs. Morris is one of the best friends I ever had. My name is Leroy Edgerton."

Bradley thrust forward his hand. He would not ask the visitor for further explanation; Matthew had found the man acceptable, and he assumed that he would learn more in good time. Leroy Edgerton did not offer an immediate accounting of himself, however, but sought approval for a closer visit to Lizzie's bedside.

"May I look upon her for a minute?" he asked. "I beg pardon for the intrusion. I only just this morning found out she's here."

Bradley stood aside. The visitor stepped close to Lizzie's bed and looked down on her intently. He stood rigidly straight, his hands clasped behind his back, his head lowered respectfully. Then he sighed and shook his head, as if in disbelief.

"You don't know who I am," he said, turning back to Jennie and her father. "It's been a long time, and I suppose Mrs. Morris probably has forgotten. But all things considered, as I explained to young Mr. Morris, she is one of the most important people in my life."

"I'm afraid I don't recognize your name," Bradley said, his tone apologetic, "but if what you say is true, Lizzie would remember you. She never forgot a friend."

"Well, she was a friend," the visitor said. "Look here, could I buy you all coffee or something? I'd love to tell you the whole story. I don't want to disturb Mrs. Morris talking here, though."

"I think we could use a break," Jennie said. "Daddy, Matt, let's all go down to the cafeteria. I'm curious to hear what Mr. Edgerton—isn't that your name?—has to tell us."

Matthew urged the others to go without him. He would stay with his mother and they could fill him in later, although he had talked briefly with Mr. Edgerton already and knew some of what the visitor had to say. Bradley and Jennie agreed.

Minutes later, settled at a table in the hospital cafeteria, coffee in hand, Leroy Edgerton began his story. He said that he learned of Lizzie's illness from his son, who was a doctor in the hospital and recognized her name because he had heard it many times over the years. "And the reason I talked about her," he said, "is that Mrs. Morris did something for me nobody else ever would: She taught me to read."

He had had but a little schooling as a child, the visitor said,

181

going to work in the cotton fields and sawmills by the time he was ten. A decade later, he moved from rural Fayette County to Memphis to try to make a better living. He got married and had five children of his own, and eventually got a job working for the city as a garbage collector.

"Could be you don't remember the big strike in 1968," he said, "but I was in it, one of the strikers."

"You bet I remember it," Bradley told him. "Jennifer here was just a youngster, but I remember it like it was yesterday."

Jennie quickly assured them that she remembered the strike, too. No one who lived in Memphis at the time and was more than a child would ever forget it, she said, and even those who were children knew about Dr. King's assassination, an indirect out-growth of the sanitation workers' strike.

"It was the strike that led Lizzie to start the literacy project at the church," Bradley said. "And that's how you came to know her?"

"Yes, sir, it was. The church women offered to teach reading. They allowed as how it didn't matter if we were young or old, rich or poor, black or white. If we couldn't read and were willing to learn, they were willing to put in the time to teach us. I went down there three nights a week at the beginning, and Mrs. Morris took as much care with us as a mother would with her own child.

"I always thought I was smart enough to read. I just never got a chance to learn. And I did learn, pretty fast. It wasn't but a few months until I was reading good enough to go to the library and get books. That give me a lot of pleasure, and Mrs. Morris said it made her feel good, too."

Jennie smiled. "I know that Mother got a lot of satisfaction out of that project," she said. "She talked about it many times through the years. She felt like she was doing something that could help even more people than the ones she taught, over time."

"And she was right," Leroy Edgerton said. "I did a lot bet-ter after I learned to read, and got a supervisor's job. Mrs. Morris made me a stronger man—gave me inner strength, I guess you'd call it. I tried to pass that along to our five children and I'm proud to say they are all educated and doing real good."

"You said your son is a doctor?" Jennie asked.

"Yes, ma'am, he is. And two of my sons are teachers. We have two girls, and one of them is a teacher and the other is a business woman."

"Lizzie would be glad to hear that," Bradley Morris told him. "I wish I could offer you some hope that she'll be well, and you can tell her all this yourself, but we don't have any reason to think that will happen."

"I can't tell you how sorry I am. Like I said before, Mrs. Morris was a friend to me. There was a lot more to it than just her helping me learn to read." He shifted uncomfortably in his chair. "I'm sorry," he said. "I'm keeping you good people. I didn't mean to keep you."

"You're not keeping us," Jennie said. "We're glad you came by. Mother always felt good about the reading project at the church, and it's really very nice to hear from someone who was helped by it."

"I think it helped Mrs. Morris, too," Leroy Edgerton said. "I don't quite know how to get into this, and I don't want you to misunderstand anything I'm going to say. One reason I consider Mrs. Morris a true friend is because she treated me with respect. Another reason is, I know it wasn't easy for her to do that in the beginning, and she was honest with me about that. We come to respect each other, if you know what I'm saying.

"I didn't trust her in the beginning—if you'll pardon me for speaking plain—but she was straight with me. What I'm getting at is this: Mrs. Morris told me early on that everything that was happening was new for her. She was talking about relations between blacks and whites. She said the signs we carried—remember the 'I am a man' signs?—she said the signs caused her to stop and think, and she knew things ought to be different. She told me flat out that there was plenty of people in the white community—in her own church, too—who still considered me a 'nigger' not worth her worrying about. And then she'd been listening to Dr.

King, and she finally decided to do what one person could to help change things. What she could do was help some of us learn to read."

Bradley, who had been studying the visitor closely as he talked, suddenly brightened. "Now I know who you are!" he exclaimed. "You're Boots! Lizzie talked about you all the time."

Leroy Edgerton smiled and said, "Yes, she would have called me Boots. Everybody did. She started out calling me Mr. Edgerton. I know that felt strange to her, because it just wasn't the custom then. But I wouldn't have it. Everybody called me Boots and that's what I wanted. She said she insisted that the church women treat us all with respect, and that meant calling us 'mister this' or 'mister that.' I told her I understood, but my friends all called me Boots. She said that would be okay, then, because she wanted us to be friends, and she'd call me whatever I wanted her to."

"She always told us how you were getting along," Bradley said. "She'd come home and report on your progress every session. And she talked a lot about you as a person, not just how well you were learning."

"And my son says I talked about her the same way."

Jennie put her coffee cup down and folded her arms across her chest, leaning back loosely in her chair. "I was a student at the University of Memphis when the strike was going on, and I'm afraid I was too busy trying to make good grades to see how important it was," she said. "But Dr. King's death shook us all to the core and brought a lot of Memphis's old racial problems to the surface. I'm sorry to have to admit that it took something like that to make us all aware of what was going on around us. When I come back now, things seem much better. But how did you hear about the reading project at Park Street?"

"They announced it at my church. But you have to understand, there was a lot of resentment. Many of the black people said we ought not to take part in that sort of thing. They felt like it was another case of rich white folks looking down on us. Some said they'd treat us men like children, and we'd have no dignity."

"But you went anyway," Jennie said. "That had to have taken a lot of courage."

Leroy Edgerton laughed. He seemed to be at ease again. "No ma'am," he said. "I don't think it was courage. I guess maybe I was desperate. How else was I ever going to learn to read?"

"You had no way of knowing," Bradley told him, "but you didn't have to worry about your dignity as far as Lizzie was concerned. She's always had a great sense of fairness. I understand your point about it being a big change for her, too. It wouldn't hardly be any other way given her upbringing, but she would never do anything to humiliate anybody."

"I know that now," the visitor said. "But at the time, I guess I didn't care. We had fought for our dignity in the strike and I was willing to carry on the fight if I had to."

"Was it really that bad?" Jennie asked.

"Yes, ma'am, it really was. We went on strike on account of our pitiful pay and the awful working conditions. But then it got to be more about how we were treated as men. It was hard for black people back then. Most of the sanitation workers didn't have much education, like me, and didn't have the skills to get better jobs. We had to make a living picking up garbage, and better pay was the only way we could make it.

"The thing that happened was, when other black people got involved—I'm talking about the ministers and teachers, even the high school students—they saw it as being more about racism. Then when Dr. King come to town to support us, that brought out a lot of folks that hadn't been involved before. And then at some point it seemed like it wasn't about money and working conditions anymore, as much as it was about our dignity as men."

Bradley and Jennie sat silently as Leroy Edgerton described how he used to come home from his garbage route, sometimes with maggots in his clothes and even in his hair, and bathe and get into clean clothes and hurry to his reading class. The class was hard for him at first, and he was embarrassed that he didn't know the alphabet, only a few letters he remembered from his early school days. It would have been easy for him to give up. But by the end of every session, Mrs. Morris had found a way to make him feel that he mattered more to her than anyone else in the world and he would be eager to return the next time.

"Mrs. Morris asked me to keep in touch after the reading course was done," he said. "I wanted to. But we lived in different worlds, if you know what I mean. No way we'd ever cross paths again.

"But I never forgot her," he said, near tears. "I wish now I could have kept in touch with her, but I hope you understand."

16

Bradley Morris got downstairs later than usual, after another restless night. He had slept soundly for a time. Then his medication wore off and suddenly he was wide awake with searing nerve pain running down the back of his shoulder. He took more Darvocet and eventually went back to sleep, only to wake again an hour or so later with a great sense of urgent apprehension, a vague perception that he needed to attend to some pressing duty.

He lay awake for a long while trying to remember what that obligation might be, and at last decided that it must be the need to make things right with Matthew. Those tensions he had worried about when they visited Matt and Sarah in Chicago were still there, lurking beneath the surface, the old quarrel over Vietnam never fully resolved.

Matt had the war dreams, too, and Lizzie would insist that Bradley do what he could to help put their son's mind and spirit at ease and bring him peace. It was up to him to initiate a dialogue and tell Matt how wrong he had been and make sure the issue never again would stand between them. He promised himself that he would talk with Matthew before the day was over and, in the early morning hours, drifted back to sleep.

Beth was the first to greet her grandfather when he went to the kitchen for breakfast.

"Did you sleep well, Granddaddy?"

"Yes, like a rock."

He was determined to put up a good front, not to let his melancholy show. He was the only one in the family who had not been able to accept the inevitable loss of Lizzie and make plans for moving on with life, and now there was the added stress of confronting Matthew over the ashes of old quarrels as well as the physical exhaustion of yet another near-sleepless night. He was weary and downhearted, but firm in his resolve that the others never know.

"And how about you?" he asked. "Did you sleep well?"

"Yes, I slept like a rock too."

"Then we're a pair of rocks this morning. What do you suppose rocks have for breakfast?"

Beth giggled. "This rock's having toast and orange juice."

"Why, that's not enough to keep a rock going all day. Busy rocks like us need bacon and eggs with our toast and orange juice. And a great big glass of milk for young rocks like you and a big cup of black coffee for old rocks like me. Is your mother up yet?"

"She went walking," Beth said. "She said she'd be back soon. Granddaddy, did you know you can't tickle yourself?"

"Well, I don't think I ever tried. But I guess you're right."

"Do you know why?"

"No. But I'll bet you do."

"It's because the part of the brain that makes you laugh when you get tickled is the same part that makes you do the tickling. It won't let you do both at the same time."

"Who told you that?"

"I learned it in science class."

"Then I guess science class is why you're so smart."

"Granddaddy, do you wear socks?"

"Well, yes. Most of the time anyway."

"Before you put them on, do you turn them inside out and check for balls of lint?"

"No, I don't think I ever thought of that."

"It's a good idea. A tiny ball of lint can make your sock hurt your feet sometimes."

"Did you learn that in science class?"

"No, I learned that from experience!"

The two bantered on, making breakfast fun. He cooked bacon and eggs, which Beth now agreed were needed by young rocks just as much as by old rocks, and while pouring himself coffee showed her his favorite mug. The beautifully cast ceramic, adorned with a simple hand-glazed pattern of flowers and leaves in subtle shades of green and violet, had been in the Kraft family for as long as Lizzie could remember and was among those little treasures she had brought to the big house after her mother died.

"This belonged to your Great-grandmother Kraft," he told Beth, "and maybe to her mother before that."

"Then it must be really old," she said. "How old do you think it is, Granddaddy?"

"I don't know. But I used to drink out of it when we visited at your great-grandmother's house in Simpson's Ridge, long before your mother was born."

Beth had a thousand questions. She was curious about everything, and Bradley relished trying to give her responsible answers. His outlook had brightened considerably well before they finished eating.

By the time Jennie returned from her walk, Catherine and Walter had come in from the veranda and suddenly the kitchen was crowded. Sarah had gone to the hospital to spell Matt, Jennie reported, and he should be home soon. That pronouncement brought a sudden quiet upon the room, reminding them why they were gathered here in the big house in the first place. Catherine said they needed to sort out the schedule so that no one would have to be at Lizzie's side all day. Watching and waiting at the medical center was beginning to tax them all.

"As long as one or two of us are there," Catherine said, "we can split up the day and night into shorter blocks of time and make it easier on everyone."

Beth said she would like to go see her grandmother again sometime during the day. She didn't care when. Jennie thought it would be better for her to go in the early afternoon, though Beth should not stay too long no matter what time they took her.

"I don't want to be a problem," Beth said. "I just want to see

Grandmama again. I wouldn't need to be there more than a few minutes."

"Of course you can see her," her mother said. "You won't be a problem. I just meant that we should plan for someone to bring you home."

They quickly worked out times and concurred in a schedule. Bradley wanted to go to the hospital right away, but Jennie said he needed more rest so he agreed to come home in the afternoon. Jennie's direction fitted his needs. He knew that Matthew, after having spent the night at the hospital, would come home and sleep a few hours, then be up and about in the afternoon. There would be a chance for the two of them to talk.

It went without saying that Catherine's plan differed little from what they had been doing all along; but the simple activity of organizing a schedule, no matter how insignificant the outcome, alleviated for a brief time the monotony of sitting by helplessly and doing nothing. They all felt better for having engaged in the hollow planning game.

When Bradley and Walter arrived at Lizzie's room, Sarah told them nothing had changed. Lizzie looked exactly the same as she had when they saw her last, pallid and lifeless, while the monitors showed vital signs no different from those they had grown accustomed to seeing. Bradley silently stooped and kissed his wife then stood at her side, without speaking, for a moment before taking a chair. It seemed ages since he had last talked to Lizzie beyond a whispered "I love you" and simple greetings and farewells, even though it could only have been a matter of hours.

Walter settled into a chair with its back against the wall near the door. Sarah and her father-in-law were seated closer to Lizzie's bedside. Walter cleared his throat as though about to speak, but said nothing. Bradley turned toward him to make conversation.

"You should have seen some of the boats we saw in Sicily," he said. "Down along the coast south of Messina. Some beautiful sail boats."

Boats was a sure topic of interest for Walter, whose proudest possession was a sleek, deep-hulled cruiser pushed at surface-skimming speed by a stout Chrysler outboard motor. He took it out of the water every winter during the coldest weeks, cleaned and polished it in his over-sized garage, then eagerly launched it again at the first sign of spring. He lived for summers on his boat, plying the lakes and rivers of western Kentucky and Tennessee. He and Bradley even had talked of an extended river trip, cruising the Tennessee or Cumberland upstream or maybe going down the Ohio and Mississippi all the way to New Orleans.

"It takes a lot of money to get into boats like that," Walter said. "I spend too much on mine, but nothing like those people do. But of course it's different when you live on the coast and the weather's good pretty much year around, as I suppose it is in Sicily."

"It was plenty hot when Lizzie and I were there in September," Bradley said. "But speaking of boats, did you get yours in the water yet? I know you've been busy."

Walter hesitated, as if he had not understood the question.

"The boat," Bradley said. "I was wondering about your boat."

Walter's tone was apologetic. "I haven't had a chance to tell you," he said, "but I sold the boat. It just seemed like the best thing to do under the circumstances."

Bradley was astonished. It was inconceivable to him that Walter would give up the single possession from which he derived his greatest pleasure. "I don't understand," he said.

"I know. We haven't told you what we're planning to do. Catherine wanted to tell you, and I probably should let her be the one. We didn't think this was the best time."

"Tell me what, Walter?"

"Well, we're planning to move. I'm also selling the business, and we're going to retire and move to Florida. I'll get another boat, but I'll want something bigger."

Bradley was stunned by Walter's revelation. He had been close to Catherine for as long as he had known Lizzie. When Catherine married Walter, he and Lizzie had been relieved to know that the young couple would make their home in Kentucky, not too far from Memphis. Then Walter started his business in Paducah, somewhat more distant than they'd hoped, but still an easy drive. The four of them had been able to visit regularly and often.

Having Catherine and Walter living close by after Lizzie was gone would have been a great comfort, one of the few remaining constants in his life. And now they would be leaving, too. He felt as if he had been blind-sided, struck from behind by a friendly assailant from whom he least expected an attack. Walter's sudden and surprising disclosure left him speechless.

"I'm sorry to tell you this way, Brad," Walter said. "Catherine had planned to tell Lizzie, but she never got a chance. Then there just didn't seem to be a good time. But we didn't mean to keep it from you, and nothing will happen for a while. Probably not until late summer."

"I'm surprised to hear it," was all Bradley could think to say.

Sarah, as if perceiving the impact of Walter's announcement on her father-in-law, even if she did not fully understand why, gamely tried to put a better face on it: "We'll all have someplace warm to visit in the winter! After another January or two in Chicago we may be ready to join you in Florida, Uncle Walter."

Sarah and Walter talked about Chicago winters. She asked where in Florida they planned to live, and he said they were not sure exactly but he expected they would be in or near Ft. Myers. They had visited friends there and always liked it. He believed Ft. Myers would be Catherine's choice and he would be willing to settle about anywhere, but in any case they had to close the sale on the business first, then get their house in Paducah on the market. Walter felt that it would be some months yet before they decided on anything definite.

Bradley was barely aware of their discussion. He sat motionless, his gaze fixed on Lizzie. He was glad she couldn't hear. She would be disappointed that her sister was moving away from Kentucky, probably forever. *I never thought this would happen, Lizzie. This doesn't leave much of the family—just you and me, but that would have been all right. Now it will be just me. . .* But he would not be able to pour out his emotions to Lizzie now, or tell her about the talk he was determined to have with Matt in the afternoon. He thought about these things, and felt great remorse for all that had been left unsaid.

17

Matthew had had only a few hours' sleep, but was up and about by early afternoon just as his father expected. He stepped out onto the veranda where Bradley sat reading a newspaper, carrying a mug of coffee. Except for Sarah, who had dedicated her afternoon to some badly neglected housekeeping chores, the others were gone. The two men would be alone and free to talk without interruption or distraction.

"I'm glad we can have some time together," Bradley said. "I've wanted us to talk."

"I'm glad, too," Matt said. "It's been hectic. You and I have not had a real chance to visit."

Despite the tension he had felt the night before, Bradley was no longer worried about confronting his son and pursuing the dialogue they never had had about Vietnam. In his heart and mind, he knew that the time had come; the last remaining gap between them was about to be closed. He already felt a sense of great relief.

"I wanted to know more about your nightmares, Matt. How often do you have them?"

"Not so often, anymore. But God knows when one may pop up, and they can be a bitch. Sarah could tell you about that."

"I know. I think I might have gone crazy from mine if your mother hadn't been there for me. She's nursed me through many a bad night."

Matthew laughed. "Something else we have in common," he said.

"Yes, but one I would be glad not to share. Are all of your

nightmares about that day the ammo dump was hit in Khe Sanh?"

"No, no. That day was the worst, and shows up a lot. But it wasn't the only bad day I had in Vietnam, not by a long shot."

"We read and heard about Khe Sanh back here, but at the time we didn't know you were there. And I'm glad we didn't, because we'd have been worried sick. And you couldn't tell us much in your letters."

"I know I didn't write as often as I should have, but thank goodness Mother was more conscientious than I was. The only good thing about Khe Sanh was the mail deliveries. We hardly ever went for more than a few days without mail. There we were, as close to oblivion as human beings could be on this earth, and we got letters from home telling us about normal things. That kept me going. No matter how bad it got, here'd come one of Mother's letters that reminded me of everything I missed back here and gave me something to live for, something to come back to."

"Your mother's letters sure got me through some bad days, too. I'm surprised you even got mail at Khe Sanh, though."

"It is amazing when you think about it. When the weather was too bad, or the shelling too heavy, they'd fly over at low altitude and drop their loads by drag chutes. One day the chute failed on a huge cargo pallet and it skidded right through the mess tent and crushed some guys eating breakfast."

"Did you see it happen?"

"No, but I was there just a little bit later. It was pretty grisly. But we didn't have accidents like that very often. And those pilots were good. We wouldn't have survived three days without them."

"We didn't really see that kind of thing, back home. Not how the supplies were flown in. We saw the bombing and strafing, the napalm. Nasty stuff if you were on the ground."

"Yeah, nasty for them. But for us, there was nothing better than the sound of a Phantom jet or Skyhawk coming in. You could always hear them first. It was a beautiful sight when they shot over a hill and swooped down on NVA about to make a run at us. But that was nothing compared to an Arc Light strike. If I could forget everything else about Vietnam, I'd never forget Arc Light."

"I don't know what Arc Light means," Bradley said.

"I'm sorry. An Arc Light strike was a bombing run by B-52's from Guam and Thailand. When these guys showed up, the earth shook and the sky lit up like nothing I'd ever want to see again. You could feel the explosions from miles away. They said the concussion from the heavy runs caused North Vietnamese soldiers a long way from the bombs to die from internal hemorrhaging. They had to call them in close enough a couple of times that it was pretty hairy for us, but God those NVA must have taken some awful hits."

"But those were enemy troops, Matt. They would have killed you if they'd had the chance."

"I know," Matthew said. "But it was an awful business. And I've never felt sure what it was all about."

"Can we talk about it some more?"

Matthew was hesitant. "It's not like I don't remember. It's just that, I don't know, it's something I'm not used to talking about." He lowered his head and rubbed a hand across his forehead, as if wiping away an invisible irritant. He looked at his father with an expression of painful resignation.

Seeing his son's reluctance, Bradley felt a stab of guilt. Over the years, by not encouraging Matt to talk about his time in Vietnam, he no doubt had furthered a tendency to bottle up terrible memories. Anyone who had not been there never could fully comprehend what it was like, but Matt surely had a right to hope that his father, who had seen war firsthand, at least might feel that they had walked in the same shoes.

"Only talk if you feel like it," he said.

"Maybe it's time. I was a new recruit as green as grass when they sent me to Khe Sanh as a 26th Marine Regiment replacement. Khe Sanh was in the middle of nowhere. God, it doesn't seem all that long ago! I can still see that place as clear as day. Every bunker, every hut, every trench, the barbed wire around the perimeter . . .

"I'd only been there a couple of days, I think, when the North Vietnamese started a big push. We were dug in, but somebody thought we ought to go out and patrol. Poke around in the jungle and try to flush 'em out. Every time my squad was sent out we got hit hard. I always came back dragging dead or wounded guys on my back. That's one thing I keep seeing in my nightmares."

Bradley sensed that Matthew wanted him to respond. "I guess they thought you had to patrol to find out where the enemy was," he said. "Fighting in the jungle like that gives the other guy a lot of cover."

"And lots of places for booby traps. I remember watching where I was about to put my boot down and thinking about old Napoleon, the way he used to hold back and pick every step coming down the stairs."

"Napoleon was just being a cat. You had good reason to watch where you stepped."

"I guess so. But you know what? Pretty soon I stopped caring. I figured I was going to get it sooner or later, no matter what I did. Patrols were a damned costly way to get information. I was actually glad I was new to the outfit. These guys weren't friends. I hadn't been around long enough to know anybody."

"Sgt. McCorkle warned us about having friends, way back at Fort Gordon. I wish I'd never been close to Carson Streator."

"Yeah, but you still have to live with those guys and depend on them. Our lives were in each other's hands, friends or not. Sometimes it didn't take long to find out a guy was a pothead or some kind of crazy, but we felt responsible for one another, especially on patrol. If somebody got hit you had to wonder if it might be your fault."

"It wasn't your fault, Matthew. What did you do when you weren't on patrol?"

"Endless guard duty, around the base perimeter. We lived like swamp rats in rifle pits and trenches, and the rain never let up. I remember thinking I'd probably not live to ever be dry again."

Day and night, Matthew told his father, Khe Sanh had been

subjected to shelling and sniper attacks. Small companies of North Vietnamese kept trying to storm the base, blasting their way with mortar and machine-gun fire. More than once the enemy had been repulsed at the last minute in hand-to-hand combat.

"I didn't know," Bradley said softly. "That had to be terrible."

"It was. But we still had it better than those poor devils on the hills outside the perimeter," Matt said. "They lived in pure hell. Always under attack and knowing they could be overrun at any minute, or cut off from the base. When they were overrun, the lucky guys died fighting. Some were dragged off to Laos and never heard of again."

"I hope it's good for you to talk about all this. I thought it would be, but the last thing I want is to dredge up painful memories that you might have been able to put aside."

"I've never been able to put any of it aside. Not yet, anyway. Have you?"

"No. Not really. And I've had a long time to work on it."

"I don't think a lifetime is long enough. It may or may not help to talk about it, but I don't see how it could make things any worse."

"If you're sure."

Matthew went on, reliving with his father scenes of blood and carnage that still haunted him. He said the stench of decaying bodies in the surrounding jungle got so strong at times that the Marines had to wear their gas masks, yet they took solace in the fact that these were enemy dead and not their own.

"We always got our casualties out, one way or another," he said. "We owed our survival to the pilots. Those guys got cargo planes and choppers in under impossible conditions and kept us supplied and took out our dead and wounded."

Matthew stopped talking. There was pain in his eyes. He looked off across the driveway and down the street toward the park at the end of the block, in deep concentration. His father would not force the conversation. He waited quietly until his son chose to speak again.

When he did begin to speak, Matt's voice was so low that Bradley had to strain to hear.

"There's no doubt in my mind that the 26th Marines would have been wiped off the face of the earth if it hadn't been for those pilots," Matthew said, picking up where he'd left off. "Except for Lopez, we never even knew their names, but I know I wouldn't be here now except for them."

"Who's Lopez?"

"He came in one day in the middle of a fire-storm, heavy with rifle ammo. We were being shelled with everything the NVA had. Lopez set his chopper down right in the middle of it, and for some reason decided to get out while the ship was being unloaded. He ran over to where my platoon was dug in and asked if we had any coffee. They had his chopper unloaded in about two minutes and he ran back to it and was about to take off when it took a direct hit and was blown to bits, all over the landing zone. All we found were pieces of his body. That one hit me pretty hard. Lopez was just a gentle young kid, out of place in a hell hole like Khe Sanh."

"Carson Streator was like that, too. But you saw so many men killed, and I don't think you can ever get used to that."

"Actually, you can. It gets to be a way of life. Every morning you start the day wondering if it's your turn. Then you feel guilty if you make it through another day and some other guys don't."

Bradley pulled himself up straighter in his chair. "It's no wonder that going through what you went through leaves you with nightmares," he said. "War is a terrible experience. I'm just sorry you had to go."

"Well, it's an experience we shared and I guess it stuck with us in about the same way. It seems kind of strange that it took us so long to get around to comparing nightmares."

"We were afraid, Matthew. Talking about our war dreams might dredge up our old quarrel, and neither of us wanted to do that. It was easier to let things lie, hidden away somewhere, than to face our differences and try to understand them. Your mother pleaded with me through the years to get it all out in the open, but I'm ashamed to say I just didn't have the courage."

Matthew put down his coffee mug. "You, not having the courage? I don't buy that for a minute," he said. "You may be strong-willed and stubborn, but you've never lacked courage."

"There's no other explanation," Bradley said. "I didn't have the courage to confront this because I would have had to tell you how wrong I was. And how sorry. Then in time it seemed like we were able to put it all behind us, leaving a lot of things unsaid. But I've been awful unfair to you, Matt. I wish I'd listened to your mother a long time ago."

"You don't have to do this, Dad."

"I know. But I want to. I did you a terrible wrong, letting you go off to Vietnam without my blessing. You did the right thing and it took a lot of guts."

"But you were so much against the war, Dad. And now it was the right thing to do? How can you say that?"

"I was against the war because I knew a lot of young men like you would die for no good reason. I didn't start out that way, but that's what I came around to. But for you and all the others who went, it was the right thing to do because you believed it was the right thing. It didn't matter what anybody else thought, except that all those protestors made what you did even more heroic."

"I never felt like a hero," Matthew said. "When I left Vietnam, I just felt like I'd been in the wrong place at the wrong time. Mostly, I felt lucky to have made it out alive. Anyway, none of it would mean much to a man of your generation. You were in the big one, that everybody supported—the war that saved the world."

"I can't tell if you're being sarcastic."

"No, no. I'm serious. It's just that your war turned out to mean a hell of a lot more than my war did. You guys were all heroes, and everybody knew it."

"It was easy for us," his father said. "We just did what everybody expected. All we had to do was get in line. You fought for your country the same as we did. Your country—people like me—let you down, but that doesn't take anything away from what you did. I was wrong, Matthew, and I've known it all these years. Will you forgive me?"

"I think we're past all that now."

"We are if you can forgive me."

"I forgive you, Dad. And I'm glad we can get by this."

"I'm proud of you, Matt," Bradley Morris told his son. "You were a good Marine. You did your duty."

There were tears in Matthew's eyes. "That means more to me than you could ever know," he said hoarsely. "I guess I've been waiting a long time to hear that, Dad."

"I'm sorry. I'd give anything to be able to go back and undo all the things I did wrong. You have to believe that."

"I believe it."

Bradley Morris wanted very much to believe that the hard feelings between them over Vietnam truly had eroded through the passing years, that this few minutes of conversation had only sanctioned what time already had accomplished. His behavior toward his son—his failure to say the things that needed to be said when it would have mattered much more—was inexcusable. He would regret it as long as he lived.

"Have you thought about going back?" he asked. "I don't have as many dreams about my war since your mother and I went to Sicily."

"I know. And I have thought about it. I'd like to go back some day and see what Vietnam's like in peacetime. There's nothing to go back to at Khe Sanh, so far as I know."

"It isn't the place that matters, Matt. It's the people. I learned that in Sicily. It took a while for me to sort it out, but that's what I came away with. When your mother and I saw the people in Sicily it wasn't just a battlefield anymore. Take Sarah and go back to Vietnam, Matthew. There are people there just like us, and that's what counts."

In the medical center that night, Bradley sat close to Lizzie's bed and held her hand firmly. "Matt and I had a long talk today," he said. "I know it won't stop his nightmares about Vietnam, but I think he feels better. You saved him the same way you saved me. Your letters gave us both something to live for and come back to. We both thank you for that."

He placed the palm of his hand on Lizzie's forehead, as if testing for fever. Her skin, as he expected it to be, was cool to his touch.

"I'd give anything if I could feel your warm body again, Lizzie, anything in this world. What is there left now? Your eyes don't see and your ears don't hear. What's left of the mind and spirit, my darling Lizzie? Where is the pretty young girl who wrote me love letters from Kentucky, the loving mother who wrote Matthew in Vietnam? Our world is so empty now, and I don't know where to turn."

Bradley settled deeper into his chair, prepared for a long watch that would be spent in silence. On this night he would not sleep.

18

His was a solitary vigil, by choice. When he insisted that no more than one person needed to be there, other family members had surrendered to his wish to spend the night alone with Lizzie, the family schedule notwithstanding. Matthew and Jennie had been the first to acquiesce, perhaps able to see through his subterfuge when he argued that they all were tired and needed rest. He wanted intimate time with their mother, private time they had inadvertently denied him while trying to carry a greater share of his burden.

At some point late in the night, Bradley left Lizzie's room and walked the hallway to try and shake off his drowsiness. The pain in his leg was always worse after long stints in a bedside chair and made walking uncomfortable enough that he would be wide awake again in short order.

He limped past the nurses' station, exchanging nods with two unfamiliar young women, and stopped briefly in front of a bulletin board where an odd mix of notices was posted. A duty roster and other important announcements were almost over-shadowed by personal items: automobiles for sale, baby-sitters wanted, apartments for rent, and so on.

Further on, he paused at the door of the family lounge. Over the days and nights he had spent at the hospital, the lounge had become a serene and inviting haven when he needed a momentary refuge. Here he could escape the monotonous electronic monitors above Lizzie's bed, which he had come to despise.

The lounge was empty, but a television set blinked out toward the corridor. Its volume had been set very low so as not to be a disturbance. A man on the television screen spoke earnestly, commanding Bradley's attention.

"Life is continuous," the man said emphatically. "The insect lays its eggs before it dies. The tree does not shed its leaves in autumn until new buds develop, ready to burst forth in the warm spring sun. It scatters its seeds each season so that generations of offspring may take root during its lifetime. Each of us carries the genes of our father and our mother, their fathers and mothers, and forebears going back through generations of ancestors . . ."

Bradley walked away from the lounge, back to Lizzie's room, considering the words of the speaker. "He made some sense, Lizzie," he said, a touch of enthusiasm in his voice. "He made some sense. We'll live on in the children—both of us."

Then he fell silent again, thinking more about what the man on television had said. Life is continuous, so how much does an individual matter? *How much do I matter? Little spurts of semen and I fathered Jennie and Matthew and passed on life to generations yet to come. But it is a ridiculous function a man performs if that's all there is to it.*

"He didn't do it justice, Lizzie. There's more to it than that, more than what he said. Trees and insects may exist just to pass on life, but you and I have loved each other. Our life together is what mattered, Lizzie. There's a lot more to two people loving and caring for each other than just passing along life. He didn't do it justice."

Who was the television speaker, and how did he presume to be an authority on such things? Somewhat agitated, Bradley left Lizzie's bedside again and limped back toward the lounge with an unclear, half-formed idea that if he could identify the messenger he might challenge the message. But when he reached the lounge the program had changed and he grudgingly accepted the fact that the man—whoever he was—would go on voicing his mis-guided theme without benefit of Bradley Morris's point of view.

The words of the speaker stuck in his mind, though, and back in Lizzie's room he kept thinking about them. Presumptions as to the continuity of life were nothing new. He'd always had a sense of one generation's blood flowing in the veins of the next. It was obvious. Jennie was the image of her mother and most people said that Matthew looked a lot like him. Beth carried traits of both sides of the family and so did Jeff and Mark. The family had branched in new directions, of course, so that the grandchildren shared bloodlines from Paul and Sarah and the generations that preceded them.

"Well, it does get a little more complicated, Lizzie," he said. "I'm sorry. You don't know what I'm talking about. I was thinking about how the children look like us, and the grandchildren. And you look so much like your mother . . ."

He still held a clear and precise mental picture of his mother-in-law, although she had been gone for years. Nola Kraft was a beautiful woman, and even when he first met the youthful Lizzie the resemblance to her mother was striking. Considering all this in the dim light of Lizzie's hospital room, he could see Lizzie's mother in his mind's eye almost as clearly as he could see Lizzie before her attack. The comatose Lizzie lying just beyond arm's length was not the real Lizzie, not the one who would live on forever in his memory.

Try as he might, he could not remember Lizzie's father nearly as well. His recollections of the Kraft family centered about Lizzie and Catherine, their mother, and Danny Boy and Butterball.

Lizzie always claimed that there was no ancestry in her family that anyone paid attention to. Her father's people had been in western Kentucky for generations—who knew or cared how many?—and her mother's family name was Brockett. She had heard that her great-grandfather Brockett's people crossed the mountains from Virginia and planned to locate somewhere west of the Mississippi, but they thought Simpson's Ridge was a beautiful place and it looked prosperous so they unloaded their wagons and settled down to stay.

"When you told me all that, we couldn't see Simpson's Ridge as either prosperous or beautiful," Bradley said, as if the thoughts in his mind were part of an on-going conversation. "We were like most teenagers, I suppose. Just about any place else in the universe would be better than where we were. We didn't see much future in Simpson's Ridge."

He recalled how Lizzie's mother had worked hard to disabuse them of such ideas. "Foolishness," Nola Kraft said. Simpson's Ridge had given the Kraft family a good life even in hard times, and as far as beauty is concerned, it's in the eye of the beholder. She was confident that others would find the wooded green hills of western Kentucky one of the most beautiful places on earth.

Nola Kraft's concept of Simpson's Ridge as "the wooded green hills" had turned out to be more accurate than his and Lizzie's limited vision of the town as merely a collection of rough streets and dingy buildings. Lizzie had missed it terribly. He had missed it, too, but not as much. His short time in an unpretentious little white frame house a block off Main Street had left him with far fewer memories than Lizzie had from her girlhood in the elegant old Kraft home in the country.

But time proved them correct insofar as the future was concerned. There was precious little to keep young people in Simpson's Ridge, a circumstance that had only grown worse in the years since they married and moved to Memphis.

"There's nothing much left of the old town now, Lizzie," he said. "But I still remember it the way it used to be, when we were young. I kind of wish we hadn't seen how it's changed."

Bradley thought back to the last time they'd visited Simpson's Ridge, a year or so—or was it longer?—before their trip to Sicily. They had been disheartened by what they found. Half the buildings left on Main Street stood empty, and the hardware store and farm supply business that were still there looked to be anything but prosperous. The old Simpson's Ridge State Bank barely clung to life. It had once been the center of commerce for the entire county, and Lizzie's father, Roscoe Kraft, had proudly served for three decades on its board of directors.

Lizzie was visibly disappointed to see that Reese's Store, where she'd bought dresses and shoes from the time she was a little girl, was no longer there. A dusty gravel parking lot spread across the site where the commanding three-story brick and limestone Reese's building used to be, attracting generations of shoppers with imposing merchandise displays in its huge store-front windows.

"Arnold Calder said there was talk that Mr. Reese burned down the building himself to collect the insurance," Bradley said, continuing his one-way conversation with Lizzie. "Mr. Reese said vandals did it. The building had been empty since the store closed a few years ago, you know, and I don't suppose we'll ever know what really happened."

A nurse slipped quietly into the room and rushed through a routine check of Lizzie's monitoring equipment. "This room feels cold to me," she said, after a cordial exchange of greetings. "Are you warm enough, Mr. Morris?" Bradley told her he was comfortable. He had made sure that Lizzie was covered by a warm blanket so that she wouldn't be cold. The nurse bid him good night and went on her way, and he returned in his mind to Simpson's Ridge and his and Lizzie's last visit.

He had become even less certain of the date, but he remembered that only the post office had shown much sign of life. The post office, next door to the bank, was one of the town's last true brick-and-mortar structures, built during the Kennedy Administration to reward loyal Democrats for consistently delivering the vote ever since the early days of the New Deal. According to Lizzie's mother, most residents considered it a step backward at the time because postal services always had been available in the back of Hazelton's hardware store and the new building meant shortened hours and generally less personal attention. But the people of Simpson's Ridge tended to make the best of such things, and Nola Kraft observed philosophically, "That's the price of progress."

Driving around town that day, they found that the old Kroger supermarket they remembered was still there, along with a newer but smaller convenience store. The venerable drive-in hamburger stand was now a shabby little café that had abandoned curb service decades earlier. And on a corner in the last block of

Third Avenue, where the street dead-ended at the only Kentucky state highway that ran through town, was Arnold Calder's garage and gasoline station.

"I'm sorry we didn't get back in the fall to tell Arnold about Sicily, Lizzie. Arnold would be more interested in hearing about our trip than anybody else I know." He took Lizzie's hand again, shook his head and smiled. "I'm sorry," he said. "You have no idea what I'm talking about. You must think I'm foolish. I was just thinking about Arnold Calder."

Bradley recalled Arnold hurrying from the back of the garage that day, wiping his palms on a soiled shop towel and thrusting out his huge hand in greeting. He pondered his relationship with Arnold Calder, an unlikely association for lots of reasons. To begin with, Arnold had come to Simpson's Ridge long after he and Lizzie moved away.

"I don't remember what happened to the car and caused me to go to Arnold's garage that first time," Bradley said. "I'm glad it did, though. There's lots of good about Arnold. And I think he loves Glory almost as much as I love you," Lizzie.

Arnold Calder's wife Glory was the faded belle of a notorious East St. Louis beer hall. She was several years older than Arnold and must have weighed close to three hundred pounds.

"Arnold always says he thinks Glory's the most beautiful woman in the world. I expect he does, too."

As Bradley Morris sat with his own beloved Lizzie, close to her bedside in the cheerless hospital room, he retraced in his mind that last visit with Arnold Calder. It seemed more momentous to him now because Lizzie had been with him and, even more important, because it was the occasion on which they had learned that Arnold and Glory Calder soon would occupy the old Kraft house—Lizzie's girlhood home.

Arnold had been bursting with pride, dying to tell, but would not breathe a word of his surprise until Glory was at his side to share in the announcement. "Come on over and have a glass of iced tea," he insisted. "Glory and I have something to tell you."

They followed him to his house, which sat on the slope of a

low bluff directly across the highway from the garage, and mounted the dozen concrete steps that led up from the sidewalk to a narrow, leveled yard and the modest but well-kept white frame home. Glory sat on a shaded front porch in a brightly painted wood-slat swing, fanning herself with a paper fan and drinking Pepsi-Cola from a bottle.

"Glory, look who's here," Arnold called to his wife.

Folds of white flesh hung limply from Glory's forearm as she reached forward to greet them, and puffy jowls almost obscured both her warm smile and her dangling earrings. She struggled up from the swing, chain bracelets clattering, and bustled inside on dainty spike-heeled shoes. Once on her feet she was surprisingly agile. She emerged just moments later carrying a tray of tall glasses of amber tea.

Arnold couldn't contain himself any longer: "What Glory and I wanted to tell you is, we've just bought the Kraft house. Missus Henderson died several months ago—I guess you know—and the place has been empty. We're moving out there next month. I promise we're going to take care of it, Lizzie. You'll be proud of what we've done the next time you see it."

The revelation was stunning. Two different families had lived in the old Kraft house since the passing of Lizzie's mother, and after the death of Ruth Henderson, the most recent occupant, Lizzie had feared it would never be lived in again. She showed little emotion when she heard Arnold Calder's announcement, but her sincerity was obvious when she told Arnold how happy she felt for him and Glory.

Later, she told Bradley that this probably was the best thing that could happen to the old house. Arnold was a proud man who was handy with tools, she said, and he would take care of things "the way Papa used to."

"I'm sorry we haven't been back to see it," Bradley said, again speaking directly to Lizzie. "I'm talking about your old home. It still looked pretty good the last time we saw it, and I'm sure Arnold's fixed it up and taken good care of it. It was always a beautiful place. Even if it hadn't been your home, Lizzie, I would have thought it was one of the prettiest houses in Kentucky."

They had driven by the Kraft house that day before they stopped at Calder's garage, and the sight left them with mixed emotions. Although the once-majestic old red sandstone mansion was in a sad state of disrepair, it still was a striking place, large and two-storied with a wide porch across the front and along one side. It was surrounded by gigantic white oak and silver maple trees. Fragile mimosa of more recent origin filled a corner of the yard, while the long path from the driveway to the front entrance was bordered by thick crape myrtle.

Bradley got up from his chair and stood over the bed, looking down on Lizzie's lifeless face. He gently smoothed the sheet and blanket that covered her and repositioned the pillow under her head, then went on with his discourse: "I've always loved the big house, Lizzie. You know that. It's been our home. But the old Kraft house had a lot of meaning for me, too. There were so many memories of you there, and Limestone Creek . . . and the old church. It hadn't changed a bit! And do you remember all the flowers?"

They also stopped by Shiloh Church on that last visit to Simpson's Ridge. The little church sat proudly on its odd-shaped tract of land, separated from the road by a wide ditch and eroded embankment. Behind it was an ill-kept cemetery, sparsely populated by tombstones of varied shapes and sizes, where they often had walked through the tall grass and weeds seeking out Kraft family graves. On that final visit, though, they settled for circling the church driveway and surveying the scene from the car.

Just beyond the church they stopped on a creaky bridge that spanned Limestone Creek. The creek traversed the old Kraft farm and ran past the church, eventually winding through the south side of Simpson's Ridge not far from the house where Bradley lived. Lizzie raved about the pretty daisies that filled a small patch of open meadow between the church and the near bank of the creek. The opposite bank rose to a steep, brush-covered bluff that stood high above the creek bed, sheer outcroppings of rough gray limestone visible at scattered points along its face and a row of tall sycamore trees marking the crest. The creek was low, typical for that time of year, with only stagnant pools of greenish water visible from the bridge.

"You always said Limestone Creek was our connecting vein. Remember when you put the note in the pickle jar and challenged me to intercept it behind our house in town? I watched all day, but I never saw it." He sat again, his chair pulled close to her bed, and again took her hand in his. "And you promised to dip your hands in the water every morning and send me a flood of love. Do you remember? I could catch it downstream. We both dipped our hands in Limestone Creek every day, all summer. And then when I was on the ship you wrote that you'd gone to the creek and dipped your hands, and you knew the water eventually would get to the ocean.

"Do you remember the little river we stopped beside just before we got to Caltagirone? I wonder if boys and girls in Sicily send their love in the water the way we did on Limestone Creek. We had such good times in Simpson's Ridge, Lizzie. I wish we could have just stayed young forever."

Bradley Morris studied his wife, lying still as death on the hospital bed. Alone with Lizzie in the middle of the night, dwelling in his mind on the days of their youth, he was a man suffering the agony of a broken heart. There was no solace, for this loss could never be replaced. He lowered his head and sobbed softly and a nurse who stopped by the room a few minutes later found him asleep in his chair.

19

In the afternoon, Anna Corydon called. She hoped there was something new on Lizzie's condition. Bradley told her nothing had changed and Anna expressed her regrets and wished him well. The Reverend Buford Acklin stopped by the big house briefly. He said he had asked all the people of Park Street Baptist Church to remember Lizzie in their prayers and please do call if there was anything he could do. Lois Burgess called. She said Russell was in Mississippi, but the last thing he said to her before he left was to please check on Lizzie today.

Walter and Catherine had stayed at the big house to be with Bradley, who worried about Matthew's time away from work. Did Walter think it was all right for Matt to be away from his job for so long? Walter said he was sure there was no problem, and as a matter of fact, Matthew had been free to go to the hospital this afternoon because he was caught up on things in Chicago.

"Matt's job isn't like working on the railroad," Walter said. "He can do most of what he needs to do from here in Memphis."

Jennie and Sarah had taken Beth shopping. Jennie was concerned that Beth had been confined to the house too much, and after the shopping trip they planned to take her to the Peabody Hotel in the late afternoon for the duck march.

Bradley recalled that Jennie had written them not to look for too many things to do during Beth's spring break visit. It seemed like only yesterday that he and Lizzie had been making plans for Beth, and he remembered Lizzie's vow that, regardless of Jennie's concern, they should arrange enough to make certain that Beth enjoyed her stay. He recalled her words distinctly; Lizzie wanted to make it "a perfect and memorable week."

When she was a little girl, Beth had loved the spectacle the Peabody created with the ducks. He and Lizzie had taken her to the grand old hotel any number of times to watch. The duck march was one of those things Memphis adults took their children to, along with visitors to town, even though they might find it somewhat ridiculous themselves. It was easy to feel embarrassed as you stood and watched a parade of trained fowl alight from an elevator and strut a red-carpeted path to the hotel fountain, accompanied by gaudily uniformed attendants and strains of John Philip Sousa march music. But the duck march was one of Memphis's best known traditions, reenacted every day for locals and tourists alike. He was glad Jennie and Sarah had included it in their list of things for Beth to do.

He also thought about their plans to take Beth to Simpson's Ridge, which wouldn't be possible now. Lizzie would have loved to do it. He could imagine her telling Beth about the old Kraft house, and how she used to ride Danny Boy down the lane and frolic with Butterball in the yard.

"I was thinking a lot about Simpson's Ridge last night," Bradley said to Catherine. "Have you heard anything about Arnold and Glory Calder lately?"

"I know they still live on the old home place," Catherine said. "I heard that Arnold was hurt in some kind of accident at the garage—a car fell on him, I think. It sounded like he might be laid up for a long time, maybe permanently. One of their daughters apparently moved back home with them with her two kids."

"I didn't know any of that."

"Walter was through there just a few months ago, hauling his boat somewhere. That's what he heard."

Walter nodded in agreement, but said nothing.

"I hope Arnold got the place all fixed up like he intended to," Bradley said. "I didn't remember that either of the daughters had children. It would be nice to see children around the old house again, don't you think?"

"Yes, it would," Catherine said. "I'd love that. But Simpson's Ridge has changed a lot. There isn't much left to go back for."

Matthew came home from the hospital late in the afternoon. They waited dinner until Jennie and Sarah arrived with Beth, who clearly had enjoyed her outing. She declared herself to have been greatly impressed with the duck march, but Bradley suspected that she was overstating her enthusiasm to make her mother feel good. He had observed a generous spirit in his granddaughter that was pleasing to see. Catherine also had seen it, and said Beth would lean over backwards to keep from hurting someone's feelings.

Talking excitedly at the dinner table, Beth had a great deal more to say about the shopping trip than she did about the visit to the Peabody. She'd found shoes she really, really liked, and her mother had bought them for her.

Beth had questions for her grandfather: When did her grandmother work at the hospital? How long? And was it really the same hospital where she was now? Bradley answered patiently. Yes, it was the very same hospital. She'd worked there for nearly twenty years, but it had been five or six years, as he recalled, since she left her job. She'd gone back often as a volunteer but that wasn't the same.

Beth said that made her grandmother a hero, too. Didn't he agree?

"Yes, I agree," Bradley said. "Your grandmother is a hero."

"I said 'too' because Granddaddy's a hero," Beth announced to the others. "We studied about World War II in school."

"Your Uncle Matthew is a hero," her grandfather said. "He was in the Marines in Vietnam."

"We didn't study about Vietnam," Beth said, then looked embarrassed, afraid she had said something wrong. "I'm sorry, Uncle Matthew, I don't know about that war."

Bradley saw a barely perceptible wince on his son's face. But Matt smiled, and told Beth, "Don't feel bad about that. Most people don't know as much as they should about Vietnam. Even grownups!"

Jennie interrupted. Bradley knew she wanted to change the subject, to get the conversation away from any discussion of

Matthew and Vietnam. Jennie always had been sensitive to the scars the war left on her brother, and no doubt wanted to spare him the discomfort.

"Before you get to feeling that the whole family is too heroic to clean up after itself," Jennie told Beth, "help me clear the table and load the dishwasher. Even heroes have to help with the housework around here."

20

The letter was addressed to Lizzie. It carried a Mankato, Minnesota, postmark and a neatly hand-printed Mankato return address with no name. It had arrived in yesterday's mail, which Sarah had left for Bradley on the kitchen table. He saw it immediately, even before he sat down to the generous breakfast Sarah had put before him.

"Mankato was Carson Streator's home town," Bradley said. "I've always remembered that. But I don't know who Lizzie would have known there."

He carefully tore open the envelope. Inside was a letter, hand-written and neatly folded, and inside the letter was a photograph and a newspaper clipping. The letter was dated just three days earlier.

"Would you please read it?" Bradley asked, passing the letter to Sarah.

"Yes, of course."

Sarah put aside the clipping and the photograph. Then she carefully smoothed the folds in the letter, and read aloud:

"Dear Mrs. Morris, your letter (enclosed) appeared in the newspaper last week. I was thrilled to hear from you, and to be reminded that there are people who still care about those things that happened so very long ago.

"Carson Streator was my brother. He was four years older than I, and I loved him dearly. I also have an older sister—Carson was in the middle. I was fifteen when he went off to the war, and I still remember the day he left like it was only yesterday. I cried like a baby and thought my heart would break. I just had a feeling that we would never see him again, and as you know that turned out to be true.

"Carson was buried overseas. It was 1958 before we were able to visit his grave. We put up a small memorial monument here in Mankato, in the little church cemetery where our mother and father have since been buried. The veterans' organizations mark it every Memorial Day with a flag, and I put flowers on it two or three times a year. Oh, I know it's been a long time, but I still feel that he deserves at least that much from those of us who are left."

Sarah paused, looking up at her father-in-law. She studied his face, as if searching for signs of emotion, unsure how he might react to the letter. He was without expression.

"Is this going to be difficult for you?" she asked.

"No," he said. "It's wonderful! But I don't understand how she knew Lizzie."

"I hope her letter will clear that up. Let me finish and we'll see."

Sarah began reading again: "We still have the letters Carson wrote from the army. Mother kept them all, and we found them when we sorted through her things after she died. Our father died a good many years ago, our mother not so long—she lived to be almost ninety! I got into his letters again after I saw your letter in the paper.

"Carson was not one to write real often, but in the last few months before he was killed he mentioned 'my friend from Kentucky' many times. It is clear that they were very close.

"I will be anxious to hear from you. I look forward to hearing all about you and your family. Especially about your husband, Carson's dear friend.

"I thought you might be interested in this picture of my grandchildren. You wouldn't have any way of knowing, but the youngest, Glenn, on the left, looks very much like Carson did at that age. I am so glad you cared enough to write. Please do write me back."

Sarah stopped reading. "That's the end of the letter," she

said. "Her name is Sharon Hammond."

She turned to the newspaper clipping. It was a letter to the editor, cut out of the Mankato *Free Press*:

> Dear Editor,
>
> I would like for you to publish this, and help me find any relatives of a young man who was my husband's best friend when he served in the army in World War II.
>
> The young man's name was Carson Streator. He was from Mankato. He and my husband, Bradley Morris, were in the 45th Division and were in Gen. Patton's invasion of Sicily. My husband was wounded, and Carson Streator was killed.

Lizzie had given her name and address, and urged any friend or relative of Carson Streator to get in touch.

Sarah handed the photograph to Bradley.

"My god," he said. "It's incredible how much the boy looks like Carson Streator. This could be him."

Bradley stared at the picture in disbelief. He was stunned by the similarity between the boy in the picture and his old friend, so long dead. It was as if Carson Streator had come back to life, to pose for a family photograph, happy and carefree. This was the way Streator would have looked at home, before the war—the way he would have been again after the war, had he survived.

"I still remember Streator so well, Sarah," he said. "When I look at this boy's face, it's just like looking at Streator. His eyes are the same, he has the same nose—even the chin is just like Streator's."

"Family resemblance can be striking," Sarah said.

"This is more than resemblance. He's a dead ringer for Carson Streator. What relation would he be?"

"Well, if he is Carson's sister's grandson, he'd be Carson's great-nephew. Isn't that right? Or is it grand-nephew?"

It was a few minutes before Bradley fully comprehended what

Lizzie had done. After all his years of wishing he knew about Streator's family but doing nothing, she'd taken matters into her own hands. She had done this for him, to try and help him find some peace of mind in regards to his long-departed comrade.

He and Lizzie had talked about Carson Streator more than once after they got home from Sicily in September. Lizzie knew he still had trouble dealing with Streator's death. A fresh look at the invasion beach near Gela, with Lizzie at his side, had been of great benefit as he tried to put bitter memories of his wartime experiences to rest. Getting close to the battlefield where he and Streator were hit gave him a new perspective, too, but his melancholy over the death of Carson Streator had not been eased all that much by his return to the island. Such reconciliation as he'd found in walking the beach at Gela had not extended to the long-standing trauma that stemmed from the suddenness and totality of Streator's fate. Nothing he saw or felt in Sicily would vindicate the loss of that vital, living human being, the gentle, innocent friend who had been erased from the rolls of mankind in the blink of an eye.

Bradley never had been certain that Lizzie fully understood the extent to which Streator's death had haunted him through the years. Perhaps he'd underestimated her in this, as in so many other things. Not only had she understood, but she had initiated this contact with Streator's family in an effort to help bring a sense of closure at last.

The picture of Sharon Hammond's young grandson touched Bradley in an unexpected way. The boy's likeness to Streator was startling, but there was no sudden shock of remembrance, nothing to invoke fresh remorse. Instead, he felt great consolation. Here, in the face of the boy, he could see the legacy of his sweet-tempered companion who was so cruelly robbed of life that awful day in Sicily. Glenn might have been Streator's own grandson, with Streator's blood flowing through his veins.

"I knew Streator had a family," he told Sarah. "I remember that he talked about his parents some, and about going on trips with his father. He most likely told me about his sisters, but I don't recall. I just had a feeling that he loved his family very much. "

"It's good to find out at last," Sarah said. "It's a wonder you remember him as well as you do."

"I'll never forget him. We thought we'd go through the war together. I don't think we ever looked as far ahead as the end of the war, but we sure didn't expect it to end so soon—for us, I mean. Streator just planned to get back to Minnesota, and I don't know what after that."

"His sister sounds like a very nice woman."

"Yes, and I'd be surprised if she wasn't. Someone must write her back. She needs to know about Lizzie."

"Of course. Don't worry about that. I'll take care of it."

Sarah had always been true to her word. Bradley knew she would write the letter, just as she promised. Responding to Sharon Hammond would be one small obligation he needn't worry about.

More than anything else, the letter from Minnesota made him eager to get back to the medical center, to be back at Lizzie's side. He put the letter and photograph aside, quickly swallowed a few sips of hot coffee, and told Sarah he was on his way to the hospital. He needed to relieve Walter, who had been there overnight; others could join him later if they wanted to.

Sarah urged him to take a few minutes to eat something before he went, but her pleas fell on deaf ears. He hurried out the kitchen door, determined to be ahead of the morning traffic.

Walter stood in the hallway outside Lizzie's room, stretching and yawning. So far as he could tell, he said, nothing had changed, and the medical staff people who had monitored Lizzie through the night had given no indication that anything was different. He had spent most of the night reading a new book on the history of World War II that Catherine had bought at a bookstore just down the street.

"I'm learning more about all you old heroes," Walter said. "When we have time, I'm going to have a lot of questions."

"It's not likely I could answer them," Bradley replied.

"You were there."

"Yes—but not for long. And I never knew what was going on. It always just seemed like one big snafu."

"Snafu? That's not a word we hear much anymore."

"Well, we used it a lot then. But you finish reading the book, Walter, and I'll ask you the questions."

Walter laughed. "I got through a good bit of it last night," he said, "but I didn't read some of it all that close. I didn't expect to be quizzed on it."

Bradley went to Lizzie's bedside and kissed her good morning. "We got a letter from Minnesota," he said. He addressed her directly, as he always did. "Streator's sister saw your letter in the paper and wrote back. She sent a picture. You couldn't imagine how much her grandson looks like him. It's absolutely amazing."

"You seem to be feeling better this morning," Walter said. "Did you get some rest?"

"I rested well. And I want you to go home and get some sleep, Walter. I can be here by myself until the others come. You must be pretty tired by now."

"I'm doing all right. I'll stay until somebody else gets here to be here with you. But I do think I'll go down and get some coffee. Can I bring you anything?"

"Thanks, but Sarah made me a big breakfast."

Walter was barely out the door when a floor nurse arrived, beginning her shift. Her demeanor was unusually somber—or was Bradley reading something into her face that wasn't there? In striking contrast to her usually brisk pace, the nurse went about her duties deliberately, almost delicately, working as if she felt like an intruder. Her routine was quite limited, given the fact that very little was being done for Lizzie, but nonetheless it took her several minutes.

She would have been briefed on Lizzie's condition when she came on duty, Bradley worried. *She must think Lizzie's time is running out. I wonder if they know something they haven't told us.*

"Has her condition changed any?" he asked.

"Everything looks about the same," the nurse said softly. "Dr. Garvey will be on the floor later today. I'm sure he'll look in on her. We've heard so many good things about Mrs. Morris. Lots of people in the hospital seem to have known her."

"Yes," Bradley said, "she's put in a good many years here."

The nurse finished her chores and left the room, reluctantly, it seemed to Bradley. He moved his chair back to Lizzie's side and, stroking the back of her hand, concentrated on the monitors. In the end, it would be these mindless electronic devices that told them when the dreadful time had come, mechanical tools replacing all human touch. He considered it a terrible injustice that a mere instrument, cold and inanimate, would be the source of the final mandate on the life of Lizzie Morris.

"I appreciate what you did for me, Lizzie, writing to Minnesota," he said. "Sarah will write his sister back. I feel better about Streator, seeing some of his family. It's almost like he was still alive, when I look at the picture.

"I told Streator all about you, Lizzie. We talked a lot when we were crossing the ocean. I had all your letters. I never read him any of your letters, but sometimes I'd tell him what you'd been doing when you wrote, things like that. I told him about Danny Boy and Butterball. I told him how much I loved you and missed you. Sometimes I felt bad, though, because he didn't have anyone like you waiting for him back in Minnesota.

"I don't think I ever told you, Lizzie, but the first time we got free in North Africa, he and I went to the edge of the ocean—it was the Mediterranean, I guess—and I dipped my hands in, just like you and I used to in Limestone Creek. I'd just got your letter, you remember, about water running to the ocean. Well, I dipped my hands in, and I really could feel your presence, just like you said. Your spirit was there, Lizzie, and I could feel it.

"You were with me during the landing, and there on the day I got hit. I had visions of you after they put me on the *Monrovia*, after they made it a hospital ship, and that kept me going. The doctors gave me credit for having a strong will to live, Lizzie, but it was you. You were there with me all the time."

Walter returned, carrying a small white paper bag in one hand and a newspaper in the other. "I brought you some coffee and a donut," he said. "I know you said you didn't want anything, but I'll bet you didn't eat any breakfast."

"Thank you very much. I should have eaten, but I didn't. Sarah fixed a good breakfast and tried to get me to take time to eat, but I wanted to get here and tell Lizzie about the letter from Minnesota."

"Well, I also brought us a newspaper. Sometimes it's good just to take time out and catch up on what else's going on in the world. I'll read the paper while you drink your coffee."

Bradley was grateful for Walter's consideration. The hot coffee tasted good. He wasn't hungry, but supposed he needed to eat. Walter's donut was not the most nutritious breakfast, perhaps, but it was more appealing to him just now than something healthy. He ate it in a few quick bites.

"You were talking about a letter," Walter said. "Something important?"

"Yes and no. It was important to me, but not really of any consequence to anyone else. I didn't know it, but Lizzie had written a letter to a newspaper in Minnesota trying to find out about Carson Streator. You know, my friend who was killed in the war."

"I know who he was. And you heard something back?"

"A letter from Streator's sister came for Lizzie yesterday. She wrote a very nice response to Lizzie's inquiry and sent a picture of her grandchildren. One of them looks just like Streator."

"It's amazing how these things play out sometimes. Lizzie hadn't told you about writing to the newspaper?"

"Not even a hint. I was taken completely by surprise, but I'm very grateful for what she did."

"I don't suppose she told anyone, then," Walter said. "Knowing Lizzie, she likely wanted to surprise you—or maybe not disappoint you if it didn't work out."

"Probably so. That's her way."

Walter gathered his things and left for the big house. He

promised to have questions about the war once he'd been able to read further into his book. First, though, he would need some sleep.

When he'd finished his coffee, Bradley began, half-heartedly, to scan the newspaper. He had ceased to concern himself with current events since Lizzie's attack; the newspaper simply was a way to pass the time. He had looked through most of the news when he was drawn to a small headline on the back page: "Detroit mobster indicted." He was astonished by what he read:

> DETROIT—John S. "Jack" De Luca, reputed Detroit Mafia lieutenant, was indicted by a federal grand jury yesterday on a number of charges.
>
> United States Attorney Daniel A. Kipling said De Luca would be charged under the federal RICO Act, the anti-racketeering law used to fight organized crime.
>
> Kipling said De Luca used his import business as a front for transporting millions of dollars in stolen art and other merchandise to world markets.
>
> De Luca, well known in international business circles, has a reputation as a "charming citizen and civic leader" which has made it difficult for law enforcement officials to get testimony against him, Kipling said.

Bradley put the newspaper aside and moved back to Lizzie's bedside. He leaned close and whispered softly in her ear. I'm glad you won't have to hear about this one," he said. "You'd be very disappointed in Mr. De Luca. I know you liked him. I did too."

He settled more deeply into the routine of his solitary bedside watch. He thought about Jack De Luca, how friendly and helpful he had been to them in Sicily. But life is full of surprises, Lizzie always said. Still—Jack De Luca, a Mafia lieutenant? He found the very idea both depressing and a little bit funny.

But he soon found his mind back on the letter from Sharon Hammond and the photograph of her grandchildren. This was Carson Streator's family, the family he always had hoped to see, and Lizzie had caused it to happen. And how simple it had been!

He felt almost euphoric, like a man who had just discovered treasure in his own back yard. He would be less reluctant to leave Lizzie's side when Sarah arrived at mid-day to take his place, almost eager to get home and look more closely at the photograph from Minnesota and, as he recognized now, the continuity of life it embodied.

21

S arah called the big house late in the afternoon. Dr. Witte Garvey had just checked on Lizzie and his report was grave: Lizzie was showing signs of deterioration and might not live through the night. Sarah believed they all should come to the medical center as soon as possible.

When they arrived at the hospital, Dr. Garvey was there to meet them. He repeated what he'd told Sarah earlier.

"I'm very sorry," he said, "but I think we're just about at the end. I'm amazed that Mrs. Morris has lasted this long. She's put up a gallant fight, but we've recognized all along that there was very little hope for recovery. You may not notice any obvious change, because the physical symptoms of her regression aren't readily apparent."

It was her electronic monitors that told the story, Dr. Garvey said. Lizzie's body was weak beyond further endurance, her vital signs degrading rapidly.

They gathered at Lizzie's bedside, where they stood solemnly over the woman who was wife, mother, sister, grandmother, the woman who had meant a great many different things to each of them.

Bradley Morris had hoped that he was prepared for this moment. He had come to accept, over time, the inevitability of Lizzie's passing—the fact that recovery was impossible and that only the life support system had kept her alive from the beginning. He had made the hardest decision of his own existence when he allowed the respirator to be removed, bowing to the judgment of those who understood substantially better than he the life forces involved, the outright hopelessness of Lizzie's circumstances. He even had begrudged the fact that death had not come immediately, once she had been taken off mechanical support, in part because he feared that prolonging her life would bring her suffering and in part because he had forced himself to give up all hope and saw a quick end as the most tolerable way out for himself.

But now there had been time in between, time during which he had relived in memory his years with Lizzie and come to treasure their years together even more—if that was possible. He was not prepared for this moment, and never would be.

He could see that the others were more accepting. Matthew and Jennie were somber, but showed no signs of the utter distress he felt. Catherine wept softly, while Walter and Sarah stood back and let the rest claim space closest around Lizzie's bed. Beth obviously did not yet fully understand the situation, though it was clear from the apprehension in her eyes that she sensed the gravity of her surroundings.

Jennie spoke first. "Come close, Beth," she said. "It's time to say goodbye to your grandmother. Then I'd like Aunt Sarah to take you home, if she will. We can't all stay."

Beth burst into tears.

"Don't cry," her mother said. "Your grandmother's had a good and full life. You'll remember all the wonderful times the two of you have had together, and how much she loved you and how much you loved her. And all the things she taught you, even when you were just a little girl. Come, say goodbye."

Beth pressed close to her grandmother's bedside. She rested her hand timidly on Lizzie's arm. "I'll always remember you, Grandmama," she said tearfully. "I love you."

Then she turned and pressed her face into Jennie's body and sobbed forcefully, her body quaking. Her mother held her tightly until the girl had cried herself out, kissing her softly on the hair and soothing her with quiet words.

"I'm all right now," Beth said at length. "I'll be all right. I love Grandmama so much. I just feel so sad."

"We all do, honey," her mother said. "We all love your grandmother and we'll all miss her. But I want you to think about the good things she means to you. Those are the things you'll never forget."

Sarah agreed to take Beth home, and Walter said he would walk them to the car. Before they left, Sarah stooped and kissed her mother-in-law tenderly on the forehead, stroked her hair, and whispered a final farewell. Beth looked back for one last glimpse of her grandmother as they went out of the room.

"Are you going to be all right, Brad?" Catherine asked, reaching toward Bradley and placing a hand lightly on his arm.

"I don't know how I can live without her," Bradley said, his eyes brimming with tears. "I just don't know how I can live without her."

"Dad, why don't you come over here and sit?" Matthew said. "There's nothing for us to do now but wait. It may be a long and tiring night. You shouldn't stand on your bad leg too long."

"It's going to be difficult for all of us," Catherine said. "I have so many memories of Lizzie. She was a wonderful big sister to me, there from the day I was born. I've been telling Walter some of the things I remember best. The very earliest things I remember all seem to center around her, even more than Mama and Papa. I think that's because Lizzie and I were always so close."

"I think you and Mother were the model for Jennie and me, Aunt Catherine," Matthew told her. "We wanted to be as close as the two of you always seemed to be."

"We did everything together," Catherine said, "except that she'd usually done it before. She always showed me the way. Oh, she got me in trouble sometimes, but I probably got her in trouble a lot more often. She always looked out for me."

"She still thinks of you as her little sister," Bradley said. "I guess she would still look out for you if she could."

In the center of the room, Lizzie lay comatose and chalk-colored. Dr. Garvey's warning had proved true; to their eyes, she looked little if any different from the way she had looked for the last week. She was alive, yet lifeless, her body emaciated and pitiful. This was not the way they would remember her, the vibrant and loving woman who had shared her life with all of them. And although they had long since moved beyond feeling self-conscious while talking about her even as she lay close at hand, they still felt the need to talk to her from time to time—a subtle challenge to the death-force that had yet to overtake her, no matter how imminent her passing might be.

Matthew had pushed a chair close to the bed and sat with his hand on his mother's arm. It was evident that he had resigned himself to what was to come, though his love for his mother would never allow him to accept it without grieving. He spoke to Lizzie as much as to the others.

"Of all the things I'll remember about Mother," he said, "her letters to me in Vietnam will be the best. When you're in a place like that, and see the horrible things you see and do the horrible things you do, you think that no one could ever understand. You think that nothing matters, because you probably won't survive the day. But then I'd get a letter from you, Mother, and know that you still loved me and everything would be all right and I had something to come home to. Your letters were like sunshine after the rain. They kept me going from one day to the next."

"I'm grateful she helped you, Matt," his father said. "God knows, I let you down."

"You don't have to feel that way," Matthew said. "It's all behind us now. And you've helped me too, in the long run."

They all fell silent. It was as if each of those gathered around Lizzie was deep in his or her own thoughts, oblivious to the others. Only the sounds of the electronic monitors invaded the stillness. Catherine moved to the foot of the bed, where she stood and looked down upon her older sister, shaking her head sadly. Then she began to smile.

"I remember how she used to pick wild cherries for me, from the trees along the lane," Catherine said. "I was too little to reach even the lowest limbs. But it wasn't long before I could climb the trees with her. We spent many a summer day climbing high in those old cherry trees, watching the world pass below us and stuffing ourselves with cherries. We'd go home with purple stains all over our clothes and Mama would say it looked like we'd been drinking ink. To this day, I still love wild cherries. You taught me that, Lizzie."

"She still likes them, too," Bradley said. "She tries to chase the birds away from the old tree in the back yard, so they won't get all the cherries."

"Is that the tree I fell out of and broke my arm?" Matthew asked. "I'd forgotten it's a cherry tree."

"That's the one," his father said. "I planted it before you were born."

"I remember that," Jennie said. "You were climbing up to get to the last of the cherries when you fell. I thought you had killed yourself!"

Catherine's opening had lightened their mood, and the atmosphere in Lizzie's room was suddenly brighter, less tense. They all had happy memories to share.

"If it hadn't been for Mother," Jennie said, "I may never have had Beth. I was nearly beyond child-bearing age when Paul and I were married, as you all know. We didn't think we would have a child, much as we wanted to. Our doctor told us the chances were very slim, but Mother kept encouraging me. She said there's a lot the doctors don't know, and if we wanted a child we just had to keep trying."

Matthew laughed. The sound of laughter, incongruous as it would have been just minutes earlier, now fit the spirit of those gathered in Lizzie's room.

"The Morris Family Proverb!" Matthew said. "Remember?"

"Of course I remember," Jennie said. She laughed, too. "Most people would be better off if they worried less about what they think they know and more about what they don't know. Isn't that it? I never knew where that came from."

"It came from Anna Corydon," her father said. "That's not exactly what Anna said, but that was your mother's variation on Anna's theme. It grew out of something pretty much like you were just talking about."

"I don't understand," Jennie said.

"They were talking about doctors. After we lost our first baby. Anna told your mother not to pay any attention to the doctors who said she might not be able to have another one. She was right of course. Otherwise, the two of you wouldn't be here!"

"I had no idea," Jennie said. "And I might add, Mother's advice didn't stop there."

"What was the rest of it?" Matthew asked.

"Maybe I shouldn't have started this. It's kind of embarrassing."

"We're all family here," Matthew urged. "What is there to be embarrassed about?"

"Okay. But it's still embarrassing. We'd been married a year and hadn't had any luck, and Mother said we were trying too hard and I was too tense. She advised that we forget about trying to have a baby and just go back to making love. She also suggested a week in the Bahamas, which we did."

"And did it work?" Catherine asked.

"All I can tell you is that I came back from the Bahamas still pale, but pregnant!"

Walter returned at that moment, surprised to hear the sound of laughter. "I don't know how much of that I missed," he said, "but you can start over if you want to."

"You didn't miss anything," Jennie told him. "It was just an 'advice from Mother' report. I think we've reached the point of recalling favorite memories. At least that's what I was doing."

"Your mother's given us all a lot to remember her for," Walter said. "If I forgot everything else about her, I'd remember her for the way she grilled me when Catherine and I first got engaged. The woman scared me to death! Young men are supposed to worry about facing their future fathers-in-law, but Papa Kraft welcomed me to the family with open arms. Then I had to face Lizzie! I got the message real fast that she didn't think I was good enough for Catherine."

"That's just because she didn't know you, Walter," Bradley said. "Lizzie had left home by then, and hadn't been around to get to know you. She's always liked you and been glad to have you in the family."

Bradley's tone of voice, unlike the others, still was altogether serious. He was surprised at what Walter had said. And concerned. Surely, after all these years, Walter understood that Lizzie liked and respected him a great deal. She had said as much many times through the years. He was sure that Lizzie never had voiced any complaint about Walter as a brother-in-law.

Walter promptly put his mind at ease. "Oh, I know that," he said. "But she was protective of Catherine, and she was going to make damned sure that I measured up. I didn't think it was funny at the time, but I do now."

"You may have seen as much of the 'tough' Lizzie as anyone ever has," Catherine said. "None of us has ever doubted she was strong, but we seldom thought of her as tough. She shed more tears than the children did when Napoleon died."

"That old cat had become part of the family," Jennie said.

"She always hated to see animals hurt," Catherine said. "Papa used to try to trap 'coons that damaged his tobacco patch, but finally had to give it up because Lizzie had such a fit every time he caught one."

The room grew quiet again. Having spent days at Lizzie's bedside, those now gathered for what they expected to be her final hours of life had run the gamut of emotions. Much of their grief was spent. They all loved this woman deeply; all would mourn her passing. Yet they would remember her in life, as they were doing now, and understand even better through the years to come that in her own quiet and modest manner she was a remarkable woman who had affected their lives in ways they were only beginning to calculate.

But Bradley could not be sanguine about Lizzie's death, as the others appeared to be. His loss would be much greater, his pain not lessened by happy memories, and as her precious life ebbed away he felt as though he were dying with her. She was his mate, and their life forces were intertwined. Surely, life without Lizzie would be perpetual darkness.

He walked to the window and looked out. People came and went on the street below, going about their affairs on what was to them an ordinary day. Little would they know or care that in this small, crowded room just above their heads the drama of a life running its natural course was being played out. Lizzie was unknown to them; they would not feel her loss.

A tiny ant crawled along the window trim, a mercurial black speck against the yellowed enamel. He watched it hurry toward a corner, then turn and retrace its steps, disoriented and confused. It moved erratically along the molding, alternately hastening forward a few inches and then stopping as if to seek its bearings—some trace of the world it knew but somehow had become hopelessly separated from—and finally disappeared from view.

He surveyed the floral arrangements on the window sill. "She loves the yellow flowers," he said softly.

"I'm sorry, Daddy, what did you say?" Jennie asked.

"I said she loves the yellow flowers."

"Oh, yes," Catherine said. "She loved the great patches of Spanish needles that bloomed along Limestone Creek in the fall. And the golden rod in the meadow. I think they were the main reason fall was her favorite season. She always looked forward to the flowers."

"And the giants," Jennie said.

"Oh, yes! I'd forgotten the giants!"

"Now you have us all confused," Walter said. "What giants?"

"She loved to make up games," Catherine said. "One of her favorites was playing giants. In the fall, especially, when the sun was low but still very bright in the late afternoons, we'd go to the pasture and pretend our long shadows were giants. We could make them do anything we wanted them to—sometimes menacing, sometimes friendly. But how did you know about giants?"

"Because she taught us to play it, too," Jennie said. "There was only one place in the park where the trees didn't get in the way. When Matt was still little, I could scare him with my shadow. Mother didn't like that, and ruled that we'd only be friendly giants. But I cheated."

"Our giants lived in the caves made by the overgrown honey-suckle during the day," Catherine said. "Then Lizzie would call them out late in the afternoon. She said they roamed the countryside at will after dark because they were invisible then. She said they never came out on a moonlit night because a Kentucky moon is benevolent and wouldn't tolerate their black spirits. On dark nights they found their way home by listening for the rustle of the leaves on the big cottonwood trees along the creek. Oh, she had some imagination!"

"She and I used to walk in the lane at night," Bradley said. "Sometimes when there was no moon it would get so dark you couldn't tell where you were, and she taught me to listen for the cottonwoods."

Talk stopped when a white-clad medical technician came, and they all watched quietly as he systematically and mechanically checked instruments and connections, with no overt concern for the patient these devices served. He worked hurriedly. He made a few cryptic notations on a checksheet attached to the clipboard he carried, then left the room with barely an acknowledgement that others were present.

Bradley was about to comment on his apparent lack of caring when an unfamiliar nurse stepped into the room. She was not assigned to Lizzie, as it turned out, but was on duty on the floor above and had simply taken a few minutes to run down and visit. Lizzie was a dear friend and she'd made it a habit to stop in from time to time.

"We all know Mrs. Morris," the nurse said. "There are still a lot of people around who were here when she worked in the hospital, and the rest of us have become acquainted with her through her volunteer work in patient services. We all just love her." It was evident that she knew Lizzie's status and had come to say goodbye, but out of consideration for the family she would not be obvious in offering her farewell.

Jennie thanked her for her kindness.

The interruptions brought a marked lapse in the amiable conversation among the family members gathered around Lizzie, and the mood once again grew somber. Few words were spoken for the next several minutes, but one by one, like mourners, they took turns standing close to Lizzie's bedside and paying silent tribute.

When another nurse, this one assigned to Lizzie, made her rounds a half-hour later, she told them there was little change. Lizzie's heartbeat and breathing were still regular, though weak. "Sometimes it takes a while," she said tenderly. "Mrs. Morris has proved to be an amazingly strong woman. It may happen soon or it may take a few hours yet. You all must be awfully tired. If you'd like to go move about a bit and stretch your legs, or go and get something to eat or whatever, I don't think you'd have to worry about being away. We'll know when the time is near."

Walter suggested that Matthew and Jennie take their father downstairs and get some food. He and Catherine would stay at Lizzie's bedside and call them immediately if there should be a turning point.

This time, Bradley agreed.

He was very tired, and there was nothing more for him to do. He had shed an ocean of tears, and grieved almost beyond human endurance. He had spent hours alone with Lizzie since she was first stricken, repeated his love to her over and over, and relived with her their decades of beautiful memories. He could not change the circumstances, could not suspend the passage of time that moved inexorably toward her final curtain. And yet . . . Lizzie was still alive. She needed him to watch over her until the end. Whether it was only a few more hours or many more, she needed him beside her, strong and determined.

"On second thought," he told Matthew, "I think I'd just like to get up and walk around a little. I'm a little stiff. But I won't be far away, and I'll be back in just a bit. Could someone come out and get me if anything changes?"

"Of course, Dad," Matthew said. "Go stretch your legs. We'll know where to find you."

Bradley paced the hallway for a time, always staying close to Lizzie's room. As he walked by the family lounge for the third or fourth time a voice from the television set caught his attention. *Another television evangelist, and they all sound alike.* Then he heard the telling words: "Listen to Brother Percy!" It was the sidewalk preacher, the little man he'd seen and heard on the street corner, mocked by the bantering teenagers.

He was surprised. He had assumed that Brother Percy was a lightweight, and certainly not a man of sufficient standing to merit an appearance on television. Television evangelists were prominent figures, in their fashion, and Brother Percy had struck him as down-and-out. The street corner, the homeless shelter, the soup kitchen—these were Brother Percy's cathedrals.

But there the little preacher was, on the screen, larger than life. His presence dominated the room.

"Jesus gave His life for you," Brother Percy said, his voice calm but his tone resolute.

There was none of the theatrical display Bradley had witnessed on the street corner. Brother Percy was a different man—not the antagonistic, Bible-brandishing showman who jousted with teenagers, but a sincere messenger with an urgent dispatch. He seemed to look Bradley directly in the eye, earnestly, pleading for attention: "We all face death, as surely as the evening must usher in the night. But let not the grave be life's goal. The body may return to dust, but not the soul."

Bradley listened.

"In my father's house are many mansions," Brother Percy proclaimed. "These are the words of Jesus. I go to prepare a place for you, that where I am, there you may be also."

Once again, the little preacher's words were familiar. His sermon was one Bradley had heard many times before, always with Lizzie at his side. The first time so long ago in Shiloh Church, yet he remembered. These were words in which Lizzie took great comfort, words on which her faith was based. She believed, and many times she had told him so. Lizzie did not fear death. In her heart and in her mind, she fervently expected to spend eternity in Paradise. Death would be but a transition.

Bradley stood in the middle of the room, transfixed, his

attention focused rigidly on the television evangelist. He heard nothing more of Brother Percy's message. He was conscious of new words, but the earlier words persisted in his mind, over and over ... *that where I am, there you may be also ... there you may be also ...*

"She's waiting for me," he said softly to himself. "You told me, Lizzie, in Caltagirone. I remember. You said you would wait until we could be together again in heaven." He walked from the lounge with new strength, as if a great burden had been lifted from his shoulders. He was ready, at last, to accept what had to come.

As soon as he entered Lizzie's room he sensed that something was different; the spiteful electronic monitors relayed an altered signal. The change was imperceptible to the others, but he knew the machines too well to be deceived. Lizzie's ordeal was at an end.

"It's time," he said quietly.

Even before the others could voice their question, a nurse rushed in to prepare the family for what was about to happen. Her trained eye had read the monitors, too, from her station just down the hall. "I'm afraid we're almost at the end now," she told them. "Mrs. Morris hasn't much time left. Would you like me to call the chaplain, or is there anyone else?"

No, they all agreed; the family was present, and there was no need for anyone else to be there. Lizzie would be surrounded to the end by the people she loved best, the people who loved her best. Those to whom she had devoted her life would be at her side in the final moments, just as she would wish. Their long vigil was almost over.

By now the change in life signs was becoming clear on the electronic monitors. They could not help but concentrate their attention on the instruments and the sorrowful message they conveyed.

"I'm going to turn these off," the nurse said. "Sometimes it's just too painful to watch."

She deftly manipulated some control and the monitors fell

black and quiet. No more impulses depicting Lizzie's waning vital signs would be seen or heard.

"I'll be right outside," the nurse said. "Please call me if you need me."

The silence was overwhelming.

"If you don't mind," Bradley Morris told the others, "I'd like a minute alone with her to say my goodbye. I won't take long."

When they were gone, he took Lizzie's hand. He spoke tenderly, but his voice was clear and firm. "We've had a great run at it, Lizzie," he said. "Weren't we a great team! But I guess we're at the end of the road now. You've been a wonderful wife, and my best friend for as long as I can remember. I wouldn't have been much without you. Thank you for all you've done for me. You gave me two beautiful children—they'll do all right, Lizzie, and they've got wonderful families of their own.

"I know there were so many times when I should have been better. You never complained, Lizzie, but you deserved better than me. Please forgive me for all my shortcomings, for all the big and little hurts I've caused you. If I could go back and live life over I'd be a better man, but we don't get that chance.

"There aren't many like you. I should have told you that more often. And how lucky I am to have you. You never gave me much to complain about. If I ever felt like you did me any small wrong, I got over it quickly. There isn't anything standing between us, Lizzie."

He paused, gazing out through the window but unaware of what he saw, contemplating his next words.

"There's not much more to say, Lizzie. I love you. I'll see you on the other side. Goodbye. Sweetest dreams."

He took a pen and sheet of paper from the drawer of a nightstand beside Lizzie's bed and wrote:

> Dear Jennie and Matthew, you have been a wonderful son and daughter. No father could have asked for more. I wish for both of you a life of love and kindness. Take care of our grandchildren for

us. I love you, and the grandchildren, very much. When your mother crosses over I want to be there to meet her, so this is goodbye. We'll look down on you from heaven and smile. Dad. p.s.—Our affairs are in order. All the papers are in the desk in the study. Please cancel my appointment with Dr. Christman and be sure and pay the newspaper boy.

He placed the paper carefully on the side of Lizzie's bed, then clasped his wife's hand and settled back in his chair, took a long breath, and closed his eyes. He glimpsed a fleeting vision of the wooded green hills of Kentucky bathed in silver moonlight. The freshening scent of willows clumped on Limestone Creek filled his nostrils. He heard the rustle of stiff Cottonwood leaves dancing in an evening breeze.

The final image in his mind's eye was that of a peaceful, tree-lined country lane. Danny Boy cantered easily toward him, with a youthful and carefree Lizzie riding happily on the horse's back and Butterball running behind.

22

The mortal remains of Bradley and Lizzie Morris were laid to rest, side by side, in the yellow clay of the old cemetery behind the Shiloh Missionary Baptist Church near Simpson's Ridge. Their fresh graves were visible from the upstairs windows of the red sandstone house where Elizabeth Kraft was born, rejuvenated now under the proud care of Arnold and Glory Calder.

The Reverend Buford Acklin accompanied the small cortege that drove from Memphis to the graveyard. Except for the minister and the family, only Russell and Lois Burgess made the trip. A large man on crutches waited at the front of the church, and introduced himself to the family. He was Arnold Calder.

Pastor Acklin presided over a brief graveside ceremony, the main funeral services having been held at the Park Street church in the city. At that earlier gathering, he had led his congregation not in mourning, but rather in rejoicing; two more souls had found their way to everlasting life in heaven.

Pastor Acklin repeated that theme in his brief final utterance at the gravesite. "Although we share the loss with their family, and we will miss their shining presence," the minister proclaimed, "we should not grieve for Bradley and Lizzie. Because I know that at this very minute they are home with Jesus. And what rewards lay in store for them there! What raptures they'll share in the radiance of eternity! So let us not grieve for Brother Brad and Sister Lizzie. If we grieve, we grieve for ourselves. The loss is ours. But for them, let us rejoice! For on this day Brad and Lizzie Morris are home in Paradise."

When the final prayer had been spoken, the family of seven adults and a lone child began to make its way back across the unkempt churchyard, slowly, to funeral cars parked under the trees, followed at a polite distance by the minister, the Burgesses, and Arnold Calder. Beth still cried softly, clinging to her mother's hand. Jeff and Mark walked behind the others without talking. Sarah slowed her pace to be with her sons.

"It's going to be hard to get back to the routine things," Matthew said to Jennie. "But life goes on, as they say. I guess we're the senior generation now."

"I'm not ready for that, Matt," Jennie said. "But you're right, and we have no choice. The first thing I have to do is get Beth back to California and back in school. Paul gets home from the Philippines in two days. Will you have lots of work to catch up on?"

"Nothing that matters much," her brother said.

Matthew looked momentarily at the old church, then surveyed the surrounding countryside. The rolling, wooded hills extended unbroken as far as the eye could see. "I have no feeling for this place," he said. "I know that Dad and Mother still loved it deeply, but I can't really understand why. It just seems to me that we're in the middle of nowhere."

"I think we would have had to live their lives to understand," Jennie said. "Simpson's Ridge meant a lot to them. This is where they met, and it's where they began life together. There wasn't any question that this is where they wanted to be buried. They're side by side, just as they were in life."

The two stopped walking and embraced. Catherine and Walter paused beside them.

"We have to keep in touch," Catherine said. "Please plan to visit us in Florida just as you would have come to see your mother and dad in Memphis."

"Thank you so much for everything, Aunt Catherine," Jennie said. "This would have been a lot harder for us if it hadn't been for you and Uncle Walter. We love you."

She hugged Catherine warmly and grasped Walter's hand.

Matthew shook hands with them both and Sarah hugged them. Catherine and Walter kissed Beth and embraced her tightly. They all paid their respects to Russell and Lois Burgess, and briefly thanked Pastor Acklin for his many acts of kindness.

Arnold Calder stood aside and waited his turn to add final condolences. Matthew and Jennie paused and expressed their gratitude to him for coming.

"Your dad was a real good man," Arnold Calder told them. "I hadn't seen him for a good bit, but I always looked forward to the days he and your mother came to Simpson's Ridge. I'm going to miss him. I didn't get to know your mother very well, but I liked her a lot. I heard so many good things about her. Glory sends her sympathy, too. She has a hard time getting around, and I didn't want her to try and come."

"Thank you," Jennie said. "And thank you again for coming. We know that Dad always wanted to see you whenever he got back to Simpson's Ridge."

"I heard that your father just willed himself to death. Is that true?"

"We think it is," Matthew said. "His death was attributed to heart failure, but he'd never had a heart problem before. It seems he just willed his heart to stop, and it did. Dr. Garvey said he was only aware of a few such cases on record, though it's not unheard of. And Dad had remarkable willpower."

"Thomas Mann explained it," Arnold Calder said. "He said human reason needs only to will more strongly than fate, and it is fate. And I can tell you, your father wouldn't have lasted long without your mother. I've been thinking about that a lot. He just thought the world of her. It's hard to lose good people like your mom and dad, but the rest of us will keep on going because that's God's way."

"Yes," Jennie said, "Matthew and I were just now talking about that."

"I wanted to give you this," Arnold Calder said as he handed Jennie a folded sheet of paper. "You can read it later. I've always liked the poems of Sir Walter Scott, and there is a verse that seemed to me to be kind of a proper tribute to your father. This is from me to him, and I wanted you to have it."

"That's very considerate," Matthew said. "We appreciate it more than I can tell you."

With nothing more to be said, the family loaded into the funeral cars and started back to Memphis. Jennie unfolded the paper Arnold Calder had given her. "To the memory of Bradley Morris, from your friend Arnold Calder" was inscribed at the top of the page, in pen and ink. Then the verse, in Arnold's rigid hand writing:

> Soldier, rest! thy warfare o'er,
> Sleep the sleep that knows not breaking,
> Dream of battled fields no more,
> Days of danger, nights of waking.

On a grassy hillside, a young girl sat astride a spirited sorrel mare and watched respectfully as the procession passed by below. The gleaming hearses moved slowly, as if picking their way carefully along the narrow country road. Their tires kicked up small swirls of yellow dust that lingered for some time after their passing, a modest tribute to the earth-warming and drying power of the afternoon sun.

Spring was fast becoming summer in western Kentucky. Already, the tiny blossoms of the redbud trees had faded to pale lavender and disappeared. The last petals of the dogwood flowers were withering and beginning to turn brown or falling white to the ground. Thunderstorms had rolled across the wooded hills often during the last week, rumbling out of blackened skies to the southwest and sweeping the land with warm rains. Graceful redtail hawks soared in widening circles above Simpson's Ridge, while the monotonous harmony of croaking frogs drifted up from the banks-full Limestone Creek. Everywhere there was new green life.

A towering thundercloud changed from white to creamy orange as the sun dipped low, then darkened to somber gray. It was almost twilight, and cool, but Glory Calder, swinging lazily on the porch of the old Kraft House just down the road from Shiloh Church, fanned herself with a paper fan and sipped cold Pepsi-Cola from a bottle.

Other Books by Robert Hays

Fiction
Blood on the Roses
The Baby River Angel
Circles in the Water
Early Stories from the Land
(editor)

Non-fiction
Patton's Oracle
Editorializing 'the Indian Problem'
A Race at Bay
State Science in Illinois
G-2: Intelligence for Patton
(with Gen. Oscar Koch)
Country Editor

About the Author

Robert Hays has been a newspaper reporter, magazine editor, public relations writer, and university professor and administrator. A native of Illinois, he taught in Texas and Missouri and retired in 2008 from a long journalism teaching career at the University of Illinois. He has spent a great deal of time in South Carolina, the home state of his wife, Mary, and was a member of the South Carolina Writers Workshop. His publications include academic journal and popular periodical articles and ten books, including his collaborative work with General Oscar Koch, *G-2: Intelligence for Patton,* and one published in paperback edition under a different title. Robert and Mary live in Champaign, Illinois. They have two sons and a grandson and share (long story!) a cat named Eddie with the family next door.

www.ingramcontent.com/pod-product-compliance
Lightning Source LLC
Chambersburg PA
CBHW021224130626
46554CB00004B/1359